Maybe a whole bunch of people would jump at the chance to legitimately run amok, to mix up in some sort of violence at the slightest excuse, to run and shoot and loot and go out in a blaze of glory. Maybe the heathen Indians had something after all, he thought. Maybe they knew that the Bible-bangers were wrong, and there is no Heaven. Maybe there was only Valhalla. Maybe the truest, the only noble human instinct, is to go down fighting.

Maybe there really is such a thing as Warrior Blood.

SOLDIER
OF FORTUNE
MAGAZINE PRESENTS:

BULLET
CREEK

L.S. CARROLL

TOR

A TOM DOHERTY ASSOCIATES BOOK
NEW YORK

BULLET CREEK

Copyright © 1988 by The Omega Group, Ltd.

A TOR Book
Published by Tom Doherty Associates, Inc.
49 West 24 Street
New York, NY 10010

ISBN: 0-812-51271-5   Can. ISBN: 0-812-51272-3

Library of Congress Catalog Card Number: 88-50632

First edition: November 1988

Printed in the United States of America

0 9 8 7 6 5 4 3 2 1

PART ONE

There are those in this world who do
not love their fellow men—
and I hate people like that.

Unknown

I.

"Let's do it," Frank Fennili said. He ground out his filter in the dashboard ashtray and reached for the ignition.

Umberto "Bertie" Rossolini grunted and stuck the Smith & Wesson .38 Special Military & Police revolver he had been playing with back in his waistband and buttoned his suit coat over it.

The black Lincoln Continental pulled out of the parking lot of the closed Sonic Burger and U-turned across the highway, the fat radial tires squealing softly. A hundred yards south from their original position they paused in the inside lane, waiting for a trailer truck to pass, then swung off the road and onto the crushed-shell surface of the used-car lot.

Ball's Used Cars was located three miles from the city limits of Lakeland, Florida. It consisted of a half acre of hard-packed sand enclosed by a chain-link fence. A mobile trailer served as an office. Next to the trailer was an open-fronted corrugated-tin shed, its space cluttered with greasy motors, tires, and car parts. There was none of the usual gay-colored bunting fluttering in the wind, and no advertising except the rented electric sign on its small trailer which, in addition to the business name, announced "Thirty Dollars a Week." The lot itself was empty of people, and contained twenty or twenty-five clunkers, most of which still carried expired out-of-state tags. The only new vehicle in evidence was a grey Corvette parked in front of the office.

Fennili and Rossolini pulled in behind it and got out of their car. They did not slam the doors.

"Fill this out, please," the woman said, sliding a W-2 form across the glass-topped desk.

Rider squatted at the corner of the desk and studied the paper for a moment, as if unfamiliar with it. Actually he could have completed it in the dark, but the hesitation was a habit he had developed. Sometimes, on good jobs, it wouldn't do to seem too practiced filling out W-2s and applications, not right after feeding somebody a line of bullshit about how he was just out of the hills looking for his first real job. He hated all the lying, but a man had to eat, and nobody hires drifters, even a crummy little car lot like this.

The secretary's looks and perfume made him acutely aware of how scruffy he must appear.

Well, two days on the road hitchhiking and a night sleeping in the sand dunes didn't help anybody look exactly well groomed. He glanced over at Joe Ball, who was reading a local paper at his desk and sipping coffee from the maker behind him, importantly ignoring the proceedings in the secretarial department.

Ball was in his late twenties or early thirties, medium height and starting to go to fat. He was dressed in tan slacks and maroon jacket over an open-collar sports shirt. His hair was styled mod and gold chains encircled his neck, expensive rings glittering from his manicured hands.

Rider started to fill out the form mechanically, trying to ignore the depression that always flooded over him in these situations. He tried not to think about how his ragged dungarees and patched army jacket compared to Ball's expensive, deodorized finery. Or how, if he was grubby now, he would look this evening after a day of fucking with greasy motors. He signed his name to the W-2 and stood up.

The secretary took it and gave him a meaningless secretary smile. Rider wondered if Ball was screwing her. Probably. They had arrived together in his car a few minutes ago. They certainly weren't married or related. A little plaque on her desk said she was Miss Cousins. Ball had called her Pat.

So he gets the pussy, too, Rider thought. I must be doing something wrong. He tried not to think about being over 40, which always depressed him, so he thought about his new job, which depressed him even more.

Ball glanced up from his paper, saw they were done, and dropped the paper on his desk. He rubbed his hands together briskly. "Ready to go to work?" he asked in a hearty salesman voice.

"I reckon," Rider said, trying to sound enthused and country.

The trailer door opened and two men came in.

Through the open door, Ball could see the Continental parked behind his Corvette. That and the fact that his visitors were dressed in suits sent the warning lights on immediately. Ball's customers never dressed or drove like that. They dressed like what's-his-name over there whom he'd hired yesterday, partly to do some much-needed cleanup around the lot, and partly to have someone to boss other than Pat, who was getting to think she owned him.

"Can I help you?" he asked, a glazed smile frozen on his face from force of habit. His mind was racing. Cops.

"Shit!" the dark curly-haired one in the brown suit said, exchanging a quick glance with the dark curly-haired one in the tan suit.

Fennili, who was in charge, was momentarily confused. There were only supposed to be two of them here, Ball and his shack job. So who was this bum? He made a quick decision. He reached around to his left side and pulled a .45 automatic from under his coat and pointed it at Ball, whose face sagged in shock. On cue, Rossolini pulled his own piece and covered Rider and the secretary.

"Is this a holdup?" Ball asked in a voice that he tried to make level and reasonable but which came out squeaky and terrified.

"Shut the fuck up!" Fennili said. "Don't move, man. Don't yell, don't run, don't talk. Just do what you're told and you will be okay. Okay?"

Ball kept staring at the weapon.

"Okay, asshole?"

"Yeah, right, okay," Ball said in a voice suddenly husky with phlegm.

"We're all going for a little ride, and we're gonna have a nice friendly talk, and if I get the right answers, then everybody gets to walk out to the highway and hitchhike home or call a cab or whatever. I don't give a fuck, as long as I get the right answers. Okay?"

"Okay." More quickly this time.

"Oh my God," Pat Cousins said on a note rising with hysteria. Her hands were pressed flat against her cheeks, hard enough to whiten the flesh.

"Shut up!" Rossolini barked, afraid of hysterics. The idea was to walk everyone out to the car quietly and unobtrusively. No muss, no fuss. Once they were at their destination, the dumb cunt could have the screaming meemies, for all he cared. Probably would, anyway.

"All right," Fennili said, "everybody out quick! Straight down the steps and into the back of our wheels. No smart-ass moves, no bullshit."

Rider took Pat Cousins by the elbow and steered her toward the door. "It's all right," he said soothingly, as worried about hysterics as the two buttonmen. He had a good idea what would happen if she flipped out. Her body was quivering with pure terror and, although Rider was afraid himself, he had a brief flash of contempt for her. "Overcivilized bitch," he thought.

He led her down the trailer steps to the Lincoln, followed closely by Rossolini, who held his revolver near his body in order to conceal it with his coat. Rider opened the rear door and helped her in, then got in himself and closed the door.

Fennili shoved Ball into the rear seat from the other side and slammed the door behind him.

The team leader slid under the wheel and cranked the car, backed it smoothly out onto the highway, and accelerated, heading south. Rossolini sat in the passenger seat, facing backward, watching the captives and playing with the revolver in his lap. They rode in silence for a short time.

Rider suddenly realized he wouldn't have to work, after all, and the thought made him almost happy. Might get killed, he thought, but no grubby, menial, boring scut work at field-hand pay for you today, Mr. Cool! He noticed that his senses were extremely sharp suddenly. He could smell the rich clean upholstery of the car, the faint odors of perfume and deodorant on his fellow passengers, and the sharper acid reek of fear. It was a beautiful Florida winter day, the air clear and invigorating, everything bright and colorful and alive. The flat scrubland flashed by, white sand and deep-green stunty pines, blue sky and puffy clouds. He was aware of the warm length of the woman's leg pressed against his, and he wondered if he was crazy. His eyes met Rossolini's, who gave him a snakelike, hard-ass killer's stare. Rider almost grinned, then remembered how the game was supposed to be played and dropped his gaze.

Joe Ball cleared his throat, then said in a plaintive voice, "Can I ask a question?"

"I ask the questions," Fennili said, keeping his eyes on the road. "The first question is, who's the overage hippie?" He jerked his thumb over his shoulder in Rider's direction.

"Just somebody I hired yesterday to work around the lot. I can't even remember his name."

"That right, sport?"

"That's right," Rider told him, keeping his head down.

"What's your name, sport?"

Rider told him.

"Where you drift in from, sport?"

"Tennessee."

"Lemme see your wallet, sport."

Rider handed his worn, shiny wallet over the back of the front seat. Rossolini went through the motel receipts, old check stubs, and wrinkled bar napkins with forgotten names and addresses on them.

"Texas license here, Frank," he told Fennili.

"What's this Texas shit, sport? Thought you was from the hills?"

"That's from a long time ago, when I was working out there. I got a license, then when I got home I didn't see no need to pay another ten for a Tennessee license."

Rossolini found a piece of creased cardboard in the wallet. "Tennessee hunting license."

"You hunt a lot, sport?" Fennili asked.

"Rabbits and squirrels and stuff."

Rossolini snickered.

"What do you men want, for God's sake?" Pat Cousins suddenly burst out. She looked around wildly, as if preparing to leap out of the car.

"Shut your fucking trap!" Rossolini yelled. He leaned over the back of the seat and slapped her in the mouth. She covered her face with her forearms and started sobbing in hysterical gasps. Ball was sitting rigid, sweat running down his forehead. His skin looked green. Rider cringed against the door, one arm thrown up for protection. "Please don't hurt us," he pleaded.

Rossolini and Fennili exchanged looks of amused contempt. They would not have been quite as amused if they knew that behind his upraised arm, Rider was grinning.

"This is it, Frank," Rossolini said. Three hundred yards beyond a green and white road sign a faint trail led off into the scrub and palmettos. They turned in and drove carefully over the loose sand ruts. Fender-high grass swished against the sides of the car.

Ball leaned forward, his body tense. "Listen, guys, this is some kind of mistake! You're fuckin' up, I swear you are. You got the wrong people. I'm not mixed up in anything this heavy! I swear it!"

He was talking fast, his words running together in a jumble of desperation. Rider could see little glints of spittle spraying from his mouth.

"I don't understand what this is all about! You better check with your bosses. I swear you're fuckin' up. All I do is turn a few hot cars and stuff once in a while. That's it. I swear it."

Fennili ignored him, concentrating on his driving. Rossolini watched him without expression, his eyes pitiless.

The sand trail disappeared at a small clearing surrounded by pine trees. They were well out of sight of the highway. There were no houses or other signs of civilization.

The car stopped.

The buttonmen got out of the front and each went to a rear door, which they opened. Fennili drew his automatic and gestured with it. "Out!"

Ball got out. His legs almost buckled as he stood. He was hyperventilating with fear.

Rossolini stood back as Rider slid out and stood up. Rossolini was so busy watching the cunt's legs as her skirt rode up while sliding over the seat that he never noticed the insignificant fact that whereas Rider had previously had his field jacket zipped, it was now hanging open.

"Go over there and sit down and keep your mouth shut, rabbit hunter," he said, pointing with the gun barrel at the base of a pine tree.

Rider went over and sat down.

Rossolini took the woman by the wrist and swung her into Ball. They both went down in a tangle.

"Please," Ball said. "Please."

Rossolini rested his haunches against the Continental's grille, gun cradled in folded arms, where he could watch Fennili work and at the same time keep an eye on the hillbilly. He didn't feature having to run him down through the weeds.

Fennili squatted down in front of the terrified car dealer and his by-now-incoherent secretary. "Now," he said, "listen real careful, asshole. I won't repeat this. About a month ago some friends of ours were driving up from Miami in a green Porsche, license number FL39291. These friends stopped in Bradenton for lunch and, when they came out, guess what? No Porsche. Some greasy, light-fingered, little fucking thief had boosted our friends' car. Can you imagine that?"

Fennili sounded almost indignant, as if he expected Ball to commiserate with him on the sad state of morality nowadays.

Ball's eyes were starting to dart to the left and right with panic. Great silver gobs of sweat stood out on his forehead.

"I knew it, I knew it." Pat Cousins started to whimper.

"You knew what, miss?" Fennili asked gently. When no one answered, he continued, "Now, this particular green Porsche has a lot of sentimental value to these friends of ours, so as a favor to them we sort of kept our eyes open for it, you know? And guess where it turns up?" When no one answered, he grabbed Ball by his styled hair, cocked the automatic, and rammed the muzzle between his bulging eyes. "Guess where it turned up, you motherfucker?" he yelled.

"Oh Jesus," Ball moaned. "Oh Jesus. Muh . . . muh . . . my place, huh? Oh Jesus. Please."

Fennili took the pistol away and rocked back on his heels. "That's right, baby. At your place," he said in a satisfied voice. "Course, we've already had a nice long talk with the greasy fucking thief who ripped it off in the first place. This punk says he turns all his car business at your place. He says he don't know it belongs to such good friends of ours, otherwise he wouldn't touch it. And he says he don't know anything about how much sentimental value this particular green Porsche has. He says he's sorry. So, anyway, soon's we find this car of our friends, we kind of checked it out one night. Looking for all that sentimental value, you know, just to make sure it's the right car. And imagine our disappointment when we can't find any. Sentimental value, I mean. In the trunk." He paused. "Are you digging me, baby?"

"Look," Ball said desperately, "we can make a deal. I've still got it. Stashed." He paused.

Rossolini could see the wheels clicking behind his eyes.

"It's with a friend," Ball said. "I gave it to him to hide for me. Even I don't know exactly where it is. I trust this guy. He'll get it for me anytime I ask for it!"

Rossolini was enjoying himself now. It was in the bag. Either this asshole had the junk or he knew where it was. Either way, as soon as he spilled his guts, they could finish up here and go get it. Shit, it was probably stashed in another car at the lot.

He kept flicking his eyes from Ball to Rider, who was still sitting docilely under his tree. Be done with this before noon, Rossolini thought. He toyed with the idea of asking Fennili about whacking these two turkeys out first and then having a little fun with the chick. The thought brought a flush of heat to his groin. He glanced at the woman, who was whimpering and moaning and showing a lot of good-looking leg.

"I swear I didn't know it belonged to you guys," Ball gasped, with the realization of imminent death in his voice.

Rossolini snickered. His eyes flicked at the hillbilly under the tree, then back to the woman's legs. He started mentally undressing her, growing more excited each second. Eyes back to the hillbilly, back to the legs—warning bells screamed!

The hillbilly was sitting as before, but now his elbows were braced on the inside of his knees and his arms were pointed in a two-handed grip at Rossolini.

A second more and Rider would have tried for a no-reflex shot, putting the round in the side of Rossolini's head directly below and behind the ear, thus severing the medulla oblongata. But Rossolini turned back just as the Ruger Security-Six .357 Magnum was coming into line, so as his eyes widened and his mouth dropped open, Rider just shot him single-action through the head.

The heavy revolver sounded like a cannon in the clearing. Birds fluttered out of the brush in panic as Rossolini took a step forward and fell down, one side of his skull distorted from hydrostatic shock. He died with an erection.

Fennili sprang up and around in panic. By the time he located Rider and thrust the automatic forward in his direction, Rider had ridden out the recoil, recocked the piece, and lined it up on Fennili. He fired, cocked, fired, cocked, fired. Rider liked single action, even at close range.

Each orange muzzle blast punched a new hole in Fennili's silk shirt. His .45 went off, blowing pine needles all over the cuffs of his flared trousers.He sat down with a thump, a stupefied, totally surprised expression on his face. Then his eyes rolled up and he fell over on his side.

Joe Ball was curled up on the ground, head tucked under his arms. Pat Cousins rose slowly from her crouch, face slack with shock. She was beyond hysterics.

Rider stood up also, ears ringing, waiting for the shakes he knew would come.

Rossolini was as dead as his partner, but was quivering and shaking as the nerves in his body ran wild in search of orders from a brain that was no longer working.

Pat Cousins looked down. She and Ball had been directly behind and below Fennili when the three 158-grain jacketed hollowpoint rounds had punched and expanded and buzz-sawed their way through him. The entry wounds were small and neat. The exit wounds were not. Pat and Joe Ball had absorbed most of this fallout. Slowly Pat raised her hands level with her eyes, staring at what they were covered with. And then Pat Cousins freaked out.

II.

Rider sat under the tree, smoking cigarettes with long, deep drags, crushing them out on the ground, and putting the filters in his jacket pocket. His mind was racing. Well, old asshole, you've stepped in the shit again. This time neck-deep. If these guys aren't some kind of undercover cops, that leaves the Mob. The Mafia.

No matter he was trying to work at an honest job. No matter he was a victim of kidnapping and attempted murder and circumstances. Forget self-defense. He could just hear the cops. What were you doing carrying a piece, Mr. Rider? Do you realize it's illegal for an ex-felon to even *own* a gun, Mr. Rider? No fixed address, Mr. Rider? Rider knew, from previous sad experience, that no matter *how* the thing goes down, the guy left standing is always the criminal. Always. Quite a history of violence you have here, Mr. Rider.

Well, fuck it.

He stood up and jammed his revolver into the inside

of his field jacket. He went over to Rossolini and rolled the corpse over so he could get at the wallet, after first drawing on the leather work gloves he'd been carrying in his back pocket.

He looked at the driver's license, hoping desperately he wouldn't find a badge. If he found a badge, he'd had it. No badge. He removed a fifty, two twenties, and a ten and transferred them to his own wallet, which had been in the dead man's jacket. He continued the body search, and was finally satisfied the man was not a cop.

He left Fennili alone. The wallet and money would be soaked with blood, anyway.

He went to the car and looked in. No registration taped to the steering column. He found it in the glove compartment. Car registered to V. Bartoli and Son's Trucking Company. Mafia, then, he thought.

He retrieved the two handguns and threw them on the front seat after decocking the automatic. He went over and nudged Ball with the toe of his work boot. "Let's go, boss."

Ball had been sitting on the ground, shaking his head and rubbing his face with hands he apparently didn't realize were smeared with Fennili's blood. It had mostly dried, though, and had left only faint streaks of red on his cheeks. It looked like rouge.

When Rider spoke, Ball's eyes cleared and his instinct for survival reasserted itself. He stood up, reflexively brushing pine needles off his jacket and pants. He looked around. "Where's Pat?"

"Over there." Rider pointed. "She got to whooping and screaming and running in circles until she got tangled up in one of them briar bushes and fell down. I suggest you round her up and we get the fuck out of here."

Now that he was thinking again, there was nothing Ball wanted more. He wanted *way* out. Somewhere like Tibet.

Between them they got the woman in the car. She was a mess, smeared with blood, her skin scratched and clothes torn from briars. She sat docilely between the two men, hiccupping occasionally.

Rider turned the Lincoln around in the clearing and headed back down the path. At the highway he headed for the car lot.

Ball put his head in his hands, then brushed at his hair, trying to arrange it in some sort of order. "God, I've got to *think*," he said.

"Never mind, boss. I've already done all your thinking for you," Rider said.

"What's that supposed to mean?"

"It means, bossman, that you stupidly ripped off some real heavy dudes and got *my* ass in a big royal sling, along with yours. So it's time for this good ol' boy to head for the hills, and since I don't feel like fooling around a bus station, and since none of that junk you've got on your lot looks like it could make it to Tampa, let alone Tennessee, I think the only decent thing you can do is drive me there." Rider paused. "For services rendered."

"What services?"

"I saved your life, you fucking idiot, and killed two men to do it, *that's* what services."

"You didn't have to start shooting. I could have talked my way out of it."

"Oh shit," Rider said in disgust.

"I knew we shouldn't have fooled with that stuff," Pat said, riveting Ball with red, accusing eyes.

"Don't start, Pat, don't start. I've got to think."

"You'd *better* start thinking," Rider said. "Your ass is in a lot deeper than mine. They don't know me for shit. They know *you*, buddy. All I want you to do is drop me off on your way to Outer Mongolia, which is where you'll be heading if you've got the brains of a piss ant."

"He's right, Joe. We've got to run," Pat replied.

"Ball's Used Cars coming up," Rider announced. "Now, listen up. We pull in. You two go in and wash up the best you can. Bossman gets his damn Mafia horse or coke or whatever the hell it is if he wants it, if it's there at the lot and doesn't take too long. Personally I think he's a damn fool if he does, but that's his business. Then me and gun-shy Pat get in the bossman's 'Vette and head up the highway toward the interstate. Bossman follows in the Lincoln. A mile or so we pull in somewhere and all pile in the 'Vette. We leave the Lincoln and head north."

Ball saw the necessity of not leaving the Lincoln at the car lot, but resented being told to drive it while a hired hand drove *his* baby.

"Fine, but you drive the Lincoln and follow us, Rider," he announced in the old boss tone of voice.

Rider swung the big car into the lot. No customers yet, thank God. "I don't have time to argue, bossman. If you think I'm going to let you two clowns drive off and leave me stranded and broke in a bloodstained Mafiamobile you're fucking crazy. Now, move, dammit!"

Ball didn't argue further. He had a sudden vision of what Fennili and Rossolini had looked like back there, and what was still in Rider's inside coat pocket.

As soon as they were both in the trailer Rider ran around behind it and retrieved his backpack, which had been left there that morning. He put the extra handguns in it and dropped the bundle behind the bucket seats of the 'Vette. Then he went in the trailer. He went in fast, in a crouch, the reloaded revolver in his hand.

Ball was standing by his desk, drying his hands on a paper towel. His face went white. "What's this?"

Rider put the weapon away and shrugged. "Just in case you had a gun stashed in here and got wild ideas."

Pat Cousins was in the bathroom dabbing at her

clothes with a wet towel. "Please," she said. "No more fighting. No more—shooting."

Rider went over to her desk and put his W-2 form in his coat pocket with the cigarette butts. As an afterthought he took the pen also, then wiped the corner of the desk with his gloves. He thought of the doorknob on the trailer, went over, and smeared both knobs. "Hurry it up, dammit!"

As soon as Ball and Pat were as presentable as possible, Rider hustled them out. He wiped the back door handle of the Lincoln, then got behind the wheel of the 'Vette.

Ball's normal assertiveness had been blunted by shock. Without realizing it he found himself in the Lincoln following his grey Corvette toward Lakeland and the interstate. He realized dimly that he wasn't thinking clearly. The tumblers in his brain were turning and clicking at a furious pace, but the usual combinations just weren't there. It was all gibberish. He knew that he was in a quiet state of panic. He squeezed the steering wheel until his knuckles were white. Think, dammit, think.

The problem was easily stated. He had ripped the Mafia off, then been involved in the death of two of their soldiers. They knew his name, they obviously knew where he worked, they probably knew where he lived. They were trying to kill him.

The solution was equally obvious. Run for your life! But that was where his thinking stalled. Run where?

He moaned through clenched teeth. Why in the name of God had he ever gotten involved in this? Why hadn't he simply left that fucking bag of shit alone? If it had still been in the trunk of that Porsche when they checked it, they would simply have taken it, assumed he was unaware of it, and left him alone. Him *and* the car. He could have turned a couple grand on the

Porsche and that would have been the end of it. Jesus, he thought sickly. I must have been crazy.

Rider was in better emotional shape than Ball. Faced with almost the same problem, Rider's thinking went automatically that one vital step beyond Ball's. Instinctively, like a pursued animal, he was heading for his bolt hole. Rider, unlike Ball, knew where to run.

They went by the I-4 overpass and into the outskirts of the city. At the first shopping center Rider turned in and parked. The Lincoln pulled up beside him, and all of them got out.

"We've got to talk," Ball said.

Rider ignored that. He pointed at Ball's car. "You got a clear title to this thing?"

"Sure, it's in the glove box. We need to go someplace and talk. Not my place. A bar, maybe. But we've got to get our shit together. We've got to get the fuck *away* from here!"

"That's what we're fixing to do, bossman. How much money you got?"

From force of habit Ball hesitated, then thought the hell with it. He felt his pocket to make sure his rubber-banded operating roll was there. "Fifteen hundred, two grand, something like that." There was $3,150 in Ball's wad, which he knew perfectly well. Old habits die hard.

Rider accepted the figure. "Okay, that's plenty. Everybody pile in, we're heading out. We'll trade this 'Vette for something a little less gaudy in Georgia."

"Whoa up, hoss," Ball protested. "It might be enough to get you to hillbilly land, but what about me and Pat? What the hell are we supposed to use for money afterward? They're not even looking for you. But they're *after* me, man. I need traveling money."

Rider eyed him. An idea had been trying to break the surface on the drive from the car lot, and now its greedy head cleared the waves. I think maybe I've found me a *real* job, he thought. "What's the proposition, bossman?"

"I need to get to my bank. First National Bank of Lakeland. About nine blocks that way." He pointed toward town.

Ball had weighed the risks. Hell, those two hoods probably hadn't even been missed yet. Odds were they worked out of Tampa, and nobody else would move on him until the bodies or the car was found, or until the hoods failed to report. Surely he had at least until afternoon before anybody started looking for anybody. And he needed that money. His thoughts had solidified to the point that he had a vague outline of what his moves should be. Get the money and run. Head north. Switch cars somewhere, preferably in some out-of-the-way hick town. Dump this trigger-happy hillbilly. Keep going, maybe all the way to Canada, Toronto or someplace like that. Use no credit cards, pay cash for everything. Get some false ID and a job selling cars. Grow a beard.

"Okay, okay," Rider said impatiently. "Let's do it, but let's do it quickly."

It was a tight fit for the three of them in the sports car, something that had not occurred to anybody until now.

Ball got in the driver's seat, Rider in the passenger seat. Rider patted his dirty dungarees and grinned at Pat. "In you go, baby. Try not to squirm around too much."

She gave him a look of disgust and squeezed in on his lap. The roof was too low, forcing her to bend her neck awkwardly. Before they were even out of the shopping center it started to ache. She could feel the gun in Rider's jacket pressing against her back.

As her shock wore off she was becoming furious with Ball. He had had no right to get her mixed up in something like this. No right at all! Her neck hurt, she was terrified, she could smell this nasty bum whose lap she was sitting on. There was blood under her fingernails. She thought of Fennili and almost gagged. It was all Joe's fault!

She had, of course, conveniently forgotten the year of easy living she'd earned collaborating with him in running stolen cars through the lot. A collaboration she had willingly entered into. Her memory was equally fuzzy about the eager greed with which they'd both examined that heavy plastic bag of pure cocaine while visions of Acapulco danced through her head.

For a second there, in the shopping center, she'd considered walking away from it all—calling a cab, going to her apartment, throwing all her clothes and shoes and jewelry in the back seat of her Maverick, and going home to her mother in Gainesville. But only for a second. They would find her there eventually, she knew. They could easily connect her to Ball, and just as easily trace her to her mother's. She remembered Rossolini's eyes and shuddered. For now she was stuck, and would have to ride it out until a better opportunity presented itself. She felt Rider shift under her, easing her weight to a different position. She gritted her teeth.

They traded the Corvette in Daytona Beach. It took no farther than that for the combination of the woman's whining and his own discomfort to convince Ball that there was no practical alternative.

A process of rationalization and common sense forced him to the conclusion that his original idea of dumping the high-profile vehicle in some out-of-the-way whistle-stop was useless, anyway. Surely the omniscient Mafia (in Ball's mind) would have a pipeline into the Motor Vehicle Bureau of any state on the East Coast. Therefore, it was only a matter of days until the pursuers had a make on his new wheels, no matter where he got them.

Don't dick around trying to be too tricky, he thought. Keep trading and keep moving. Drawing his money from the bank had been quick and painless. This current transaction cost them more time and a lot more of Ball's sweat. He was very conscious of the eccentric image they presented. A slightly disheveled but well-dressed couple, obviously from out of town but with no luggage, accompanied by a hippie with a backpack, and trying to make a fast deal at a used-car lot was hard to explain.

After mulling over a number of explanations to casually lay on a lot owner, none of which rang true, Ball in the end used none. They simply drove into a lot on the outskirts of Daytona Beach and told the "I'm a good old honest country boy" owner that they were making an unexpected and necessary trip (very true) north and needed a larger car.

The honest country boy's natural suspicions were allayed by the obviously proper title Ball had and the scent of a quick and large profit.

After a perfunctory haggle over price and a quick check of the new car, Ball returned to the man's cluttered office to complete the necessary paperwork while Rider transferred his pack to the blue '81 Ford LTD.

"Don't forget my toolbox," Ball called out the door while the man was notarizing the title.

Rider unlocked the Corvette trunk. It was empty except for a new spare tire and jack and a red toolbox. On a hunch he opened it after glancing around, his movements hidden from casual observers by the trunk lid. The tray contained the usual assortment of tools, all brand-new and unused, which further confirmed his assessment of Ball's character and life-style. Prick probably ain't had his hands dirty since he was riding a bicycle, he thought. He lifted the tool tray out and was not really surprised to see, instead of more tools, something wrapped in brown paper which filled the box almost to the level of the tray. He worked his finger under a loose flap of the paper and felt smooth plastic over some sort of powder. Wonderful, he thought in sour amusement. He hefted the toolbox, estimating its total weight; then replaced the tool tray, closed the box, and carried it over to the Ford. He toyed with the idea of waiting until Ball came out and then pretending to trip and spill the thing, or putting it on the ground and forgetting it, just to get a rise out of Ball, then decided it wasn't the time for silly games. Pat Cousins, leaning against the fender of the Ford, watched him with ill-concealed tension as he put the toolbox in the trunk and slammed the lid.

"Don't worry, sweetie," he said, "I didn't spill any." She turned her head and ignored him.

They made another stop on the far side of town for gas and oil, and then Ball and Pat went to a Wal-Mart and bought clothes, toilet articles, and some cheap luggage while Rider waited in the car.

When they came out, he sent Ball back in to the sporting-goods section where Ball used his driver's license to purchase a box of .38 Special, a box of .357 Magnum, and a box of .45-caliber Colt automatic-pistol ammunition.

Then they headed north. It was two-thirty in the afternoon.

Winter twilight was fading into darkness as they bypassed Jacksonville, heading west on I-10 for I-75 North. Traffic was not heavy and they made good progress. Ball drove, with Pat in the front seat next to him.

Rider was sprawled across the back seat, drinking beer as he fiddled with the automatic and his own weapon. He put the .45 in his inside coat pocket and the Ruger in his backpack. The .45 fit the pocket better, although he was slightly wary of having to depend on a weapon he had not zeroed in personally.

He popped the top on another beer and lit a cigarette. "Got any idea where you two are going to end up?" he asked the front seat.

"What do you care?" Ball said. "All you've got to do is sit on your ass back there and swill beer until we get to Hicktown. They're not after you. We'll worry about ourselves. Don't sweat it."

"God, let's stop at a motel soon. I've got to have a shower and some food," Pat said.

They ignored her.

Rider drank beer and leaned his arms over the back of the front seat. "You're wrong there, bossman. I *do* sweat it. I'm sincerely concerned that you and this sweet thing make out all right. The reason I'm concerned is that they might not be after me *now* but, if they catch your ass, how long is it gonna be before they squeeze you like a sponge and you start puking up everything you know? From what I saw in the clearing back down the road, not long. I figure you'd sell me down the river before they even asked."

"Well, I guess you better hope real hard we get away," Ball said.

"Bullshit! I'm not hoping shit because I already *know*. You're gonna get caught, baby, you can put that in the bank. I bet I can even guess what you figure on doing."

Rider paused for a swallow of beer. When Ball said nothing he continued.

"Doesn't make any difference *where* you go. Wherever it is, it'll be some big city, because you're a city boy, and you can't live without your shopping centers and central heating and sissy clothes and dry cleaners. You don't even know there *is* anything else but a big city. Just a whole lot of nothing out there, woods and hills and hick towns or something. It's a grey area in your head, just space between the places where all the cool people live. Between the cities."

"So what?"

"So when you get to your city you get a job doing what you know how to do best, which is sticking it so far up the poor man's ass his ears wiggle. In other words, being a used-car salesman. Am I pretty close, bossman?"

"You could be," Ball said, slightly shaken.

"So the idea did occur to you, huh?" Rider asked sarcastically. "Just keep in mind that if this ignorant hick can figure all this complicated shit out, so can the guys you ripped off. And the guys you ripped off, buddy, *live* in the city. They *thrive* in the city, like fucking cockroaches."

He drained his beer, threw the empty on the floor, and ripped another from the sodden paper sack.

It was completely dark now, and signs flickered by in their headlights.

Rider lit another cigarette and leaned over the backrest again. "And I bet the next thing you do, Mr. Ball, sir, is try to turn that bag of shit you got stashed in your toolbox. Which will be really fucking dumb, because you don't know what you're doing. I could hope the locals would just dump you in a ditch after they ripped you off, but I can't count on it. The word might be out on you, and they might just string you along while they called Tampa or Miami for instructions. Those instructions might include finding out how a pussy like you managed to get the best of two experienced soldiers. And then they've got *my* name, and description, and general location, which they might be real interested in for a number of reasons. General principles, maybe. It doesn't show much respect to go around whacking out their people, and I understand that they're real big on respect. So I *do* sweat your plans, Mr. Joe. I sweat them a lot."

Ball's instinct was telling him that all this was leading up to something, but he couldn't figure out what. Just for something to say, he asked, "By the way, what were you doing with a gun this morning? You usually start a new job armed to the teeth?"

Rider laughed and slouched back in the seat. "Maybe I was gonna rob you."

"Guess today just ain't my day," Ball said.

"Actually, bossman, I slept on the beach last night, and I like to keep something handy for sea serpents and stuff. I was planning on pawning it to you until payday. I hadn't got around to unloading it yet."

"Jesus," Ball muttered. He was thinking about coincidence and life and death. They drove in silence for several minutes.

Rider watched the road signs marching by. Ball watched the rearview mirror, his stomach tightening every time a car passed them, his foot tensed to smash down on the brake at the first sign of a gun thrust through a window. Pat Cousins sulked, intermittently demanding that they stop at a motel.

Rider spoke from the darkness of the rear seat. "When they find you, boss, and they will sooner or later, it'll be real easy to take you in the city. You have no real defense, you know. Too damn many people in the city. Strangers coming at you from all sides, crowded sidewalks, dark alleys, hell, you can't watch everybody. Nobody could. One day, after you've started to relax, you'll be coming out of some fancy restaurant and all of a sudden realize somebody's behind you. Whack, a sap over the head, they roll you onto the floorboard, cover you with a rug, and you wake up tied over a barrel in some warehouse with your pants around your ankles while they heat the poker."

"Do you realize how gross you are?" Pat asked.

"Not near as gross as that dago I shot in the head would have been," Rider told her. "The main reason I managed to take them was because he was too busy trying to look up your dress to keep his mind on business. I bet he would have come up with some real interesting games before he used the wire on you."

She had made up her mind to ignore him, but now twisted in the seat to confront the shadowed form.

"Wire?"

She saw the beer can tilt up, lower. "That's right. I found it when I searched him. A garrotte, a piece of piano wire with handles or a loop on each end. A strangling wire. You hold a handle in each hand, then cross your arms to form a loop. You put the loop over the head and pull tight."

He reached in a jacket pocket and there it was, dangling from his hand in an obscene coil.

She stared at the thing, unable to force her gaze away.

"I'm told a strong man can actually cut the head clean off with one of these things," Rider said. "Maybe brown suit was one of them guys who like to choke 'em while he's doing his thing."

"Knock it off, Rider," Ball said in a strained voice. "Please. You keep on and she's going to get hysterical and we don't need that."

"Right." Rider put the garrotte back in his pocket and popped the top on another beer.

Pat stared at Rider for a while, taking deep breaths. Finally she faced forward, staring out the windshield.

Ball drove on in grim silence, thinking about the garrotte, his crotch damp with sweat.

The trucking warehouse on the outskirts of Tampa was closed for the night, its huge rolling doors shut. The parking lot's security lights revealed three luxury cars parked in front of the modern brick office built onto the side of the warehouse.

Inside this building the lights were all on in the rearmost suite of offices.

Bobby Bartoli was mixing his first drink of the day, a rum and Coke in a Styrofoam coffee cup, when the phone on his desk rang.

Al Mewson, one of the firm's numerous lawyers, who was sitting on the corner of Bartoli's desk, picked it up. The two soldiers watching television at the other end of the room turned the volume down and looked around expectantly. Mewson spoke a few quiet words into the instrument, listened a second, then held it out to Bartoli. The eldest son of Vito Bartoli took his drink with him and lowered his considerable bulk into the desk chair, which sighed in pneumatic protest. "Yeah?"

The voice on the other end was terse. "Not good, Mr. Bartoli. We found them about fifteen minutes ago, about eight miles from the car lot, at the end of one of them dirt tracks. Both shot. No sign of the wheels. Somebody took their pieces or threw them in the brush. They ain't around the bodies."

Bartoli's face remained expressionless as he listened. He took a sip of the lukewarm drink, grimacing at the watching men.

"Okay, now listen careful, Tommy. Leave the bodies. Don't fuck with them, it's not worth it. There's nothing on them that can connect us. But we've got to find the wheels. Because they *can* connect the wheels to us, and they might be able to connect the bodies to the wheels. You follow me?"

"Yes, sir!"

"Okay, good. I'm going to send Carmine and Petey and a couple more guys over to help you look. Carmine will have a set of keys that fit Frank's wheels. Look down back roads, look in shopping centers. Check the airport; that's the first place to look. When you find it—uh—wait a minute." Bartoli stuck the phone under his chin and rummaged around on his desk until he came up with a legal pad. "Tommy?"

"Yes, sir."

"Check the lot where fuzzy nuts banks. It's the First National of Lakeland. I don't have the address, you can look it up. When you find the wheels, drive them back here and we'll clean them up if they need it. In the meantime, check that dirt road again, on foot. Make sure you didn't leave any tire tracks or anything."

"No sweat on that, Mr. Bartoli," the voice assured him. "That sand's so fucking loose it just runs back in the tracks. We're cool on that."

"Okay, Tommy. Get to work. Find me those wheels."

"Yes, sir, Mr. B."

Bartoli hung up and took another drink. He looked at the lawyer and the soldiers. "You guys follow that?"

"We follow, Bobby," Mewson said. "The question is who—and why? I don't read Ball like that. You know we tossed his house the other day. No gun collections or kung fu suits. He's nothing but a punk. Started out selling insurance on a debit route in niggertown. Got into the used-car bit, then into the hot-car bit. Hell, the guy even spent his service time in the air force gassing jets in Georgia or something. We're not dealing with some closet commando here."

Bobby Bartoli had taken over the family business from Vito Bartoli less than a year ago. He was well aware that he was on probation, and could almost feel Vito's heavy garlic breath on his neck. He was sure that the old man, supposedly retired and sitting on the beach down in West Palm, had already been informed in minute detail about this latest fuckup. Several pounds of pure-dee uncut coke worth a cool million missing, Christ knows where, and now two of his people whacked-out like common street punks. Pretty soon the cops would be crawling over everything like fucking maggots.

Bartoli was in his early thirties, with a large square body and even features. His expensive dental work and dark curly hair complemented his carefully cultured tan. His clothes were well tailored and in the best of taste. He always made a point of remaining cool and collected. He never yelled at his people or threatened them. But those close to him knew that beneath the cultured veneer Bobby Bartoli was capable of the most extreme viciousness. The giveaway signal was the vein on his neck which began throbbing whenever he was angry or under stress. It was fluttering now, Mewson saw, right next to the obligatory gold chain around Bartoli's throat.

"Okay, then," Mewson said. "Bobby, a few suggestions. First thing in the morning we toss Ball's car lot. We toss it good, all the cars, the trailer, the sandlot in back, everything. There's no reason for any stress from the law, they don't know Ball isn't there, or anything's wrong. We can dress our people up like customers or workmen or something. That sound okay?"

"Yeah, that's cool. We better cover all bases."

Mewson sat down and pulled a notebook from his pocket and began making notes. "Also, we need to get in touch with our contact in the DMV. Even an asshole like this guy Ball isn't stupid enough to stay with his Corvette. He'll trade it, and we need to know who he traded it to."

Bartoli leaned back in his chair and sipped his drink, content for the moment to let someone else work on the fine details. He started to calm down.

"And I'm going to get Porky McConnel on this guy's trail. You remember him? He's the P.I. who used to be a skip tracer up in Jax. That dude can find anybody!"

"Yeah, I know him," Bartoli said. "He does damn good work. Put him on this full-time. With bonus if he comes through."

Mewson paused in his note-taking. "A bonus?"

"You heard me," Bartoli grated. "A big bonus. It ain't even the shit so much anymore, Al. Some motherfucker is dicking with us. I don't know if it's Ball or somebody else, but I'm gonna teach 'em some fucking respect. You can count on it." He tilted his head back to swallow the last of his drink, and Mewson saw that his vein was ticking away again.

III.

By eleven o'clock the adrenaline and the emotional shock had worn off the three fugitives, and mental and physical exhaustion began to take its toll.

They stopped at a Jiffy Market and bought sandwiches and more beer for Rider, then began watching for motels.

Ball was groggy with fatigue, and it took a conscious effort to force his eyes open. Rider was starting to reel from a combination of not enough food and too much beer. Pat Cousins had subsided into dazed silence, half-asleep as she slumped against the door.

They settled for one of those food/gas/lodging complexes somewhere well south of Atlanta on I-75. The buildings were situated on a group of low hills well off the interstate, which gave the two men a reasonable sense of security. The only thing that could be seen by anyone looking for them on the expressway was the large neon sign rearing its orange glow a hundred feet into the night sky.

The gas station and restaurant area were brightly lit and busy with trailer trucks and travelers. There were a substantial number of assorted vehicles parked in front of the two-story motel.

Ball limped stiffly into the office and rented a double on the second floor. They parked the car and carried the pack, food, beer, and new clothes up to the room.

It was a typical middle-class motel room: two double beds, table and chairs, color television chained to the wall, and a large vanity/bathroom area with too many mirrors.

Rider went straight to the bathroom and unloaded his bursting bladder. As he was relieving himself he studied his image in one of the mirrors. The bright fluorescent lights emphasized his scruffiness, the beard and mustache badly in need of attention, the oily hair poking from under the watch cap in untidy clumps, the crow's-feet and faint scars on his forehead and nose, the eyes wide and glassy-looking. Can't wait 'til tomorrow, he thought, because I get better looking every day. He grimaced in disgust, zipped up, and got his pack and threw it on the bed closest to the back of the room. In case they had visitors, the space between the bed and the brick wall might come in handy. Unless, of course, the visitors smashed the big floor-to-ceiling window and threw in a half pound of C-4. Fuck it! He couldn't cover all the possibilities under these circumstances, and he was too damn tired, dirty, and drunk to worry about it.

He sat at the table and ate several sandwiches, washing them down with beer, while Ball and Pat took turns using the shower.

She came out of the bathroom while Ball was shaving at the vanity. Her dark blond hair was plastered to her head and she was wrapped in one of the bedspreads. She looked much younger without makeup.

"Feel better?" Rider asked in a halfhearted attempt to be pleasant. She ignored him. Fuck you, then, he thought. I'll go back to being my usual nasty, ungentlemanly self.

He dug his spare clothes out of his pack and went into the bathroom to shower. He took all the weapons with him, laying them on the closed commode seat and covering them with a towel against the steam. He had no intention of being caught in a shower, deaf from water noise, blind from soap, naked, and unarmed in the bargain.

Pat was sitting on the edge of the bed drying her hair with a motel towel. When Ball was finished in the vanity he collapsed on the other side of the bed with a groan.

Rider came out of the shower in fresh clothes. He shaved, trimmed his beard, and brushed his teeth. Then he replaced his toilet articles and two of the guns in the backpack and finished dressing. He lay on his bed with the automatic and an ashtray next to him, opened a beer, and lit a cigarette.

"What the hell am I supposed to do without a blow dryer?" Pat asked no one in particular. "Or makeup? Or anything?" She swung her legs up on the bed and sat cross-legged, facing Ball. "What are we going to do, Joe?" she whined.

Ball sat up with a tired sigh and lit one of his little cigars, which he had always believed complemented his macho mustache and rugged good looks. Right now he didn't feel so macho. He was scared shitless and confused. All he could think of was to run and keep running. All he wanted to do was sleep, a deep, untroubled sleep in some warm, dark, completely safe place, a place he knew didn't exist. The fear was like a greasy ball of ice in his stomach, a constant state of near nausea, threatening to explode into panic at a knock on the door. And his cigarillo tasted like shit!

"Well?" she asked.

Oh God, he thought. The rent's due, all the kids are sick, we're broke, and you don't have a job. What are we gonna do, you useless bastard? "I don't really know, Pat," he said.

She hugged the spread around her and started a little rocking motion. "I *knew* you shouldn't have fooled with that junk. God, I knew it. I knew it. I knew it."

"Oh shit!" he exploded, suddenly in a rage. "Don't give me that shit! You were right there with me, figuring up how much it was worth, pricing fucking new cars and calling travel agents and shit. I could see the cash register clicking. I could see you drooling, you greedy little bitch. Don't start on me, Pat. Nobody twisted your arm. Don't start on me."

She was groping for an angry retort when Rider yelled, "Shut up, dammit, both of you! Listen to me."

They glared at him with flushed faces. He sat up in bed and swung around to face them, legs crossed. Before they could transfer their anger to him, Rider said, "I've got a proposition!"

"We're not interested in any propositions from you," Pat said, all cranked up for verbal combat.

"Just listen a minute, okay?" Rider replied. "You people have fucked up bad. Doesn't make any difference whose fault it was, what's done is done, and you're both in the same boat, and the boat is sinking. That right?"

Ball was ready to listen to anything. He didn't have to go along with it, but he could listen, and as his brief flare-up of anger faded he welcomed a diversion from Pat's nagging. "Okay, you're right, I guess. We're in trouble, no shit. I'll admit that. What's your idea?"

"The way I see it," Rider said, "you need a place to hide. It's as simple as that. If you keep moving, you leave a trail, you spend money, you get worn out. You need a place where you can go to ground. A place where you can rest, where you can make some plans while things cool down and the trail gets cold."

Two words that Rider had said kept repeating themselves in Ball's mind. The words were *rest* and *plans*. That's what he needed, all right. Some rest and a little time to figure things out. He nodded in agreement and Rider went on, warming to the scenario he had finalized on the drive from Florida.

"You two screwed up, all right, but you lucked out, too. You must have a gold horseshoe up your ass, bossman, because you ran into yours truly, just at the right time. Just in time for me to pull you out of a bad scene down there. And I'm the man with the plan, folks, because I've got the place you can hide out."

"Where?" Pat asked skeptically, but Rider saw she was interested.

"Way the hell and gone up in the hills." He grinned. "Mountains, really. So far back up in the woods they have to pipe sunlight in."

"I don't know," Ball said, but his pulse was starting to speed up. Safety. Plans. Sleep.

"It's cool," Rider said. "Isolated. No people. Or rather, only people I know. Any strangers sniffing around, I'll get the word. You guys couldn't find a better deal if you had a million dollars and connections."

He drank some beer. "Think of this, Joe. All those Mafia people are city guys, just like you. They'll figure you'll head for a city. They'll look for you in the city. Shit, man, it'll never occur to them *not* to look in the city."

Ball said nothing, thinking.

"Did it ever occur to you *not* to go to the city?" Rider asked.

"Okay, I'll think about it," Ball said.

"You do that."

Ball lay back, his mind working. He reached up and turned off his lamp and closed his eyes.

Pat Cousins started to fluff her pillow, then paused. "You always sleep in your boots?" she asked Rider, who had stretched out on his bed.

"Only when I might have to kick my way through a bathroom window on short notice."

A little later, when they were both snoring, Rider finished his beer and turned his own light out. Before he drifted into sleep, a thought presented itself. He reached into his jacket and got the garrotte and put it on the nightstand between the two beds. It wouldn't hurt to have them see it first thing in the morning. Just a reminder of the shit they were in. He wondered if he would ever get around to telling them that he hadn't really found it on Rossolini. It was his own.

After a quick breakfast, they were on the road again before eight o'clock.

Rider hadn't eaten much. He was suffering from a pretty good hangover and was working on a can of V8 juice as they pulled back onto I-75.

The early morning air was much colder this far north, and the sky was dim and grey, promising rain.

Ball switched on the heater and radio. Luckily the heater worked. The radio didn't. After fiddling with the knobs for a while he gave up and settled down to the serious business of building distance between himself and the shadowy threat behind him.

In a little while the car warmed up and Pat Cousins felt her shoulders start to unclench as she relaxed. She turned in the seat to face Rider. "What kind of a house do you have, Mr. Rider?"

Christ, he thought. She picks eight o'clock on a shitty, hung-over morning to start being pleasant. As far as he could remember it was the first time she had spoken to him without whining or hostility. It occurred to him that her motives were less than unselfish.

He regarded her from bloodshot eyes. "It's just a small log cabin. One big room, a shower stall in the back, and a front porch. Pretty humble, I guess. I can guarantee you'll find it inconvenient. But it's safe. I can guarantee that, too."

"Speaking of guarantees," Ball said. "Assuming you remember what you were talking about last night, I've got a couple of questions."

Rider finished his V8 and threw the empty can into the clutter of beer cans and crumpled cigarette packs that had magically accumulated on the back floorboards. He wasn't really ready for this. What he was really ready for was a beer. There were three full cans left from yesterday, but he knew how bad it would look if he started this early. They might get to thinking he was an alcoholic or something, and lose confidence.

Nevertheless, he reasoned, it had been proven in coordination tests, utilizing a Link Trainer, that a mildly intoxicated individual functioned significantly better than one with a hangover. And, anyway, he couldn't think worth a damn like this, and probably couldn't shoot, either. He needed to get his head straight, and that was no shit. He popped a top and chugged half a can before he could change his mind. "Questions? Okay, bossman. Shoot."

"Since your head is probably a little bleary this morning, I'll keep it simple," Ball said. "Assuming we decide to take you up on your offer of a hideout, what's in it for you? What is it going to cost me?"

Rider chocked the rest of the beer down and lit a cigarette. He started coughing, partly from necessity but mostly to stall for time. Coming up for air, he said,

"That's a good question, Joe. Shows you're thinking. What do you think would be fair?"

Now they were on Ball's home ground. Some people have the personality to be successful businessmen and some don't. Ball did. "Well, I figure we'll need at least a month to let things cool down. I don't know what rent on a log cabin runs, but a decent apartment, like the one I have, runs around eight hundred a month. I'll add a little kicker. I'll give you a grand for a month. Okay?"

Rider would have much preferred to postpone this until later, but it had started now, so, so be it. He let a flash of natural anger flush away a good portion of his hangover. "Bullshit, man! B-U-L-L-shit! You shut up and listen to me, and you listen good. All my goddamn life I've been screwed by people like you. Bosses, pawnshop owners, bankers, bondsmen, and, yeah, used-car dealers!"

"Look, if you—"

"Shut up, Joe! I've got something to say, and you shut the fuck up and listen!"

Rider had forgotten the unopened beer in his hand. He threw his half-smoked cigarette on the floor and ground it out savagely. "There's people like you, and there's people like me. People like you run this world, and people like me get screwed. Always! And the difference is that people like me are simple. We don't have those complicated brains all ate up with success and phony facade and money. We don't spend ninety percent of our waking hours dreaming up ways to fuck everybody. We don't have time to practice in front of a mirror smiling and looking sincere. We don't bother perfecting those honest, solid handshakes and hearty backclapping and weasel wording. All we want to do is live decent and drink a little beer and screw the old lady and maybe get stoned and contemplate the stars on a summer night. We say what we mean and stick by our friends and keep our word, and we don't stand a chance with you pushy cocksuckers!"

"Okay, okay, settle down," Ball said, realizing that Rider was working himself into a tirade.

Rider yanked the top off his beer and drank, foam dribbling down his chin. "I'll settle down when I'm finished, Ball. You still think you're back in your car lot but you're not. You aren't paying one hundred dollars for an eight-hundred-dollar car from some poor son-of-a-bitch who's up against it, and then reselling the same damn car for fifteen hundred to another poor son-of-a-bitch. You aren't selling a life-insurance policy to some ignoramus who can't read the fine print. You aren't bonding some screwed-up jerk out of jail on a pure-profit, no-risk deal. You aren't standing behind the counter of a pawnshop telling a guy who's got a wife and five kids stranded in a strange city that all you can loan him on a two-hundred-dollar watch is fifteen dollars. Not today, pal. Not this time. This time we make a fair deal or we don't deal. You keep driving this thing north for another two hundred miles and I'll get out along the side of the road and sayonara, son-of-a-bitch. You take your chances, and I'll take mine. Good luck."

"All right," Ball said. "I'm not selling cars now. I'll admit I need a place to stay for a while. Now that you've got that out of your system, let's settle down and talk business, okay?"

Rider fumbled for his cigarettes and lit one. His hands were shaking. "All right, Joe. It's not out of my system, but okay. I'm not going to get something out of my system in five minutes that's been building up for years. I don't fit in, somehow. All everybody else is interested in is playing the phony, artificial game in order to reap the phony, artificial profits. If that's your bag, fine, but like I said, this time it's gonna be an even deal. I'm not working for field-hand wages, not this time!"

"All I want to do is rent a place for a month," Ball said. "Nobody's talking about working."

"That's where you're wrong. I've *already* worked for *you*. I went to work for you yesterday morning, and I killed two men before nine o'clock. If they find us I might have to kill more. I might get killed myself. We ain't talking about renting a cabin here. We're talking about a *hideout*. We're talking about mercenary work. You went to the big time when you copped that bag of dope, Joe, and you've got to expect to pay more than minimum wage. So quit thinking you're hiring me to vacuum out cars. It's a whole new ball game, man. Get used to it."

Ball sighed. "Okay, Rider, quit bullshitting around. What do you want? Keep in mind I've only got a couple thousand dollars."

"I know what you've got," Rider said. "But I realize you need most of it for operating money when you leave. So all you have to do is buy us some groceries. No cash. You keep it."

"Then, what? The dope?"

"Not all of it. Just a quarter of it," Rider replied. When Ball said nothing, he went on. "I can't turn it any better than you can. But I'm not in a big sweat, either. My life-style isn't predicated on a thousand dollars a week for fancy clothes and hair spray. I can sit on it for years, or deal it a gram at a time. That way, I'll have an income forever. Kind of like a retirement fund."

Ball had long realized that anything he did with the coke would involve skirting the periphery of organized crime, at the very least. The thought of that started the sweat oozing again, and since he had been prepared to bargain all of it away in return for a way out of this nightmare, Rider's price didn't seem unreasonable. "Fine, I'll go along with that. You've got a deal. I buy the food and cut you out a quarter of the coke. We get a place to stay. You stay sober enough to make sure nobody comes nosing around. In a month, we leave. You never heard of us. That it?"

"Except for a few details," Rider said.

"Details?" Pat asked. She had a fleeting thought that he was going to demand bed privileges.

"You get more for your money than a hideout," Rider told them. "If they find us, and that's a possibility we have to consider, then we'll have to fight. In order to do that, I've got to make a few preparations and I'll need some help from you, Joe. Brush clearing, stuff like that."

"I guess," Ball said dubiously.

"No guessing, dammit! We're in this shit together, and we'll need teamwork. I've got to make the place defensible, and that means a little work. Clearing lanes of fire, digging fighting holes, stringing wire. I'm not going to bust my balls while you two sit on your asses."

"He'll help," Pat told Rider. "So will I. I used to be a pretty good cook, back home."

"Okay, okay," Ball answered. "I'll clear brush and dig holes and Ms. Home Ec here can cook and clean up a storm and we'll all live happily ever after. But I said I had a couple of questions for you, and the second question is this: What's to keep us from getting back up in those hills and having an accident? That way you get to keep it all, friend. The dope, the car, the money, all of it. I'll bet people have been known to disappear up there for a hell of a lot less than two thousand dollars and half-mil' worth of drugs."

"I kind of figured that would come up," Rider said, opening another beer. "Look at it this way, troops. Number one, I might be a stone killer, but I'm not into murder."

Nobody said anything.

"There *is* a difference, you know. It might have been all gruesome and traumatic down there in Lakeland, but by God, that is the way violence is. When the killing starts there's gonna be a bloody mess, and I can't help that. But no matter how bad it looked it was *still* self-defense. Those guys were gonna punch our ticket, believe me. It was us or them. I'm not into murder."

"I've got to consider something like that," Ball said. "I hope you understand."

"Anyway," Rider told them, "I need you people. I've got two dead bodies back there and you two are my only proof it was self-defense. You think I'm stupid enough to bury you around *my* turf? If and when any cops come around I need two live talking bodies, not two more corpses. Shit, Ball, give me credit for a little sense."

"Yeah, well, people get greedy," Ball said. "Sometimes they don't think too clear."

"Tell us about it," Pat Cousins muttered.

The Drunken Chief carefully eased his ancient bones into the equally ancient rocking chair. He surveyed the sweep of valley which stretched in descending levels from his front porch to the winding gravel road far below. The gravel road was as grey as the hillsides, where the drabness of winter hardwood and dead wet leaves formed a dreary contrast to dark conifers and patches of snow.

The old Cherokee snugged his handmade blanket tighter against his shrunken shoulders and smelled the air. As grey as the sky was, even a fool of a white man would know that it would soon rain. But none of them could be certain that the rain would turn to snow before dawn. Only an old Indian.

The Drunken Chief chuckled and reached down for the plastic gallon jug by his side. He raised it in both blue-veined, unsteady hands and took a deep drink of the corn whiskey, shuddering with pleasure as it spread runnels of warmth outward from his stomach.

He put the jug down and lifted the German naval binoculars from the nail in the porch post. He focused quickly, as the heavy instrument tired his fragile arms in a very short time. Nothing moved below. No smoke from the dozen or so cheap modular homes and old trailers scattered along the road and half-hidden by the trees. No smoke had risen from them for a long time now. One by one the families who once lived in them had given up and left for the cities and jobs. Now they stood empty, windows smashed in and senselessly vandalized by the same people who had ripped out the plumbing and well pumps.

The only signs that anyone had ever used them for homes were the random rusting corpses of junked and cannibalized cars. The Drunken Chief raised the binoculars slightly. Halfway up the short little valley and separated from the other houses was a projection of fairly level ground which sloped gradually down to the road. A small log cabin, much like the Chief's own, was built there. A rough driveway, prickled with pine stumps, connected the cabin's front yard with the road.

A dented Chevrolet pickup stood sentry duty in front of the porch. It had been covered with a torn and rotten tarp. A front tire was flat. Although this building also appeared abandoned, the Drunken Chief knew this was not so. He knew the Crazy One who lived there would return. Every winter the Crazy One left for better hunting grounds, and every summer he returned to shoot at targets and climb the hills and sit on the porch and drink vast quantities of cheap beer and smoke the leaves of the hemp plants he grew in the woods. Sometimes the Crazy One would have other people at his cabin, and then there would be great leaping bonfires and much shouting and laughter and loud music. But mostly he was alone. Several times the Drunken Chief had seen the Crazy One sitting on his porch, watching the Drunken Chief watch him.

Maybe the Crazy One would come earlier than usual this year, because—

The Drunken Chief lived alone on his mountain, and although he was content to do this, with only the whiskey and his huge color television, sometimes people came. Mostly they were young people, wearing a city white man's idea of outdoor clothing, and sweating under massive loads which they carried on their backs, like mules.

These people always seemed fascinated by the Drunken Chief, and sat around his feet asking stupid questions, like how old he was and had he ever fought the white soldiers. Yes, the Drunken Chief would tell them, he had fought many battles against the soldiers. He never told them the soldiers were Germans and the battles were in a land across the sea. Sometimes, when he had drunk too much corn whiskey, he would tell them other things.

He would tell them of the spirits of the mountain and the wind. He would tell them that he was a man of power, and could see the shape of things to come.

They were always polite and listened, but he could tell that they didn't believe.

The Drunken Chief lowered the binoculars to his lap. It was cold out here, and normally he would have been inside by his fire. But last night he had had a dream.

He had dreamed of fire and blood. He had seen many soldiers and much death. The Drunken Chief had seen a vision of war. He raised the binoculars again, focusing on the cabin of the Crazy One.

Waiting.

IV.

Pat Cousins sat up in the seat, her stomach rolling with motion sickness. She rubbed the sleep from her eyes.

Rider was driving, a cigarette in one hand and a beer between his legs. It was dark out, and the headlights cut a tunnel of brightness through the pitch black of country night.

"Where are we? What time is it?" she croaked.

"It's nighttime, and we're in God's country," Rider told her, wheeling the car around a hairpin curve, tires squealing.

Pat's stomach gave another lurch as she caught a fast glimpse of a steep drop-off to her right. The opposite side of the road offered a view of ancient black cliff, slick with moisture. "God's country," she moaned. Pat Cousins had never been out of Florida except for a two-week vacation in California one summer.

The contrast between glaring level sands and smooth straight roads she was used to, and this . . . this *wagon track* winding and dipping through a dripping, primeval forest truly frightened her. She wished they would at least pass a house so she would know they weren't on Mars. Instead, she saw a sign that said, "Be Careful of Falling Rocks."

"It looks more like Transylvania than God's country," she commented.

"Want some food?" Ball asked from behind her. He dropped a cardboard bucket of fried chicken over the seat.

"No thanks," she said. "I feel like barfing from this roller-coaster ride. *Can't* you slow down a little, Rider?"

"Heading for the barn, ma'am. Never fear, Rider is here. I know what I'm doing."

She saw that he was drunk again. Her acid retort was interrupted violently as he suddenly jammed down the brakes. The car slewed sideways, tires squealing. She had been turned sideways in the seat, facing Rider, so her shoulder took the punishment as it slammed into the padded dashboard. Ball came lunging halfway over the backrest. "Jesus Christ!" he sputtered.

"Sorry about that, folks," Rider said. He eased the car onto the shoulder and around a forty-foot pine tree, which was stretched across the right-of-way. "When it rains a lot, or freezes and thaws, the banks get soft and the trees along the road fall down sometimes," he said.

"Jesus Christ!" Ball snapped. "Look out for the rocks! Look out for the trees! What else do we have to watch out for? Flash floods? Jesus Christ!"

Rider's adrenaline had surged from the near miss. It was mixing just fine with the alcohol. "Oh, quit complaining. Hell, I spilled beer all over my lap, and I'm not complaining. And anyway, did you see those reflexes? I bet you people didn't even *see* the goddamn thing."

"Just slow the fuck down a little, okay?" Ball mumbled. He was beginning to regret letting Rider take over the driving.

They went by a small community, several houses and a combination gas station and country store. The lights were all on, and Pat glanced at her watch in the glow. Seven o'clock.

"How much farther?"

"Sixteen miles," Rider said without hesitation. "Anybody need anything? Cigarettes, chewing gum, Tampax? Last chance until tomorrow. We'll go shopping then."

"I guess not," Ball said.

Presently they turned left onto a narrow steel bridge which spanned a wide, shallow river. They could see rapids glowing against the blackness of water. Another store, apparently closed for the winter, advertised rafts for rent. Everything looked cold. "Hiwassee River," Rider said in a tourist-guide voice. "People come from all over the world to ride these rapids. This is where they filmed *Deliverance*."

"Bullshit," Ball snorted. "They filmed that on some river in Georgia. That's a fact."

"Well, they should have filmed it here. Shows they're all ignorant bastards."

"How much farther?" Pat asked again, rubbing her shoulder.

The road began to have more uphill than downhill. It got rougher, the car's suspension taking greater punishment. At some point, everybody's ears popped. The rain started again, a fine mist at first, which soon turned to hominy snow, glinting tiny particles which flashed back into the headlights.

Rider turned the car again, over a small concrete bridge and onto a narrow gravel and mud road. There was more mud than gravel. They went several miles, twisting and climbing constantly. Occasionally the tires spun briefly. "City car," Rider muttered. He stopped the car at a level stretch and got out, slamming the door.

Ball cracked his door, flinching at the bitter mountain air which swirled in. "What's wrong?" he shouted.

Rider was at the back of the car, legs spread. "Prostate trouble," he said, throwing his empty can into the bushes.

"How much farther?"

Rider zipped up and came back, his collar turned up against the blowing snow. He was grinning. He pointed at a level section cut out of the low dirt bank. "That's my driveway. We're here."

The Drunken Chief was watching television. He was watching Bo and Luke Duke exceed the speed limit, run stop signs, operate a motor vehicle in a reckless manner, force police cars into lakes, and leap huge chasms, all without getting arrested, getting killed, or even losing their license. He laughed a lot. The only show he enjoyed more was *The A-Team*, a series about a group of professional mercenaries who were always screwing up and getting captured by the bad guys so they could escape by converting a farm tractor into an M1 battle tank with welding machines that were always conveniently at hand. The Drunken Chief had once seen a few Tiger tanks, so he could appreciate the realism of that. Sometimes he wondered why no one was ever hurt during the obligatory car chase, with all that automatic gunfire spraying and ricocheting around the city streets, but he didn't wonder much. Surely the people who made the shows knew what they were about. Maybe all the people went inside at a certain time of day so the police and gangsters and commandos could chase and shoot at each other.

The Drunken Chief didn't know, and he didn't really care. He just enjoyed comedy shows on television.

Suddenly, in the middle of a belly laugh, he stopped

and raised his head, like a wild animal that has caught a strange scent. He sat motionless for a moment, then slowly got up and pulled his blanket around him. He limped to the door, removed the bar, and pulled it open.

The valley below him was a void of darkness except for the glow of headlights, muted by a curtain of falling snow. A car, stopped in the road by the Crazy One's cabin.

The Drunken Chief smiled. Let the young, polite ones scoff. Let them think he was a foolish old Indian. Was he not really a man of power?

Had he not had a dream?

Porky McConnel was tired. His rump hurt from too much time in office chairs and car seats. His belt cut into his sagging, massive stomach, which was growling with indigestion. He blinked his eyes against the glare of night traffic and sighed with exhaustion.

His people, well, Bartoli's people, had found the Corvette earlier that evening. It was simple, really. All it had needed was manpower and money. Operating from his office in downtown Tampa, McConnel had tacked a huge road map of Florida on one wall.

Anyone with the Mob after them and any sense at all, he reasoned, would head north. East and west was ocean, south was Mob country, pure and simple. Ball would realize this. Hell, he had to go north. But where would he ditch the Corvette? Once out of Florida, it was a whole new ballgame. Then he could point his scared-shitless ass in any direction, and Porky McConnel would have had to work for his money. But Ball hadn't. Instead, he had stupidly traded the conspicuous grey Corvette while still in the state.

McConnel had spent the entire day in his office, coordinating the search by telephone, sticking colored pins in his map as the negative reports came in. When you mean to cover ground, you use the interstate. From Lakeland you could go northeast and pick up I-95 at Daytona Beach, or west and get on I-75 at Tampa.

If you need to trade cars in a hurry, you go to a used-car dealer or a new-car dealer who handles used ones. You don't get off the expressway and drive thirty miles on secondary roads looking for one, either. You take a downtown city exit and get on one of the main drags, which are lined with dealerships. You pull into the first one you see, make a quick trade at a loss, and get back on the interstate. It was simple, really.

Put two guys in a car, one to drive, one to look. Send several teams east and several more west, with instructions to follow the interstate, taking exit ramps at all major cities and towns. Cruise a mile or so down each thoroughfare, looking, then cruise back checking out the opposite side of the street. There were a lot of towns along the interstate, and a lot of used-car dealers, but the thing had been accomplished before dark on the same day.

Of course, it had been a long shot. There was a large amount of luck involved. Ball could have purposely picked a dealership in an out-of-the-way place miles from the interstate. Or he might have decided not to trade at all, although that was highly unlikely, as McConnel now knew: it must have been pretty crowded with three of them in a Corvette.

If nothing had turned up by the close of business this evening, he had been prepared to institute a phone search in the morning, having the callers request information on a 1983 grey Corvette from every dealership in the state. But something *had* turned up. Money and manpower, he thought with satisfaction as he took the exit ramp for Sea Wind Avenue, only a mile from Bartoli's office and his scene of triumph.

All detective work—police, private, insurance, or

whatever—was basically legwork. Sure there were tricks of the trade, shortcuts and connections, but basically it was legwork. Given unlimited manpower and a little luck, miracles could be accomplished. Bartoli had furnished the manpower and Dame Fortune had provided luck in abundance.

He had driven to Daytona Beach, racing against the car lot's closing time, mentally rehearsing his cover story for a detailed search of the 'Vette. He decided to use his Insurance Investigators ID and a fifty-dollar bill, but it hadn't been necessary. Thinking he was just a customer, the dealer had been eagerly accommodating. When he popped the trunk lid to demonstrate the absence of saltwater rust, McConnel had spotted the slip of paper immediately. A glance at it and a few minutes' casual conversation with the man had been enough. Ball and a good-looking woman. And some scruffy dude with a hillbilly accent. A Tennessee accent, the owner had assured him, proud of his ability to recognize regional dialects, having become accustomed to matching them with license plates.

McConnel pulled into the Bartoli and Son's parking lot. The lights in the office were burning, as expected. He patted his breast pocket in reassurance. The paper was still there, as he knew it would be. The paper that was going to earn him a generous bonus for services rendered. A W-2 employee deduction form, with a name and address on it.

A Tennessee address.

V.

Rider woke a little after daylight. It was very cold. He had been too drunk and tired last night to fool with splitting kindling and prying the frozen logs from the woodpile outside.

Ball and the woman had collapsed in Rider's double bed without bothering to undress. Now they were two motionless lumps under a huge pile of quilts. The only thing Rider could see when he looked across the single large room was a small bit of Pat's blond hair poking like a rooster tail from under the covers.

Rider grimaced as he threw the sleeping bag aside and swung to a sitting position on the old couch. His head was splitting and his mouth tasted foul from cigarettes. He could see his breath and, although he was longing for a drink of water, he knew that whatever water he had left when he went to Florida would be frozen solid in the milk jugs outside. He dressed quickly and took a hatchet and ax from behind the huge, old-fashioned wood cookstove that squatted against the back wall.

He went onto the porch and urinated, shivering. The ground was covered with a light drifting of snow. He raised bleary eyes halfway up the steep side of the foothills which blocked the end of the valley and saw a thin plume of smoke drifting from the Chief's cabin. I'm back early, you old bastard, he thought by way of greeting.

He split kindling and pried a number of red-oak logs from the pile and carried them inside. When the fire was roaring, he put several of his plastic water jugs by the stove to thaw, then found a bottle of aspirin and washed four of them down with the can of beer he had slept with.

By the time Pat woke up, the cabin was warm and Rider had thawed enough water to make coffee. He had also managed to thaw his last three cans of beer. Pat sat up in the bed, hair tousled and eyes puffy. "Do I smell coffee?"

Rider nodded toward the stove. "Over there. Give Sleeping Beauty a shake. It's ten o'clock and we've got to get to town. I'm starved and the cupboard is bare."

While they were getting ready, Rider went outside and got a shovel from under the house, which was built on cinder-block piers. He went to the rear of the building and a short way down the slope opposite the road and began digging. The ground was frozen only on the surface, and he had no trouble breaking through to the fifty-five-gallon drum buried horizontally in the side of the hill. He cleared the dirt from the lid and removed it.

When he came inside, Ball was sitting on the side of the bed, drinking coffee and looking grumpy. Pat was brushing her short hair in front of the camping mirror on the wall.

"Where's the john?" she asked.

Rider grinned. He had been anticipating this. He dumped his blanket-wrapped bundle on the couch and put the .50-caliber ammunition box on the floor next to it. "Out the door, off the porch, and sixty paces to the left. You can't miss it."

She looked at him, confused. "I beg your pardon?"

Rider took her by the elbow and led her out the front door. Standing on the porch, he turned her in the right direction and pointed.

"Oh Lord," Pat said in a small voice.

"Look at it this way," Rider said. "No pipes to freeze. No water bill. And cold like it is, no smell. Summertime I have to use wood ashes for the smell."

After watching her carefully thread her way down the icy path, tottering on the stylish high-heeled boots, he forced his way past the cold-stiffened tarp over the pickup and, after several attempts, succeeded in jerking the door open. He was not particularly surprised when the motor would not turn over. He got out and manhandled the heavy canvas off the truck and raised the hood. He went back inside and opened another can of beer.

Ball was standing with his back to the stove. He eyed the beer in Rider's hand and looked at his watch. "Jesus Christ, fella, at ten-thirty in the morning?"

Rider drank some beer. "If you take it like medicine, it's all right. Don't sweat it, boss. I need the keys to the car. You can change a flat tire when you get warm."

Ball tossed him the keys. "Going somewhere?"

"I need to jump my truck so we can get to town," Rider said. "Unless you want to starve to death. I'm not a great hunter."

"Why don't we just take the goddamn car?" Ball asked irritably.

"Because the goddamn car is big and shiny and *strange*, that's why. This is a little country town. All people got to do all day long is sit outside the store and gossip. I pull in there in a big fancy car with a rich city guy and a classy woman, they'll have plenty to gossip about, all right. Anybody comes nosing around, all they'll have to do is buy one of the local yokels *one* damn beer and they'll know exactly how many bugs are smashed in the grille and what color Pat's eyes are. Good God, Ball, think a little."

"How the hell are they supposed to find us, anyway, if this . . . this *chateau* is so far back in the woods like you told us?" Ball said, spilling coffee as he swept his arm to indicate the room.

Rider avoided Ball's eyes by taking another drink. "Shit, I don't know. But this is serious business, so let's act serious, okay? We just don't take any unnecessary chances, is all I'm saying."

When Ball didn't answer, he took the opportunity and went outside. Pat Cousins was coming back from the outhouse, looking miserable. Rider cranked the Ford, which they had left in the road, and coaxed it up the steep driveway. He attached jumper cables between the vehicles and after some trouble got the pickup running. While it was warming up he went inside and unwrapped the bundle on the couch.

Ball came in, washed his hands, and poured himself another cup of coffee. He and Pat watched as Rider removed the weapons, wiped them with an oily rag, and loaded them from the ammo box. He put the shotgun and rifle under the bed and inserted a thirty-round magazine in the M2 carbine, seating it with a sharp tap.

"Is all this necessary just to go to *town?*" Pat asked.

Rider produced a Bianchi shoulder holster from under the couch and put it on. "Baby, I go to town armed when the Mafia *isn't* after me." He jammed the Magnum in the holster and put his field jacket on, putting the .45 in the side pocket, picked up the carbine, and grinned at them. "Ready to go shopping?"

"All you got to do, Tommy," Bartoli said, "is get up there to this town. Rent a motel room. Get you some clothes like the locals wear. Go to the post office, give them a song and dance about how you are thinking about buying some land that was advertised in the paper. Find out where it is. Is it a good neighborhood, that kind of shit. Be smooth."

"Yes, sir," Tommy Bocca said. He was sitting in the chair by Mr. Bartoli's desk, outwardly calm, his hands resting in his lap, fingers intertwined. Inwardly he was seething with excitement. He wanted a drink. He needed a cigarette desperately. This was the big chance. Years of skirting on the edge of the big time, running errands, collecting drops, all the odd jobs. Breaking a leg here and there on welchers and all that petty shit. But no more. This was the big time. When this was over, it would all be different.

Tommy knew he'd handled the Fennili-Rossolini business cool, and because he had he was getting a chance to really prove himself. If he pulled this one off, no more gopher work for Tommy Bocca! He snapped out of his daydream.

"I'm sending Pete Tammi and Johnny Blue Eyes with you," Bartoli was saying. "But you'll be in charge, Tommy. You know what you got to do. You're clear on that?"

"Oh, yes, sir. What I do, I locate these people. They live out in the country, so we slide in there and take them. We search the car and we search the grounds for the stuff. If we can't find it, we use the pliers. When they tell us where it is, we dump them and split. We go to Knoxville and drop the car and iron at, uh, River Salvage, then catch the plane back."

Bartoli got up from behind his desk and picked up a small expensive suitcase, which had been resting by his leg. He put it by Tommy Bocca's chair. "Bring the coke back in this. You put the suits on at the junkyard. I don't have to tell you not to get nervous about dope as long as you aren't at an airport of entry."

Tommy laughed. "No, sir. As long as we ain't got iron we can carry anything, long as we look respectable and got credit cards."

Bartoli extended his hand. "Gene's got your iron in the shop, along with a suitcase to carry it in. The pistols can't be traced. They're already taped to be on the safe side. So—good luck, son. Do me a job!"

Tommy took the extended hand in a firm grip. "Yes, sir, Mr. Bart, we will. I won't let you down." He picked up the suitcase and left, his heart thudding with anticipation and determination.

Bartoli made himself a drink and sat back down behind his desk. There was no way on God's earth they could trace anything back to him. Once more, he ticked the items off on his large blunt fingers.

Tommy Bocca and associates could not be connected to him. If they were caught, they would never (*never*) talk.

All the weapons, which had originally been stolen from armories, were untraceable and, anyway, as soon as the job was finished they would be turned into lumps of slag by the cutting torches of River Salvage, Inc. The car the team would use had been purchased in Miami by an Argentine businessman. From Argentina it had been shipped back to Miami. All factory registration numbers had then been further confused by more experts. Bartoli's friends always had vehicles and weapons laid back for little emergencies like this.

He took a swallow of his drink. He was covered from asshole to appetite, he thought with satisfaction. If the worst happened and Tommy fucked up, well, he just fucked up, is all. Bartoli was still cool. But no way Tommy was gonna fuck up.

Bartoli raised the blotter on his desk and slid the W-2 form out and smiled. How cool can a guy be, leaving his name and address right where somebody can find it? This hillbilly asshole, whoever he was, was in for a rude surprise, by God.

What could possibly go wrong?

It was thirty-two miles round-trip to town and they made it back by two o'clock. While Pat and Ball put away groceries, Rider went down the road and filled his water jugs at the spring, which ran into an ancient rusted iron cistern sunk into the side of the hill below his cabin.

It had turned into a beautiful day, the sky clear and blue. The light snow had melted, turning the road to a paste of mud. It was almost warm out, and Rider breathed deeply of the clear mountain air as he loaded the heavy containers into the truck. When he got back, Ball helped him carry them to the porch.

Pat was warming a frying pan on the stove. "I've never cooked like this before," she said, slicing a tube of sausage.

"You'll learn quick enough," Rider told her. He poured lemonade mix into a gallon jug of water, added sugar, and shook it. When he saw Ball watching in distaste, he picked up the other plastic jug and snapped it with his index finger. Beads of alcohol, visible through the thin white plastic, coursed to the top. "Mixes good with moonshine," he told Ball.

Ball, who was becoming more paranoid with each beer his host and erstwhile bodyguard drank, groaned. "Where in Christ's name did you get that?"

"Found it by the spring," Rider said. Actually this was the truth. It had been sunk at the bottom of the cistern, icy cold in the running water. Rider had left his twenty-dollar bill under a flat rock, silently thanking the Drunken Chief, whom he had never met. Once he had taken his jug and sat on the rock, drunk until morning, waiting on the old Indian. The Drunken Chief had never shown up for his money. Rider had staggered up the road, cussing him for an unsociable old bastard who deserved to die alone. Now he went outside and sat on the steps working on his drink and enjoying the weather.

Fuck the city, he thought, listening to the silence. A few birds fluttered in scrub brush. Far above, a crow barked over a distant winter cornfield. Water dripped from the back of the cabin. "Let them come," he mused. "There is no way they can move unless I hear them." In this he was right. City people do not realize how quiet the woods are. There is noise, but it is *familiar* noise.

And there is only so much familiar noise. Birds. The small rustling business of animals. In extreme cold the crack of frozen trees popping. In autumn huge stiff leaves fluttering to the ground. But all familiar—all of it. And the ear gets used to these noises, ignoring them.

But let a car drift down the hill, motor off, in clear air. The crunch of tires on gravel carries for miles. Let an intruder cough on a still morning, or breech a weapon. Let someone stumble and curse. As the animals knew, and Rider knew, you don't look. Or even smell. You listen to the silence.

He drank his moonshine.

After they ate, Rider showed them how to work the faucet connected to the rain drums in back of the cabin, and after Ball and the woman had used the antique tub, Rider heated his own water and bathed. Then he pulled a battered steamer trunk from under the bed and got dressed.

When he came out on the porch they stared at him, in the early evening light, amazed.

"My God!" Pat Cousins said.

Rider was wearing army-issue camouflage. A web belt, loaded with extra magazines for the carbine, encircled his waist. The revolver was in the shoulder holster, overlapping the assault suspenders, with the attached combat knife riding upside down on the right shoulder. "Never fear, Rider's here," he said.

Feeling more foolish as they continued staring at him, Rider mixed a drink of shine and lemonade and sat down on a plastic milk crate. "Might as well be ready," he said. "How the fuck am I supposed to be dressed? In a goddamn business suit? With sissy city shoes? In a tie?"

"It's just . . . well, *unusual*," Pat said.

"This ain't a *usual* situation. We're in the country, and we could be in a combat situation at any time. What am I supposed to do, wait until they pull up out front and then go inside and gear up while they wait?"

Pat could see Rider's embarrassment. "It's okay," she said, "I understand."

"Hell, no, you don't. If we got to go to war this is the shit to do it in. This is my poaching gear, but it works for war, too. Blends with the terrain. Damn near invisible at night. Don't shine." He pointed to the web gear, sloshing his drink. "Everything's here where I need it. No fumbling around in the dark. No falling out. Just snap and it's in my hand." He propped the rifle back in the corner and snaked the knife from the shoulder rig. A quiet pop and ten inches of 440C stainless-steel, Teflon-coated blade gleamed softly in the evening sun.

They stared at it.

"It's like a goddamn razor," Rider said. He stood there a few seconds. When nobody said anything he replaced the knife and sat down. "Fuck you," he told them. "Kiss my ass." He sat there and worked on his drink, keeping guard. After a while, they both went back inside.

Rider sat on the steps of the porch, rifle between his legs. It was getting cold, but not nearly as cold as last night. He could see his breath, and stars sprinkled the depthless sky. A hunting moon was coming up over the ridge to his right. He had the portable radio playing softly. He killed the last of a coffee cup of mix and was trying to muster enough energy to get a refill when he heard a log thump into the stove.

The door opened and closed, and Pat Cousins came out, bundled in her inadequate coat. She sat down on the step next to him. He saw she had a coffee cup of her own. "Pretty good stuff once you get used to it," she said.

"You'll be sorry in the morning."

"I might not live 'til morning."

"Oh hell, I imagine you will," Rider said. He got up, went inside, and mixed another drink. When he came back he noticed a lump in one of his voluminous pockets. Investigating, he found a Baggie of last summer's grass, rolled together with several withered papers. "Well, no shit. What we got here?"

After Rider fumbled the dry grass around for a while Pat took it from him and rolled a joint. "Do you really think they'll find us?" she asked between drags.

"Don't know," Rider said, hacking on the harsh smoke.

"God, I'm scared. I've never seen anybody die like that." She took another drag. "I've never seen *anybody* die. I'm not ready for this, man." She began to cry.

"People die every day," Rider said. "Most of it's enough to gag a maggot on a gut wagon."

"I know! I saw it, goddamn you! I don't want to hear about it! I don't want to see your fucking knife, either!"

"Sorry," Rider said.

"I just want to go home," she said miserably, tossing the wasted roach into the yard. After a while, she wiped her nose on the back of her hand. "I burned half your sausage, you know? The stove gets too hot."

"Don't worry," Rider replied. "Ball can afford a little sausage while you're learning."

"Who lives in the house up there with the light on?"

Rider cleared his throat. "That's the Drunken Chief. That's where your booze came from."

She looked up at the hill awhile. "Do you really like it up here? It's so *quiet!*"

"It's supposed to be quiet. I can stand the quiet because I don't have to put up with any city bullshit. I don't have to cut my grass unless I feel like it. I can drag any kind of junk I want into my yard and park it there until the next fucking ice age. I can target-practice anyplace I feel like it. I can get drunk and bay at the moon if I want. I can pee in a ditch when I need to, instead of running around with my bladder bursting, kissing some son-of-a-bitch's ass to use his nasty bathroom."

He leaned back against the porch post and watched her a minute, studying the pixie sort of face framed in the short blond hair. He found her eyes particularly attractive, not so much for the brown color, but because they had a slight downslant, almost a reversed Oriental look. "You know," he said, "you're a fine-looking female, Pat. It's a shame you're such an asshole."

She rounded on him, "And you wouldn't be too bad-looking if you had some teeth!"

Ready for battle, she was surprised when Rider threw back his head, laughing in honest delight. "Keep coming up with stuff like that and I'll have to change my mind."

"You've lost me, sport," she grumbled.

"Hell, woman, you came at me from the left flank on that one. You were supposed to get all ladylike and insulted, like you get most of the time. Instead you shot me down. Maybe there's hope for you yet."

"What's so awful about being a lady?" she asked.

"Not a thing wrong with it, if you *are* a lady. But most of you people are fucking guys for money. Pure and simple. I don't care if you marry a doctor or just shack up with somebody because he's got a nice pad and a shiny car. It's still basically for *money,* which makes you a guess what?"

"Now wait just a goddamn minute, buster!"

"And then," Rider continued, warming to his subject, "you work at some gravy job, making more money than you're worth because your ass looks good. Generally, for some outfit that makes its money ripping off the public. Insurance agencies, loan companies, banks, used-car dealers. That makes you at least unethical, if not crooked."

"The hell with you, Rider." She stood up, face tight with anger.

"And then you have the gall to ride around in a fancy car with your nose stuck up in the air, like you was a *lady* or something. Which makes you a phony."

"You're weird, you know that?" she said, turning to the door.

"So what we end up with is a phony, crooked, uppity whore," Rider told her retreating backside.

She slammed the door on him. He sat there, drunkenly pleased with himself, even though he knew he'd blown a possibly pleasant relationship. He really didn't give a shit.

VI.

Tommy Bocca was driving. Pete Tammi was sitting next to him, fiddling with the Mossberg riot gun. Johnny "Blue Eyes" Avilla was riding in the back seat, the M16 cradled in his lap, smoking and looking out the window. The twisting, roller-coaster road was making him sick to his stomach. He cracked a rear window, letting the cold air blow against his face.

"There it is," Pete Tammi said as they topped a rise and saw the country store squatting where the road forked. He consulted the paper with its crudely drawn map. "Bear left here."

Bocca swung the Pontiac station wagon past the cinder-block building, eyeing the structure. The green paint was old and faded. The front of the place boasted a sagging porch roof over a chipped and grease-stained concrete pad, which was littered with a lawn mower and a variety of rusting farm equipment. Faded metal signs advertising different brands of soft drinks and chewing tobacco were tacked up haphazardly. The only signs of life were two mangy-looking dogs which lolled on the ground in front of the porch. They raised their heads tiredly as the vehicle swept past.

"A real fucking supermarket," Tammi sneered. He consulted the map the woman at the post office had obligingly sketched out for him a little while ago.

They had arrived in the small town early the previous evening, only to discover that there were no motels there. The jerk they had asked at the one gas station that was open had laughed at them. That, and having to drive an additional thirty miles to find one, had not sweetened them on life.

After checking in at a Ramada Inn, they had located a Wal-Mart, where they all bought work clothes, hunting boots, and heavy jackets.

They had driven back to the whistle-stop early this morning, parking in front of the post office, waiting for it to open.

"Why, I guess that's the Bullet Creek community you want," the old postmistress had told Tammi. "Not many people up there no more."

"Really? Why not?"

"No work," she answered. "People can't pay on their houses, they go where the work is. It sure ain't around here." She'd ripped a sheet of paper from a pad on the counter and had drawn him a map to Rural Route 1.

Now, looking at it, Tammi said, "Supposed to be another country store, closed up, six miles on the left, right at the top of a long hill. We pass that, go another mile or so, then take a right over a little concrete bridge. Supposed to be a sign there says 'Bullet Creek Baptist Church.' Church is closed, too."

Bocca grunted. The unaccustomed wool shirt he was wearing was scratching the back of his neck, and he was nervous. These two clowns hadn't seen what Fennili and Rossolini had looked like, but he had. And he kept noticing the signs.

He cleared his throat. "Okay, here's how we work this. I don't know nothing about the layout of this place, so when we get on this Route 1 thing, you guys look sharp, but don't stare. Just look casual, right?"

"Got it," Johnny Blue Eyes said.

"I wanna locate this place first. I wanna drive past and size it up. There should be a mailbox with a name on it. Or look for the car they got in Daytona."

Pete Tammi glanced at his watch. "Shit, it's only nine-thirty. They might still be crashin'."

They went by the last store, on the left where it was supposed to be, then slowed, searching for the turnoff.

"Shit," Johnny Avilla said suddenly, breaking a tense silence. "This'll be a milk run. No cops or other people to worry about, like in town. Just us and them, and they won't know what hit 'em."

Tommy Bocca sincerely hoped so. He had almost convinced himself that there was no other way it could possibly go, when he saw another sign.

This one was like the rest, a large, diamond-shaped, faded-yellow road sign, its heavy steel dented and dimpled and punctured by every kind of small-arms ammunition sold in the Free World. This particular specimen had an added fillip. Someone had leaned out of a car window and placed a 12-gauge rifle slug dead through its center. The hole was a good one and a half inches in diameter, its jagged edges curled out the back. Tommy Bocca's stomach tightened convulsively.

Pat Cousins sat on the side of the bed, putting on her shoes and shivering from the morning chill. The fire had gone out sometime in the night. Ball lay on the other side of the bed, an anonymous heap of blankets, snoring. She tied her laces and glanced over at Rider, who was sprawled on the couch with the carbine propped against his leg. His feet stuck out from under the sleeping bag in a totally relaxed sprawl.

"Jesus," she said. "My two manly protectors." She hadn't been able to take the pounding headache another minute. Her mouth had a funny, unpleasant taste, and something was wrong with her eyes. Everything was sliding into everything else in a subtle, disconcerting manner. All she could think of was some exercise. She washed two aspirin down with a glass of spring water, shrugged into her coat, and went outside.

The valley was damp and still, the dark green mountains rearing fog-shrouded above the road. A thin grey finger of smoke wound from the Drunken Chief's cabin, remote in the quiet morning air. She went down the driveway and started walking toward the cistern, her feet crunching the gravel. Somewhere, far off, a dog began barking.

"There it is!" Pete Tammi exclaimed. It wasn't hard to miss, being the first house they had seen since passing the church.

Tommy Bocca had a fleeting, peripheral vision of a log cabin, up on a hill to his left, with a pickup truck and the target car parked in front. "Got it," he snapped. From what he had seen, it looked quiet. No movement.

They would drive on past for a mile or so and park. He would think the situation over. Maybe they would drive back up, park again, and sneak through the brush. Kick the fucking door in and take them. He thought of dogs. "Anybody see any dogs?"

"Naw," Johnny Avilla said.

"Didn't see none," Pete Tammi agreed.

But maybe dogs were there, anyway. Laid up under the house or something. Maybe they'd drive past again, after a while, and lay some real plans. Finding the actual place was a big step. Or they could come back, power up into the driveway, and barrel out, come crashing in. Couldn't be many people there, not with just the car and a pickup.

Plans were flashing through Bocca's brain as he drove, possibilities and probabilities and problems. He'd just made up his mind to play it cool, to park farther down and give the deal some real thought, when he saw, with sudden clarity, that it wasn't going to be possible. The road came to an obvious dead end less than five hundred yards farther on. And he realized, without looking, that their car was visible from the cabin—the entire length of it.

"Look," Tammi said, leaning forward.

Almost at the end of the road, alongside what appeared to be an old watering trough sunk into the hillside, was the unmistakable figure of a woman, striding briskly along.

Bocca knew instinctively that it was the woman they were after. Effectively boxed between the unknown enemies on the hill behind him and the single female enemy in front, his foot made the choice before he had time to think. "Get her," he barked, the car picking up speed.

She looked around, face going slack with a half awareness of what was happening as the vehicle skidded to a stop behind her. She started to run.

Johnny Avilla threw his rifle on the seat and was out the door before the car had stopped moving. He caught her at the edge of the road, jerking her back from the briars she was tangled in, and rabbit-punched her behind the ear. She sagged, momentarily stunned. He grabbed her by the coat collar and threw her sprawling into the back seat. As soon as Avilla piled in on top of the girl, Bocca rocketed the car forward with enough violence to slam the door shut. He slid to a stop at the end of the road and began backing and filling, trying to turn the heavy machine.

His mind was racing now. It was happening too fast,

and it wasn't his fault. He would have preferred to think the thing over, make a leisurely approach, with all the odds on his side. But here he was, exposed to them on the hill, with the bitch flopping around in the back seat. He wanted to stop and slap her silly, find out who was in the cabin and what they had, but as the car came around he looked up and saw a figure standing on the porch, and he began to understand what being in command meant.

Rider woke to the crunch of tires on gravel. He lay a moment, trying to assess the gravity of this morning's hangover, listening to the sound fade on down the road. Still half-asleep, he forced himself to a sitting position with the guilty realization that the Grateful Dead could have held a midnight concert in the room and he wouldn't have known.

"They got her!" a male voice screamed from the porch. Rider swung off the couch as Ball burst in the door, puffy-eyed from sleep, his fly gaping open. "Down the road! Jerked her in the car! I was piss—"

"Shit!" Rider exploded. Adrenaline surged through him, washing out the poisons, as he leaped to the open door, knocking Ball out of the way.

A station wagon was accelerating up the road, dust boiling behind it in a chalky cloud.

Rider spun back into the house, snatching the carbine and looping the sling around his neck in a combat carry. He dived at the bed, clawed the rifle with its 10-round magazine from under it. Thought of more ammo. No time! No time!

He raced outside in his stocking feet, the carbine clanking against his chest, and the world geared down for them all in a slow-motion dream as . . .

Pat Cousins' head cleared and she understood where she was. She thought of torture to make her tell about the dope and started fighting against Johnny Blue Eyes, who was bouncing around in the back seat trying to jack a round in his assault rifle, and Pete Tammi, who had no idea what Bocca was going to do but was nevertheless rolling his window down so he could shoot out of it, and Tommy Bocca, who was floorboarding the car back up the road watching Rider run down the driveway and stop, kneeling and facing them as Ball ran in the house looking for a weapon and changed his mind and started to run out the back door to safety until he remembered there was no back door, and still in slow motion . . .

Rider screwed the Heckler & Koch SL7 into his shoulder and took a sight picture on the right front tire, trying to control his breathing. Almost a no-deflection shot, lead just a cunt hair, lead and squeeze and squeeze and blam!

The weapon went off and the 7.62 NATO round blew the tire open and the front of the car slewed around a little and kept coming, power steering compensating for the flayed tire as Bocca churned forward mindlessly, all plans and ideas long gone, operating on instinct alone.

More deflection now as Rider rocked back down into the firing position and shot again, taking out the other front tire of the insolent chariot which still hurtled toward him, vibrating on its shattered rubber.

Pete Tammi leaned out his window and fired ahead through the dust, the number 4 buck booming into the ditch at the bottom of the driveway.

Rider shot into the radiator, pumping rounds in as water sprayed up from the impact, coating the windshield in a greasy mist of oil and antifreeze.

As they roared by the driveway in their crippled machine, Johnny "Blue Eyes" Avilla butt-stroked the woman clawing at his back, pointed the M16 out the window, and squeezed the trigger. The high-velocity rounds sprayed the hillside, ricocheting off rocks, cutting down bushes, pulverizing the headlights of Rider's truck in a geyser of powdered glass.

As the back of the car presented itself Rider shot out a rear tire, aimed at the last one, fired and missed and fired again, blowing it almost off the rim in a flapping tangle of synthetic and wire. The car slid into the ditch, uncontrollable and dying, as was Johnny Blue Eyes. The round that missed the tire hit a rock, ricocheting into the differential, and ricocheting off that through the bottom of the car, tumbling its still-supersonic way into the left buttock of Johnny Blue Eyes, shattering his pelvis and sweeping through his stomach to exit out his right side, below the rib cage.

Johnny Blue Eyes wondered why he was numb and sick and dizzy, and where the sudden stink of shit was coming from.

As he sagged back with his mouth open, Pat Cousins came scrambling out of the car, her mouth dripping threads of blood, located Rider, and headed for him.

Tommy Bocca didn't really know what to do. He had been slammed into the steering wheel as the car hit. With his side numb from the impact, he grabbed his own weapon, a MAC-10 submachine gun. Bastard in the road behind him with a rifle that could shoot clean through a car, and no cover anyplace, so it's gunfight at the O.K. Corral and he rolled out the door onto the packed-dirt road and pointed and squeezed.

Rider, who had run to the bottom of the driveway, waited a precious second to let the stupid cunt blocking his line of fire get clear and put his last round dead center in Tommy's chest. At the same time the MAC-10 went off in a sustained burst, spewing .45 ACP slugs down the road in a line of flying dirt which passed Rider by three feet.

Tommy Bocca sat spraddle-legged next to the open

car door, one hand resting casually on the rocker panel, the other limply grasping the gun in his lap. There was the most horrible combination of pain and numbness in his chest that he could ever have imagined. It was so bad that he leaned forward to escape it and vomited a great gout of dark, syrupy blood all over his hand and the gun. He suddenly realized he was dying and that nothing could stop it, not prayer and not God and not his mother, not anything. All he wanted was to get it over with, to have an end to the naked terror that coursed through him. He leaned forward even more, seeing the unbelievable amount of blood pouring from his mouth, splashing in his lap and between his legs on the gravel of the road. He gritted his teeth against the bitter copper taste and repeated soundlessly, Let it be over. Please, God, let it be over, please.

Pete Tammi was down on the floorboards, battle-shocked and frozen over his shotgun. He could taste the floor dust in his mouth and saw in minute detail all the detritus before his eyes: lumps of dried mud, pop tops, gum wrappers. He couldn't believe this was real. There must be a mistake. It wasn't supposed to go like this, not at all like this, and he didn't know what to do.

Maybe he could surrender.

Rider laid the SL7 down against the bank and unslung the carbine. Pat Cousins was halfway up the driveway, squatting down with blood still dripping from her chin.

Ball was up on the porch, holding on to a post with one hand, Rider's shotgun in the other. "You get 'em?" he yelled down.

Rider had an almost uncontrollable urge to shoot Ball off the porch, but was afraid to turn away from the car in the ditch. He had no real idea how many people were left inside. He would have liked to ask Pat, who should know, but decided quickly that the information would not be worth the effort.

He slammed a three-round burst from the carbine through the back window and yelled "Every mother-fucker outta there with your hands on your head!" He was surprised when a voice replied, "Okay, don't shoot. Here I come!"

The front door on the ditch side eased open and a roly-poly, half-bald, smudged-looking character in stiff new work clothes slid out, stumbling on the uneven ground. His hands were elevated as far as the stubby arms would allow.

Rider wanted to shoot him, too, but needed to know how many more were in that damn car, which he was afraid to check.

"Everybody else out, too, goddammit!"

"Nobody left," the roly-poly guy said. "They're all dead." He talked fast, his face white.

Rider thought a minute, then came up with an idea that would save him from having to check personally. Recon by fire. The old artillery-in-the-ville-first meth-od. "Ball!" he yelled, glad he hadn't shot the asshole.

"Yeah!"

"Look up on the porch, behind that pile of wood. Should be a yellow jug. It's marked 'Gas.'"

Ball searched, held it up. At Rider's direction, he brought it down the driveway, set it in the ditch halfway to the car, and retreated.

Rider gestured at Pete Tammi with the carbine. "Come get it, ace."

Tammi wobbled down the ditch, hands still up. He picked up the plastic jug reluctantly, as if afraid Rider would shoot him for lowering his arms. Following orders, he carried it back to the car and poured the mixture of gas and chain-saw oil over the front and back seats. The reeking liquid washed some of the blood down Johnny Avilla's side in a diluted pink stream. "Nobody in here, man. All dead, I swear to Christ, brother."

"Then they won't mind," Rider said. "Back off and light it."

Pete Tammi could see that Johnny Blue Eyes, slumped in a pool of blood out of Rider's view, was still alive. Dying, but alive. He thought wildly of denying he had any matches. He thought of running. But he stepped back up on the bank, dug in his pocket, and came up with an expensive lighter, a gift from Bobby Bartoli.

"Light it," Rider ordered.

Tammi looked down into the car from his vantage point on the bank. Johnny Avilla had rolled his face around so that he could watch Tammi through the rear window. The blood-caked mouth moved, quivered, subsided. The eyes, still alive enough to react to the stink of raw gas in the car, pleaded with Tammi.

"Look," Tammi said desperately. "I think the guy in the back is still kickin'. He's hurt bad, but I coulda swore I just seen him move."

Rider leveled the carbine on Tammi's chest. "Motherfucker, you can't have it both ways. You told me a minute ago wasn't nobody alive in there. Swore to Christ. Now you tell me there is. I hate a fuckin' liar! So if you lied before, I'm gonna shoot you. Right now. And if you didn't, then *light the goddamn thing now!*" Rider was almost hysterical.

Pete Tammi snapped the lighter into life, looked into the flame as if searching for his soul, and flipped it into the front seat of the car.

There was a huge *whoof* of fire, followed immediately by a similar explosion as the back seat ignited. Tammi stumbled away, his legs singed, as the car disappeared in a raging column of black-laced orange, its paint starting to blister.

An unearthly, quavering, keening cry cut through the air from somewhere. Tammi desperately wanted to believe the noise was nothing more than super-heated air, forcing its way through the punctured cooling system. The heat was stunning, even this far away. He turned back to Rider and saw what was going to happen next. "Ah, no, man," he cried. "Please, man. Don't. Wait. I—"

Rider held the carbine low and fired a five-round burst, letting the kick of the weapon walk the rounds up his target.

Pete Tammi grabbed a small sapling with white-knuckled hands, swaying with impact as he was struck progressively in the groin, the abdomen, the chest, and the throat. The fifth round went wild. He fell back slowly, still gripping the tree, which bent with him all the way to the ground. The ringing echo of the shots was punctuated by the sound of his relaxed bowels breaking wind.

It was ten minutes after ten.

The Drunken Chief sat on his porch with the binoculars, watching. He had overslept this morning because he had stayed up too late last night, watching celebrities plug their latest book or movie on the Johnny Carson show.

The popping of small-arms fire had brought him out of his warm bed a short time ago. Now he could see the twisting column of rubber-fed smoke rising from the road below.

It all reminded him of the big war against the Krauts. After a while, the wind blowing up the valley brought him a smell he also remembered. One he associated with burning tanks, dripping the melted fat of their incinerated crews out the bottom in blue-flamed puddles.

VII.

They squatted on the hillside staring at the billowing flames of the station wagon from eyes vacant with shock. Then the wind changed, blowing the smoke uphill toward the cabin, and Pat Cousins stumbled away from it, gagging and rubbing her eyes.

Rider took Ball by the sleeve and led him up the hill to the truck, where they picked up the largest pieces of headlight glass to avoid flats. Then they got tools from under the porch and went to the lower part of Rider's property, a large area cleared of trees and covered with waist-high, brown winter weeds.

"Start digging," Rider said.

Ball stared at his shovel for a second in dismay, dreading not so much the physical labor as the realization of what the digging was for. Then he gritted his teeth and pushed the point of the shovel into the soft, damp earth.

"This used to be a garden," Rider grunted as they worked. "All the roots and shit already plowed up.

Thank your ass for that, bossman. This is easy work. You should try digging in the woods sometime."

He continued a soliloquy of inane remarks as the pile of dirt slowly grew.

Ball worked in a daze. He felt trapped in a nightmare that wouldn't end. Less than a week ago he had been living in moderate luxury, eating in fine restaurants, driving an expensive car. He had been hanging out in high-class lounges, dressed in tailored threads, his hair styled and his fingers heavy with masculine jewelry. He had money in the bank and a classy shack job, and people treated him with friendly respect.

And now here he was. His classy shack job was up on the hill puking out of a blood-smeared mouth while he dug a mass grave in some godforsaken field at the direction of an uncouth maniac. His face was smeared with a mixture of sweat, dirt, and a film of greasy smoke. The smell of burning meat blended with the sour-milk odor of freshly turned earth, making his stomach churn. His hair hung down in untidy strands, his back was aching, and the rough shovel handle was rubbing his palms raw.

And over it all was sickening, constant fear. The sure knowledge that people were out to kill him, that people were actually seeking to do to him what Rider had done to that little fat guy. It was unbelievable. It wasn't fair. He caught himself whimpering in self-pity, turned it into a groan, and took a fresh grip on the shovel with his blistered hands.

Two feet down they ran out of plowed dirt and hit compacted red shale, which had to be broken out. Rider used the pick to gouge the material up, then Ball shoveled. It was slow, painful work.

Rider was sweating out the by-products of gallons of beer and moonshine. It oozed from his pores in the distinctive smell of all drunks. In spite of this he would have enjoyed himself, watching Ball suffer from the unaccustomed labor, if he hadn't been worried about the tableau at the bottom of his driveway. Nobody ever came down this dead-end road, but it was possible. Somebody lost, or looking for investment property. Somebody from the bank, checking on the abandoned houses below. Or a county mountie, cruising on the state road at the foot of the mountain, attracted by the column of smoke.

Rider could imagine explaining the bullet-riddled, burning hulk, surrounded by frying corpses, to one of *those*. No, they had to clean this fucking mess up as fast as possible, and they might as well be digging graves while the car was cooling.

When the hole was four feet deep Rider called a halt. He would have liked it deeper, but Ball was starting to stagger, his own hands were blistered, and the station wagon had finally burned out.

They trudged back up the hill under a warming noontime sun. Rider cranked his pickup and backed it down the driveway, easing it up to the blackened wreck. The heat from the cooling metal was still intense. He could feel his eyeballs start to dry out as he dropped the logging chain around the rear bumper and made the connection fast. Now comes the fun part, he thought grimly.

"Come on, Ball. Let's do it."

Ball could think of no way out, no excuses.

The corpse was splayed out in the road next to the car, its back propped against the open front door. The body had swelled from the heat, the skin blackened and shiny like an overcooked sausage. All the clothes and hair were gone, the eyes dehydrated to marble-size lumps in the gaping sockets. The skull had cracked, giving the distended head the shape of a dropped pumpkin.

Ball felt the bile rising in his throat. He fought it down, clenched his jaw, and grabbed the ankles.

"Christ, it's hot!" he choked, snatching his hands away.

Rider ran to his truck, rummaged behind the seat, and came out with several mismatched pairs of work gloves. In a frenzy now to get this over with, he threw a set at Ball and donned another pair.

In order for both of them to get at the body it was necessary first to drag it away from the door so that one of them could lift the shoulders. Rider took hold of the ankles and pulled. The carcass came away easily, thumping on its back in the road. Part of it still stuck to the door, a section of skin and back fat, welded there from heat.

Ball gaped at the sight, the memory of a time long-past blooming into life: a picture of a barbecue in someone's manicured backyard, well-dressed, laughing, civilized people, and the pieces of butchered chicken, left too long on the grill, tearing away no matter how daintily the host tried to turn them. Ball lost it, spewing bitter vomit all over his muddy shoes, all over Tommy Bocca's head and shoulders, the final indignity.

Rider waited for him to heave it all up, gagging and wiping his streaming eyes, then said harshly, "Let's get it, man. Quicker we get this over the better."

They succeeded in getting the steaming obscenity onto the bare springs of the front seat, where it sprawled grotesquely, like smoldering rubbish.

Ball tried to avert his eyes from the thing in the back seat. Johnny Avilla didn't look nearly as bad as Bocca did. Unlike Bocca, who was only half cooked, Avilla was just about totally cremated, having been in the heart of the fire. There was no humanity left to him. He simply resembled a charred, child-size mummy.

Rider tried to kick the front door shut, but it bounced back, warped from the heat. "Get on this motherfucker," he panted. They both put gloved hands against it and shoved. It clunked shut.

As they were lifting Tammi's body in from the other side of the car, Ball noticed a wallet drop out of the blood-soaked pants pocket. They threw the body in on top of Bocca. When Tammi landed, the impact squirted blood out of all his bodily orifices, natural and otherwise, and Ball felt like fainting. Without really thinking, he bent down in the ditch and picked up the dead man's wallet. The expensive, zippered leather was sticky with blood, and, forgetting the gloves, he thought of fingerprints. He decided to burn it later, in Rider's stove. He stuck it in his front pocket.

"Stand clear," Rider shouted. He put the pickup in gear, took up the slack in the tow chain, and started dragging the station wagon backward down the road. When it was even with the garden where they had dug the grave, he stopped and locked the emergency brake.

He produced a piece of half-rotten canvas tarp from the junk in the back of the truck and spread it on the road by the station wagon. With a considerable amount of grunting and sweating they rolled the bodies one at a time out of the car onto the tarp and dragged them up into the field, tipping them into the hole.

Pete Tammi's arm, already stiff with rigor mortis, stuck up over the edge, and no amount of pushing or prying would get it down below ground level. Rider, sweat pouring off his face and stinging his eyes, seized the pickax and beat the recalcitrant member down where it belonged.

This isn't real, Ball thought. This isn't happening.

"You cover it up," Rider said, his chest heaving. "I'll get rid of the car."

"I don't feel so good."

"Goddamn you, I said cover it up!" Rider shouted hoarsely. His eyes were wild.

Ball cringed, then began shoveling the soft dirt into the hole.

Rider went back to the truck, remembered he was unarmed, got the carbine, then returned to the truck and started to pull the wreck again.

The gore didn't bother him all that much. He'd seen plenty of that in 'Nam. It was this business of cleaning up afterward that was getting to him. Nasty, filthy, backbreaking work, all the time expecting a carload of fucking tourists to come sight-seeing down the road with their fancy cameras.

In 'Nam, by God, you left 'em where they fell. Or somebody else cleaned the mess up, generally with bulldozers or a backhoe. Fuck this shit!

It didn't take long to drag the station wagon down to the overgrown logging road, and up that to the top of the low ridge. Rider positioned it, unhooked his chain, then nudged it over the edge with the truck.

It slid, started to roll, then jammed upside down against a tree halfway down. Now it was just one more stripped, junked vehicle, pushed over into a hollow and forgotten. There were plenty of them around here, and nobody would give it a second glance. In a week, any gore inside would be cleaned off by the forest nightlife or birds, and by spring it would be covered with weeds and vines, invisible even from the logging road.

As he turned back onto the dirt road, Rider glanced to his right at the faint footpath which led up to the Drunken Chief's cabin. There was no doubt the old bastard was taking all this activity in, but Rider wasn't even slightly concerned about that. He was confident the Chief would mind his own fucking business.

Once every two or three months some of the Chief's

relatives, or somebody, drove down to the trail and backpacked supplies up to the Chief. They then left immediately. He had no other visitors. He certainly had no phone. It was obvious to Rider that the Chief gave not shit one as far as what anybody else did, as long as they left him alone, which Rider was perfectly happy to do.

When he got back, Ball had the mass grave covered and was sitting on the mound of dirt, filthy and exhausted, his head in his hands.

"Come on," Rider told him, in a better mood now that the job was almost done. "Let's get Miss High-class to help us clean the road up a little bit."

Later that afternoon they sat on the porch, exhausted from physical and mental stress. It had turned into a warm day for that time of year, and the air was almost mild.

All three were working on the moonshine, starting to relax as the alcohol loosened muscles and partially blotted out the morning's horror.

Ball looked at his hands. Even though he had scrubbed the grime away in Rider's tub, he couldn't seem to stop searching for minute specks of blood or flesh. He forced his eyes away. "I can't understand how they got on us so fast," he said.

"Beats me," Rider answered. He was slouched on the front steps, dressed in clean cammies, a glass in one hand and a cigarette in the other. The carbine was in his lap, extra magazines stuffed in his cargo pockets. He had cleaned both weapons and put the SL7 back under the bed, with an extra ten-round magazine held to the stock with heavy rubber bands.

"I'm just glad to be alive," Pat said. "We could all be dead right now." She shivered. "Maybe we should leave here now, hide somewhere else. They obviously know where we are."

Rider laughed. "Nobody could be dead now, except them guys. They were a bunch of clowns. They didn't stand a chance."

Pat's voice rose in agitation. "Clowns? Are you crazy? Those were hit men. Mafia hit men. Professional killers, for God's sake!"

"They were a bunch of clowns!" He turned to face her and Ball. "Look. You guys remember Crazy Joe Gallo, up in Brooklyn?"

After a moment of silence and blank looks, Ball nodded. "I guess I remember that, yeah."

"Well, there was a story in *Playboy* about it. I forget the name of the piece. They got Gallo in a place called Umberto's Clam House. Three of them walked in and shot him. He ran outside and died."

"So?" Pat asked. "They got him, didn't they?"

"Yeah, they got him, all right, but you know what his so-called bodyguard was doing? He was sitting there with his thumb up his ass and a .25-caliber automatic in his pocket. A *.25-caliber* automatic! A fucking ladies' gun! Shit! A fucking clown!"

They both stared at him, not quite understanding.

"A .25-caliber automatic," he continued in a quieter, reasonable voice, as if explaining to children, "is useless. It's good for nothing. It doesn't have enough power to shoot through a heavy coat. It *might* kill somebody if you jammed it up against his throat and emptied the magazine, but for a stand-up gunfight, against another person with a real gun, let alone three people, it's a laugh. You'd do better to throw it and run like hell."

"Fine," Ball said. "What's-his-name's bodyguard didn't know his job. Big deal. *These* three guys today had the real shit. What's your point?"

"The point is that the bodyguard was a clown. You ain't heard the best part yet. The three guys that hit Gallo, they knew where he was, okay? They headed over there. They unwrapped their guns, which had been stored in some fucking cellar or something. They unwrapped them and guess what?" Rider paused for a long drink.

"Yeah, okay," Ball prodded, not really interested.

"The fucking guns were too fucking rusty to work! They had to go back and get more. Jesus Christ! Here's your professional *Mafia* hit men, and they ain't even got guns that work! Guns they ain't familiar with. Guns they ain't zeroed in. Chee-rist!"

"The guns these guys had sure as hell worked!" Ball said.

Rider snorted in disgust. "Hell, yes, they worked, but did they hit anything with them? Are we fucking dead? Are *they* dead?" He swept his arm out to indicate the garden below them, and Ball winced and involuntarily looked at his hands.

"Fucking clowns. They came in cold. No recon. They had no idea what they were up against. It could have been you and me, or it could have been you and me and fifteen of my relatives. They had no idea what the terrain was like. They didn't know if I was up on a hill with cleared lanes of fire and a machine gun, or what the approaches were like, or the quality of the opposition, or *anything*. They just came dancing in with their—I bet—unzeroed, unfamiliar weapons and thought they could walk in and take us, like they do those jerks they fuck with in the city."

"I guess," Ball said, remembering how he had tried to squeeze behind the woodpile on the porch when the M16 cut loose.

"Listen to me, Ball," Rider said earnestly, seeing he wasn't getting through. "These guys are used to running around wasting little Jewish storekeepers and pimps and shit like that. It's all shake the guy's hand while your partner stabs him in the back. It's all intrigue and double-dealing and back-shooting. It's all in the city, against people who are so fucking ate up with the godlike Mafia image that they don't even try to fight back. All they do is run and hide and wait, like a bunch of fucking rabbits."

He paused for a breath, then went on, "They don't know how to *fight*. If those guys today had spent some time in the service, instead of draft dodging, they might still be alive. But instead they spent it being cool and breaking drunks' legs and bragging to people in bars that they were connected. A bunch of fucking clowns, Ball." He took a drink, then said, as if it was the greatest sin possible, "And they can't fucking *shoot!*"

Pat listened in amazed silence. Rider was crazy, of course. A frothing, certified maniac, but what he said was making some sense. There *had* been a lot of shooting, and nobody was really hurt, except those in the hole down the hill. She ran her tongue over her swollen lip, which had been cleaned and treated with Anbesol.

"So what happens now?" she asked, addressing no one in particular.

Rider smiled, rubbing his hand lovingly over the smooth finished wood of the weapon in his lap. "Why, I imagine that now they'll send in the A-team."

After supper Ball remembered the bloodstained wallet. He went over to the pile of dirty clothes in the corner and fished it out, grimacing with distaste. The blood had long since dried, leaving the surface of the leather smooth and shiny. Maybe there was money inside. He unzipped the wallet and removed several hundred dollars in twenties, putting them in his own pocket. He glanced over at Rider, who was on the couch, snoring. He removed the few papers the wallet contained and glanced at them. A couple of receipts, some business cards with telephone numbers scrawled on the backs. A W-2 form. Ball froze, staring at the name on the document. After a few seconds he threw the wallet and its contents into the stove, with the exception of the W-2 form. He glanced again at Rider. Still satisfied he was asleep, Ball carefully refolded the paper and put it in his shirt pocket. He went over to the bed and sat down, staring at Rider, thinking hard.

Once again, the lights in the Bartoli trucking company office were burning late.

Bartoli had been pacing the confines of the room for hours, but now sat slumped in his swivel chair, staring morosely out the window at the sodium-illuminated parking lot.

Across the room in the easy chair, Al Mewson looked at his watch and cleared his throat. "Uh, Bob, it's past two."

Bartoli glanced at his own watch and grunted. Then he stood up, stretched, and rubbed his stubbled face. "That's it, then," he acknowledged in a resigned voice.

Both men glanced at the phone sitting silently on the desk. They had received a check-in call from a motel late the night before but nothing since. They had spent the day waiting for the call from Knoxville, and as morning turned into early afternoon with no word, Bartoli had become increasingly curt with his other business calls. Finally he had instructed his secretary not to accept any more calls unless they were from Knoxville. At six that evening, unable to control his patience longer, he had called River Salvage and been informed his people hadn't shown up. By now, early in the morning of the following day, it was painfully obvious that they would not ever hear from them.

If Bocca and his team had been arrested for any reason they would have called by now. Lawyers were available for this eventuality. If they'd been involved in a traffic accident, all three men carried numbers that authorities could call to notify bogus next of kin, who would in turn notify Bartoli.

Since they had not surfaced anywhere, there was only one conclusion possible. One that Bartoli had trouble accepting.

"It probably won't do any good," Mewson said, "but in the morning I'll report the station wagon stolen."

Bartoli glanced around from the bar, where he was mixing a drink. "Is that smart?"

Mewson shrugged. "Can't hurt. The thing's perfectly legal and can't be connected to you, anyway. If it turns up abandoned somewhere full of bullet holes and *hasn't* been reported stolen, the front guy might have to answer some embarrassing questions."

"Yeah, I can dig that."

"And who knows, Bob. They might be stupid enough to go driving around in it. I really doubt it, but they might."

Bartoli's heavy face lost some of its gloom as he contemplated that idea. "Jesus, yes! The cops pick 'em up in a set of hot wheels. They notify your front guy and he tells us, and I send somebody up to post bond, and when they walk out the front of the jail, bam!" He drove his balled fist into his palm with a meaty smack.

"Don't count on it. Nobody's really that stupid. It's just a remote possibility, kind of covering all the bases, you know?"

"Well, now," Bartoli said, still clinging to the idea because of the satisfaction it gave him. "They can't be too fucking bright. That W-2 form in the 'Vette's trunk wasn't a real smooth move."

Al Mewson leaned back in the chair and studied his wing-tip shoes. "I wonder," he mused.

"Uh? Wonder what?"

"Nothing," Mewson said, not yet ready to verbalize his ideas. "What's important now is what you're planning on next."

Bartoli, who had the coffee cup of whiskey halfway to his mouth, paused in astonishment. "What the fuck you *think* I'm planning to do next? I'm going to run these fucking greaseballs down and I'm gonna make a real Technicolor example out of 'em!" He finished his drink in one gulp and crushed the cup. "*Nobody* fucks with me like this and gets away with it. Nobody! I'll find them, and then, baby, it's the meat hook and cattle prod and blowtorch, just like the old days!"

"What makes you think you've got to find them again?"

Bartoli started to reply, then changed his mind. He quickly turned to the bar and mixed another drink with fingers beginning to tremble with rage. In a few seconds he felt calmer. He took a drink and sat down behind his desk. He lit a cigar and regarded Mewson through the expensive smoke.

"Okay, Al," he said. "We've worked together a long time and you've got some kind of rocket up your ass about this thing. Some idea I'm not following. So spell it out. I'm listening."

Mewson leaned forward, his expression intent. "This is just an idea I've got, Bob, a feeling. I could very well be way off base, but—" He paused, then plunged ahead. "That damn W-2 form! It's just too pat. You were right when you said it wasn't a smooth move on this Rider's part. As a matter of fact, it was very dumb, or very sloppy. And a hell of a piece of good luck on our part. Christ, it led us right to him!"

"Go on," Bartoli said when Mewson stopped to organize his thoughts.

"My point is, they were just too sloppy, or we were too lucky. You know I gamble?"

Bartoli nodded.

"Well, I don't have a gambling *problem*, and it's not a problem because when I gamble, I win. And I win because I don't believe in *luck*. And I don't believe in coincidence, either. What I do believe in is the old saw about beware of Greeks bearing gifts."

Bartoli puffed on his cigar, thinking. "What you're trying to say is that paper wasn't left in that trunk by accident? That these fucking people rip me off and kill my people and then fix it up so I can *find* them?"

"It has occurred to me."

"That's fucking crazy," Bartoli snorted.

"The world is full of nuts, Bob. Individual nuts and groups of nuts. The guy who committed suicide by drilling holes in his head. Hinckley. Jim Jones. The Moonies. Hell, half the world is crazy, and the other half is stupid. Maybe you can't see that so good because wise guys like you have a grip on reality. You know what the world is like and you know how to make it pay."

Bartoli shook his head. "I just can't see Ball pulling this."

"I agree. Ball is a known quantity. A greasy little punk who let his greed get in the way of his common sense. The woman is nothing. But this other one, this hillbilly."

"Yes," Bartoli said softly, squinting through smoke. "The hillbilly." He took a drink and then said slowly, thinking as he spoke, "Who fills out a W-2 form, anyway? A guy who's just got a job, that's who. A guy who could have been in that office when Frank and Bertie waltzed in."

Mewson nodded, relieved that Bartoli seemed to be following his thinking. "In which case they would have dragged this guy along for the party," he said. "And somehow he gets the drop on them, and then sells Ball on the idea of hiding out in the mountains, and then Christ knows what happened when Tommy and the boys got up there. He might have sixty relatives that thought they were revenuers. He might have been waiting and just ambushed them. He damn sure knew they were coming."

"If you're right about this," Bartoli said.

"If I'm right," Mewson agreed.

After a short silence, Bartoli said, "So you think they're still up there?"

"Ball and the woman might panic and run. Depends on how heavy things got yesterday. But Rider? Yes, I think he's probably still there, waiting."

"Then, by Christ," Bartoli growled, reaching for the phone.

Mewson held up his hand in a restraining gesture. "Uh, Bob. I've got a suggestion."

Bartoli drew his hand back from the instrument, waiting.

"I don't know what went on up there in Tennessee," Mewson said, "but I've got an idea that Tommy didn't have much of a chance. You send more boys up there, the same thing could happen. It could get real messy. For all of us."

Bartoli's face started to darken. Before he could reply, Mewson went on quickly. "You can't send a team of hit men out in a black Caddy for that kind of job, Bob. Not in that country. I was raised in Oklahoma, and I know, believe me."

"Then, what?" Bartoli asked in a low, ominous voice. His hand still rested on the desk, halfway to the telephone.

"All your boys are city boys," Mewson said. "When you've got a problem in the city, they can handle it fine. But it's different terrain up there. Things work different up there. Nobody around here has any experience at it. No reason they should, the money's in the city, not up in the mountains. If you send anybody up there they'll stand out like ratshit in a sugar bowl. They'll get spotted and they'll stumble around and they'll make a mess and they'll get wasted. This is an unusual problem for us. I'm suggesting we handle it in an unusual way."

"We haven't got nobody local," Bartoli said.

"True. They've got their own brand of corruption out in the sticks, and they don't like strangers and we let them have it because it's not worth the trouble to move in. We don't want gang wars over peanuts."

"I know all this shit," Bartoli said. "Tell me something I don't know, Al, or let me make a phone call."

"All right," Mewson said. "This is more like a military problem than a business problem. I'm suggesting we simply use a different kind of talent on this one. It'll cost us, and it'll take a little time to set up, but the job will get done right."

"If I go along, it better," Bartoli said, finally drawing his hand back from the phone. "What kind of talent you got in mind?"

Mewson smiled and leaned back in his chair, starting to relax again. "Ever heard of a mercenary?"

VIII.

Ball's mind had been spinning with indecision since he opened his eyes that morning. He wanted out, pure and simple, but was afraid to broach the subject to Rider directly. Ball was positive that Rider was insane. There was no telling what someone like that would do if Ball tried to get in his car and leave. Christ, he might shoot them both for desertion or something!

Ball had lain awake for hours last night, thinking about that W-2 form, and had come to the only possible conclusion. He was certain he had seen Rider go over to Pat's desk, back in his office, and put the paper in a side pocket of his army jacket.

So Rider had it when they left Lakeland, and now it turns up in what's-his-name's wallet. That explained how their hideout had been discovered so quickly. The question was, then, how had it gotten from Rider's pocket to the fat guy's wallet? Since there hadn't been time for Rider to *mail* it back to Florida (and why would he do that?), the only answer was that he had left it somewhere along the route. Ball thought that probably it had been left somewhere in the Corvette, which their pursuers had surely found and searched. Where it had been left wasn't really important, though. How and why it had been left were the important questions, and their answers were what had his mind whirling with wild fantasies of escape and flight.

He was sure that piece of paper could not have fallen or bounced or blown out of Rider's coat pocket. That field jacket had deep, wide pockets. So what was left, logically, was that Rider had purposely left the form in the Corvette for the mob to find.

Even if it *had* been an accident, the damage was still done. This place was known, it was blown, it was marked, and Ball wanted out. He wanted away from this insane situation and the crazy over on the couch who was sitting there bleary-eyed, watching Alka-Seltzer dissolve in a glass of water.

Rider drank his medicine and grimaced sheepishly at Pat Cousins, who was trying to fry bacon on the huge old wood stove. "Plop, plop, fizz, fizz," he told her. She glanced at him without expression and went back to prodding the bacon with a fork.

Rider turned to Ball, who was sitting on the edge of the rumpled bed. "Somebody needs to go into town this morning," he said.

Ball's breath caught in his throat and his pulse surged, but he kept staring into his coffee cup, as if Rider had not spoken. When he felt that he could control his expression and voice, he looked up. "Well, I'm not stopping you," he whined.

"I'd rather not, Ball. I'm not expecting any company today, it's way too soon, but you never know. I'd rather be here and let them come to me, if they come. I don't feature driving back and having to check this place out for ambushes and booby traps."

"But it's okay if I get caught in some ambush coming back up the mountain, is that it?" Ball said, cautioning himself not to lay it on too thick.

"Jesus Christ, nobody's laid up in the bushes all night waiting on your fat ass! Take my truck if you're so worried," Rider said in exasperation.

Frightened that he'd talked himself into a corner, Ball stood up in feigned resignation. "Oh, shit, all right. I'll take the car. I don't trust the brakes on that rattletrap of yours."

"Considering your previous occupation, you oughta know all about rattletraps," Rider sneered. He handed Ball a shopping list. "I need ammo. Don't buy it all in one place. I don't want them getting the idea we're planning on fighting a war. There are three hardware stores and a Western Auto in town. Get about four boxes in each place. The wire and crap you can get at the Farmers Co-op. There's a couple of gas cans on the porch. Pat can get the clothespins and tacks and groceries in the supermarket. Okay?

"Oh, by the way," Rider said, "don't go the way we went; instead, take a left at the bottom of the mountain and follow it to the interstate, about thirty miles. There's a bigger place there, which we came through on the way in, if you remember."

"I think I can handle it," Ball grumbled to cover his rising excitement. He tried to remember what he would be leaving behind. A few clothes and toilet articles, nothing that couldn't be replaced easily enough. His foot itched to be pressing down on the LTD's gas pedal, heading away from here. Away from these gloomy mountains, away from this primitive shack, away from those bodies down the hill. Away from Rider. He'd take his chances with the Mob somewhere else. Let Rider get off fighting his crazy one-man war against the big timers, by God. Mrs. Ball's son was going to be long gone.

Trying to conceal his nervousness at the proximity of escape, he casually finished his coffee, stood up, and put on his coat. "You ready, Pat?" he asked.

Pat, who was by now sitting on a wooden chair by the stove nibbling halfheartedly on a piece of burned bacon, looked up. "You go on," she said in a take-it-or-leave-it voice. "I've got another hangover and that twisty road makes me sick."

Ball was shocked at this—something he had not anticipated—but only for a second. No way was he going to make a big thing of it and risk Rider getting suspicious. Fuck her, then. Excess baggage, anyway. All he needed was a set of wheels, the money belt around his waist, and his dope, which was in the toolbox in the back of the car. Rider had taken his share last night and stashed it somewhere. "Well, guess I've got to do it all, then," he said in what he hoped was a disgusted voice.

He went outside, got in the Ford, and started it after some grinding on the starter. He let it warm up for a minute, then reached for the gearshift. The passenger door opened and Rider slid in beside him, the .45 stuck in his waistband. "One little thing," Rider said, as Ball felt his testicles shrink with fear. "Not that I think you would, of course, but just in case you got any wild ideas about keeping the pedal to the metal all the way to Arizona, I think you better leave us some cash to operate on, bossman."

Ball felt the sweat pop out on his forehead. "That's my money," he said weakly. "This wasn't the deal."

"It's still your money," Rider told him. "I'm just gonna hold most of it until you get back." He laid his hand casually on the pistol butt. "Cough it up, bossman."

Ball felt like screaming in frustration and disappointment. Instead he gave Rider a rigid, humorless grin, unbuckled the money belt, pulled it out through his shirt front, and threw it on the seat between them.

Rider unsnapped one of the flap pockets and extracted a thick wad of twenties. He tossed it in Ball's lap. "Must be over five hundred there, which is plenty for what we need. Any left over, you can treat yourself to lunch at McDonald's." When Ball didn't say anything, Rider grinned at him with genuine mirth, took the money belt, and slammed the door closed. "Have fun," he told Ball.

As Ball pulled out of Rider's driveway, Al Mewson was nursing his third cup of coffee in a Washington, D.C., restaurant. He was groggy from lack of sleep and jet lag, but Bartoli's impatience had allowed no delay. Now, after a hectic flurry of phone calls, packing, and the night flight up from Florida, he sat regarding the man facing him, wondering if a change to booze would help him shape up.

Harrison Smith studied him sympathetically while he lit a Kent. "Al, you look like you been shot at and missed and shit at and hit. This must be important."

Mewson shrugged. "I've got people on my ass, Harry. They want things moving."

Smith leaned back in the soft cushions of the booth and wondered in what way he could help Mewson get things moving. If it was the usual type of business, he stood to make some money, possibly a lot of money.

Smith was a sleek, florid, middle-aged man who looked like a successful executive, which in fact he was. He had met Mewson back in the Cuban days, when Mewson's "business interests" and the CIA, which Smith then worked for, had similar concerns on that troubled island.

Since then, Smith had left the Company, and was

now associated with a large, semi-legitimate arms dealer located on the outskirts of the nation's capital. Several times in the past, Mewson had come to him with requests for "specialized equipment," items that were exotic, or illegal, or both, and Smith had filled these orders through a careful, clandestine juggling of paperwork. There was so much inventory in the arms dealer's acres of warehouses that the relatively tiny amounts of ordnance requested—explosives, silencers, LAWs (light antitank weapons), automatic weapons, and infrared devices—had never been missed.

So it surprised him when Mewson leaned forward and said, "I need a contact for a job."

Smith knew immediately what Mewson meant, of course, but the request was so unexpected that he wanted time to think. He motioned to the waitress, at the same time looking at his Patek Philippe watch. "The hell with the sun over the yardarm and all that shit, Al," he said. "You look like you could use a jolt, and so can I."

They both sat without speaking until their drinks arrived, then Smith took a sip of his, frowning. "What kind of contact are you talking about, Al? I was under the impression that you had all the talent you needed already on the payroll."

"Not quite," Mewson told him. "This is something unusual. The problem is way the hell and gone up in the backwoods. All our people are city guys. What we need here is more in the military line. A small group of people, say half a dozen, who can operate in the backcountry, get in and do the job, then get back out." He paused. "And keep their mouths shut, of course."

Smith allowed himself a tight little smile. "Of course."

"I figure either you know somebody who can do us a job, or you know somebody who knows somebody,"

Mewson said. "Just tell me what you think a fair price for a name and phone number is, okay?"

"All right," Smith said, suddenly businesslike. "I might just have a man for you. However, I'm going to need a little more intelligence on your problem." He waited until Mewson nodded. "This *is* domestic?"

"Yes."

"From what you've already said, I'm assuming it's short-term. Now, I need straight scoop on this, Al, because if it isn't straight the whole thing could backfire on all of us. The types we're dealing with here sometimes have funny ideas about certain things."

"Oh?" Mewson said, raising his eyebrows. "What kind of funny ideas?"

Smith paused to formulate his thoughts so that Mewson, and Mewson's people, would understand what he was trying to tell them. "Al, the people you work for, and the people I used to work for, operate on a set of ground rules pretty much alike. Diplomacy and intrigue and, uh, disinformation."

Mewson smiled. "Disinformation," he repeated, pronouncing each syllable separately. "You mean lying."

Smith shrugged. "Call it what you want. The point is that the people you say you need for this job aren't connected, and they aren't spooks. They're *soldiers*, and that means you have to play it straight with them. No lying about the situation, no setups, no bullshit. The guy I have in mind knows how to mind his own business, he won't ask anything that isn't essential to the job, and if he says he'll do the job, he'll do it. But you've got to deal up front with him."

Mewson felt a twinge of anger tighten his belly. "Maybe you better make it clear to this fuck who *he's* dealing with!"

Smith took a drink and sighed—for him, a sign of

tension. This was delicate ground he was on now, but it was absolutely essential that Mewson's people understand the possible consequences of any kind of double-dealing. "Don't get your ass up, Al," he said reasonably. "I'm simply trying to point out the type of mentality you're going to be dealing with. If you play it straight, everything goes smooth. If you don't, these people might act stupid, and it'll just be a fucking mess for everybody. Including me. Including *you*."

"Nobody's stupid enough to play games with us, not if they know who we are," Mewson said petulantly. But even as he spoke he thought of the faceless figure back in those Tennessee mountains, the reason he was here in the first place.

Smith sighed again, this time more in exasperation than nervousness. He signaled the waitress for two fresh drinks. When they arrived he took a swallow and lit another Kent. "Al, this 'fuck,' as you call him, operates on a certain set of principles. They might be weird principles, by our standards, or society's, but to him they make sense. They're *practical*. They're as necessary for his line of work as it is for your people to wax a snitch. So I'm just telling you, if you tell him the target involves five guys and it turns out the target is a blind man and three little old ladies, he's going to cause trouble. Not that he's necessarily got any qualms about wasting old ladies, I don't know one way or the other, but because you *lied* to him. Because you purposely gave him bad intel." Smith paused for breath, then said, almost pleadingly, "Can you understand that?"

"All right," Mewson conceded. "Nobody's gonna feed any bullshit. This is a straightforward, in-and-out deal. No funny business necessary. Satisfied?" He was still thinking of Rider.

Smith was ready to drop this line of conversation, so

he nodded. Suspicious by training and inclination, this whole business was making him nervous. It wasn't his bag anymore. Back in the old days there was a lot of shit like this going down, but then he had the Company covering his ass. Now his ass was alone and waving out in the breeze, and he had no way of knowing if Mewson was leveling with him. This might be some weird kind of setup, something to get him involved in something else, something he might not touch otherwise. Both Mewson and Smith spent a good deal of their time weighing possibilities, figuring angles, trying to smell out the setup or the double cross.

"Okay," Smith said, smiling. "Just needed to get that straight, Al. Now, let's see, one or two more things I need to know."

"One thing *I* need to know," Mewson said. "How much is this name going to cost?"

Smith waved his hand in dismissal. "Hell, Al, no problem there. You might not even be able to do business. If you and my contact get together and things work out, just send me whatever you think it was worth." He gave Mewson an old-buddies smile. The truth was, he did not really know what information like this was worth. He also did not know how Mewson's people would react if Parsons fucked the job up. All in all, it seemed safer to let things run their course on this one. That way, if things went wrong between Mewson's people and Parsons, they couldn't come back on him for selling them a bum product. This way it would just be a favor. Hell, it wasn't his line of work, anyway. And maybe there would be an under-the-counter arms deal in it for him. Smith was greedy, but he had survived until now by not allowing his greed to cloud his caution.

"Okay, that's fine with me," Mewson agreed. "What else do you need to know?"

"Just one thing, actually. This job is in the family, right? I mean, it's not Red, and it doesn't involve any kind of law? My men won't touch it if it does."

Mewson thought a minute. "It's not *in* the family, but it is family business. No, it doesn't involve politics or the law. None of that."

"Well, that does it, I guess," Smith said. He finished his drink and looked at his watch. "Where are you staying?"

Mewson grimaced. "Shit, not anywhere. I haven't been off the fucking plane two hours."

"Why don't you go find a motel, get some sleep, and call me this afternoon?" Smith said. He reached for the check.

Mewson brushed his hand away from it with a gesture. "I've got it, Harry. I'll give you a buzz about two, let you know where I am."

"Right, then," Smith said. He stood up and put his coat on. The two men smiled meaninglessly at each other and Smith left. They did not shake hands.

Ball was parked in the shopping center, chain-smoking. For the third time he counted the money Rider had left him. Over eight hundred dollars. It would have to be enough, because Mrs. Ball hadn't raised her boy to play any more crazy, dangerous games in the middle of nowhere. It was time to get out. There was enough money to get him somewhere. Anywhere away from here would do, then he could sell the car and make a fresh start. Screw the rest of the money, screw the bitch, and screw Rider. He had his ass and more than half the dope and that was enough. But there was one thing he had to do first, and even the thought made his bowels feel loose.

Ball had a pocket full of change from a laundromat coin changer and a name that Rider had mentioned on the trip up. He got out of the car and went into the phone booth, closing the door tightly behind him. He fed a coin into the instrument with nervous, clumsy fingers and dialed long-distance information. His heart was pounding and he was sweating.

"What city, please?"

Ball wet dry lips and spoke in a hoarse voice. "Tampa, Florida, please."

Bartoli was talking to Al Mewson, who was calling from a pay phone in a motel lobby, when his intercom buzzer sounded. "Hold on a minute, Al," he said, and flipped the switch.

"Mr. Bartoli," the secretary said, "there's a Mr. Joseph Ball wanting to speak with you long-distance. Are you in?"

Bartoli started to grin. "Oh, yes, I'm definitely in to Mr. Ball. Put him right on." "It's Ball, hold on," he told Mewson in a tight voice. Then he punched the blinking button and said, "Bartoli here."

The voice came in a frightened rush, obviously rehearsed words almost running together. "Mr. Bartoli, I guess you know who I am, but I don't expect you to admit that over the phone, so please just listen." A pause, then, "Mr. Bartoli, I had nothing to do with your property. It was all Rider's doing. I hired him to clean the cars and he must have found it. When your men came he killed them, and he practically kidnapped us to his place here, and now he's got your stuff, and he's got my money, too, and the woman." Ball sounded like he was ready to cry. *The little fuck*, Bartoli thought contemptuously. Aloud, he said, "I don't know what you're talking about, ace."

"Yessir, yessir," the frightened voice babbled. "I understand that. I just want you to know I didn't have nothin' to do with this whole mess, Mr. Bartoli. This

Rider guy's crazy. He killed the three men you sent up here, and I'm getting out before he kills me, too. I'm just trying to explain I didn't have anything to do with any of it. I'm running now, Mr. Bartoli, and I'm begging you to leave me out of it."

There was a short pause in Ball's frantic delivery, and Bartoli tried to think of a way he could find out anything useful without admitting he even knew what the conversation was about. Before anything occurred to him, Ball got his second wind.

"You want Rider, he's up there, Mr. Bartoli. Just him and the woman and your property. Please, just forget about me. Please!"

The phone clicked as the connection was broken. Bartoli sat for a minute, smiling, then punched Mewson back on the line. "Al? Looks like the rats are starting to leave the ship."

When Ball hadn't returned by early afternoon, Rider wasn't surprised. He also didn't blame Ball. Running was what any sensible person would have done. And Ball was next to useless in any kind of fight. Rider hadn't needed Ball, but he had needed Ball's cash. Wars cost money.

He dressed in dark city clothes, put his shotgun behind the truck seat, and stuck the automatic in his waistband, buttoning his jacket over it.

With Pat cranking and Rider fiddling with the carburetor, they managed to get his pickup running. It took almost three hours to reach the small city, a trip Ball had accomplished before in half the time.

They stopped at a garage and had the headlights replaced. The mechanic studied the damage. "Bullet holes?"

Rider shrugged. "Kids!" he said in a disgusted voice. The mechanic nodded in sympathy.

Rider took care of the ammunition and hardware

supplies while Pat shopped for the rest of the things on Rider's list.

When the truck was loaded he headed downtown instead of back the way they had come. He turned into the parking lot of Trailways and stopped. Pat turned to him in puzzlement.

Rider took a thick wad of bills from his pocket and threw them in her lap. "That's half of what's left, sweetface. I split it up while you were in the Supergiant."

"I don't understand," she said.

"It's simple. We're clearing the area of noncombatants. Ball showed good sense, although I can't say much for his chivalry. Anyway, take that and hole up in some little town for a month or so. By then all this shit should be over, one way or the other. Then you can go somewhere and start over. I doubt if they're really interested in you."

Pat picked the money out of her lap and looked at it, then looked at Rider. "You're just letting me go?"

"Why not? I've got what I want. A war and enough money to fight it with. Let's face it, Pat, you might well be great in bed, but in this business you'd just be in the way."

She started shaking her head from side to side. "God, I knew you were weird, but I don't believe this. You actually plan to take on the Mafia single-handed? You *want* to take them on? Who the hell do you think you are, that Mack Bolan guy?"

Rider laughed. "That's fiction. I know I don't have a chance in hell, but this is my turf up here, and I figure I can give the bastards a real run. One they won't by God forget for a while."

"But why?" she asked. "Do you want to spend the night with me?" she said all in one breath.

Rider missed a beat. It was just for a second, his face wiped blank with surprise, but it gave her a perverse sense of satisfaction. Then he grinned his crazy grin. "What's this shit, the fair maiden giving the brave knight a going-away present?"

"No," she said. "It's not that, I don't think you're a brave knight. I think you're a goddamn crazy fool. And I'm leaving, don't worry about that. It's just . . . well, I had something to do with getting you in this mess, and you just gave me a lot of money when you didn't have to, so this is the only way I have to pay you back." She paused. "And don't remind me about the whore business, either, you bastard. Maybe I am, but I'm an honest whore, so if you want to put this wreck in gear and head for that motel we just passed, do it. If not, say so, and I'll see you around."

Rider felt a surge of satisfaction and lust. Who gives a rat's ass what her stupid motives are, he thought. Don't look a gift horse in the mouth and all that old shit. Just don't fuck it up now. "Just promise me you'll still respect me later," he said, pleased that he hadn't turned the truck off.

It wasn't a bit awkward. She was well practiced, and Rider was fatalistic. It either worked or it didn't.

Rider rolled over and took a drink from the whiskey bottle and lit a cigarette. "Answer me one question," he said.

"What?"

"Who's bigger, me or Ball?"

Watching him as he spoke, she knew how to reply. "He's longer, you're thicker."

"Okay, then who's better?"

She smiled. "Well . . . Joey is. But he isn't always drunk like you are. If you'd sober up—"

"Listen," Rider said. "My daddy always said, 'Son, you can be a lover or a drunk, but you can't be both.'"

Pat, who had climaxed, more from the last week

than from Rider's technique, laughed. "Okay, Joey's a lover. You're a drunk." She rolled over and took a cigarette from the pack on the nightstand and lit it. "Can I ask you a serious question now?"

"Sure," Rider said.

"Why?" she asked. "I mean, seriously, what in the name of God is motivating you in all of this? What are you getting out of it? You're not crazy, not really. At least you don't *seem* crazy. But what you're doing *is* crazy. Really I've got to know, Rider. Please tell me if you can. In God's name, why?"

Well, shit, Rider thought. Here you go letting the old ego take charge, starting to think that this good-looking whore is interested in you, because you're a real man, truly macho, that she could see beyond your teeth and clothes and poverty, but the only reason she's in the sack with you is simple woman's curiosity.

"What's wrong now?"

"I'm thinking," he said, and thought, So tell her. Tell her why you're in this. She won't understand, of course. She might nod her head and ohh and ahh but it's all bullshit. She won't understand, and she's got plenty of company, plenty. Come to think of it, who *would* understand? And the answer was, he knew, just you, Rider. Just you.

"Christ!" Pat said. "You look mean one second, now you're grinning. Christ!" She sat up in the bed, then as an afterthought pulled the blanket chastely over her breasts.

Rider took another drink, then sat up facing her. "One thing," he said, "is this. I've been bored ever since 'Nam. *Bored!* You understand that?"

She nodded, wide-eyed and attentive.

"I mean, shit! I hated 'Nam. It was hot and sweaty and useless and I was scared shitless all the time. But . . . I came back to finish my time in the world and guess what? I got bored. The same shit all the time. The same routine. The same—" Rider stopped, at a loss. He took a lumberjack-size slug of whiskey and grinned, embarrassed.

"I shipped over," he said as if ashamed and amazed at the same time. "Christ, I *still* can't believe it, I shipped over for another tour in that *shithole!*"

Pat Cousins said nothing, listening.

"The second time, there was a little incident. Things kinda got out of hand. I fucked up, I guess." He shrugged.

"What happened?" she asked.

"It's got nothing to do with what we're talking about. The point is that they shipped my ass home and I've been bored ever since. You always remember the good stuff and forget the bad stuff. I *know* I was bored there, too, and hot and cold and miserable and wanted to come home, but I can't really remember that part. Can you understand *that?*"

"What happened?"

"Ah shit," Rider said, exasperated. "Will you listen? All I can remember is the excitement, the . . . the uncertainty, the *adventure*. The kick I got from doing something I was *good* at! Everything else is dull. Fucking dull!"

"But what happened?"

"Jesus Christ on a crutch! The little psychoanalyst! Nothing happened! Nothing that's got a fucking thing to do with what you asked me originally. Okay?"

"I'm sorry," she said.

Rider turned the plastic motel cup up and discovered that he had never filled it. He started to, then thought the hell with it and drank from the bottle. "Big deal, okay? I was standing in front of battalion headquarters one day and three dinks came out, been interrogated or something. Hands tied behind their backs." Rider hiccuped. "Came down the steps, and three or four KIAs laid out next to the steps, all covered with ponchos, all you could see was the boots, you know, and the motherfucking flies trying to get at them and everything, and these three dinks kinda paused, you know, and one of them *spit* on the . . . the. . . *corpses*, spit on those dead grunts, you know, and I took my trusty, gas-operated, magazine-fed, selective-fire M14 and put the motherfucker on rock and roll and blew all three right into hell."

"Oh, how awful," Pat said insincerely.

Rider laughed bitterly. He shook his head. "Darling, I don't know why I'm bothering. That wasn't a traumatic experience. Hell, I'm *proud* of it! The only thing I regret was that some fuckin' reporter got wind of it and I got my ass shipped home."

"Then I still don't understand."

"Understand what? Are we off all the psychoanalyst-search-for-traumatic-past-experience as the key to why I'm committing suicide?"

"I guess," Pat said. "I don't know." She started to cry. "I don't know anything. I've never been into this sh-sh-shit! I don't know what's going on. Oh God, I'm so damn scared!" She rolled away from him and curled up sobbing, fists bunched under her chin.

Rider, annoyed at the display, sat uncomfortably through it. When it subsided, he said, to her and to himself, "I knew you would never understand. That big goombah down there in Florida is the way he is and Ball is the way he is, and I'm the way I am, and there's no mystery to it. Some people like the color red and some like the color blue and there's no rhyme or reason for it." He paused, then continued, in a subtly different tone, his voice a shade tighter, "And it's also that I resent a bunch of people coming into this country with their secret signs and foreign ways trying to throw their weight around with people who settled this goddamn place. I resent it. Who the fuck do they think they are? Everybody's supposed to squat every time they holler shit, just because they're willing to kill? Maybe it's time they found out it works both ways!''

IX.

Mewson had no preconceived notion of what to expect when he opened the motel door that evening, but the person standing on the other side was a distinct letdown. He must have been at least fifty years old. Clean-shaven and of average height and build, the mercenary called Parsons was dressed in a nondescript open-throated shirt, slacks, and nylon rain jacket. His greying sandy hair was cut short, and he wore glasses and a hesitant smile.

"Mr. Mewson, I believe we have a mutual friend whose name starts with *s*."

"That's right," Mewson said. "Come on in." He turned and went to the liquor cabinet.

"Drink?" he asked as he heard the door close.

"Please. Scotch with a dash of soda. No ice."

Mewson felt a twinge of annoyance. He had just ordered a fresh bucket of ice a few minutes ago. He mixed the drinks and brought them across the room to

Parsons, who had sat down in one of the straight-backed chairs furnished with the room.

They made small talk about the miserable Washington weather while they sipped the drinks and sized each other up.

Shortly the conversation petered out and they eyed each other, waiting for somebody to get down to business. Presently Parsons spoke. "Lay it out for me, Mr. Mewson," he said tersely. "No names, no places. Just your own words on what's going to have to be done. I'll ask questions about details later on." He took a drink, set it on the arm of his chair, folded his hands in his lap, and waited.

Mewson set his own drink down and gave an abbreviated version of the problem. He represented sponsors from whom a certain individual had stolen something valuable, and the sponsors wanted it back, not only for its monetary value but as a matter of principle. This individual had killed two of the sponsors' people when he heisted the goods, and three more of the sponsors' people had disappeared trying to get the goods back. This individual was holed up in the backwoods and, since none of the sponsors' people were any good at this sort of thing, they had decided to try hiring professionals. The law couldn't be involved. Nobody knew what kind of backup this individual had, in weapons or people. All they had was an address and a name. The job would involve first wasting whoever was on the premises and then trying to find the property and returning it to its rightful owner. Payment would be more if the property was recovered intact, but the primary mission was to secure the area so representatives of the sponsor could institute their own search at leisure. Mewson drew a breath. "I think that covers the basics," he said. He picked his glass up and took a drink, watching Parsons.

Parsons had slumped down in the chair seat during

Mewson's recital. His eyes were almost closed and his hands still rested in his lap, loosely clasped. Mewson noted a bulge of fat below and over the man's belt buckle. Jesus Christ, he thought.

Suddenly Parsons' eyes opened. "Is it dope?" he asked.

Mewson's first reaction was to lie. Then he thought of Harrison Smith's advice, and he thought of the futility of lying, since, after all, he was hiring Parsons to *find* the stuff; so he said, almost instantly, "Hell, yes, it's dope!" He hoped he had put the right amount of exasperated annoyance in his voice.

Parsons smiled and nodded. "Okay," he said in a satisfied tone. He sat up in the chair. "It *had* to be dope. Nobody else has this kind of money to throw around. So that means the Mob, right?"

This time Mewson waited a second before answering, then said, "Does it make a difference?"

"No, it really doesn't," Parsons answered. "I've never actually signed a contract where I knew who the hell I was really working for. They can *say* it's the Pooh-Bah of Punjab, but it might really be Standard Oil. Or they can *say* it's the CIA and it might be the goddamn KGB. Or the Mafia. Or Christ knows." He picked his drink up and put it back down. "We don't have any way of finding out, you know. All we can go by is the nature of the contract. I mean, if the CIA tries to hire me to overthrow the government of El Sal, I gotta know it's bullshit, right?"

"This is private," Mewson said. "As I'm sure our friend explained to you. There isn't any of this written-contract business."

"No, of course not. Not in this kind of deal." Parsons sat up in the chair. "But you understand, in that case, everything's up front. In cash."

"That's smooth," Mewson said. "As long as you understand that we expect satisfactory results from cash rendered." Then his annoyance surfaced at Parsons' appearance. "So you'll be paid, but you better come through. Is that understood?"

Parsons laughed—a rich chuckle of amusement. Then he stood up and reached for his belt buckle.

For an instant of panic Mewson thought he was going for a gun, but Parsons loosened his buckle and pulled a tiny piece of rubbery material from between his shirt buttons. "This is a disguise, Mr. Mewson. An overweight, four-eyed square selling encyclopedias. You think I want people describing how I came to see a *known* rep of the Mob? Shit. If you think I'm out of shape, get down and do as many push-ups as you can, then I'll do double, with you on my back!"

Surprised, Mewson said nothing, as Parsons rebuckled his belt and sat down. He picked up his drink and rolled it in both hands, then met Mewson's eyes.

"You ready to get down to business?"

It wasn't an all-night session because Mewson didn't have that many answers to begin with. When he found this out, Parsons skipped around. He wanted every detail Mewson had about Fennili and Rossolini. How good they were. What they were armed with. Where the wounds were. What caliber. How far apart the bodies were. Whether they'd got off any shots. Also questions about Bocca's crew. Some of the answers Mewson had, some he didn't. Parsons told him to use his contacts to gather any kind of background they could get on the primary target. Check Rider's military and police records, old school history, physical description, anything.

When they were finished Parsons smiled one of his tight little smiles and shook his head. "No wonder your people didn't get back. No recon. No intelligence.

They just waltz in up there cold and expect to take names and kick ass. Christ! Civilians!"

"All right," Mewson said testily. "We fucked up, and we know it. That's why you're here. Do you want this or not?"

Parsons picked up his warm drink and finally finished it, to Mewson's relief.

The lawyer stood up with both glasses. "Refill?"

Parsons refused, then said, "I don't know if I want it or not. I don't even know if I can handle it. I don't have anything to go on, which, as I've already pointed out, is where you people went wrong."

Mewson was still standing, empty glasses in hand. He started to speak but Parsons held up his hand. "Don't get excited. I didn't say I wouldn't take the job. I just said I don't know yet." He paused, then said, "I'll do a recon. It'll take maybe three days. I'll charge only expenses, and for that I'll want five thousand up front. If I decide I don't want the job, you get back what I didn't use and you've got a wad of information you didn't have before. If I decide to take the job, I keep what's left out of the five thousand and we renegotiate on the actual contract. Fair enough?"

Mewson thought a minute. "If you do decide to go in, how long will it be before you can, uh, complete the actual contract, and how much money are we talking?"

Parsons shook his head, as if exasperated at a stubborn child. "Mr. Mewson, when you take your car to the garage, do you expect the mechanic to quote you price and time before he even looks under the hood?"

Mewson said, "The last time I took my car to the garage the charge for the estimate was twenty-five dollars, if memory serves me right. We're in a little different league here, Mr. Parsons."

Parsons folded his hands again. "So we are, Mr. Mewson, so we are."

They locked eyes for a second, then Mewson realized he was still holding the two empty glasses, and he felt slightly foolish. He turned and took them back to the liquor cabinet and mixed himself another drink, his back to Parsons. Let *him* hang for a while, he thought, taking his time. When he came back he brought his briefcase from the double bed and put it on the carpet in front of his feet when he sat down. He took a drink, put his glass on the arm of the chair, and snapped open the case. He was hoping that Parsons would at least lean forward in order to see over the top of the open lid, but Parsons just sat there, relaxed, with his hands clasped in his lap and his face expressionless. Mewson reached under a layer of shorts and T-shirts and extracted two slim sheaves of bills, by feel. Each sheaf was held together by a red paper band and contained twenty-five used one-hundred-dollar bills. He handed them to Parsons.

Parsons took the money, put it in a jacket pocket, zipped it closed, and stood up. "Where will you be in three days?" he asked.

"Right here, waiting on you," Mewson said, thinking of the reasonably warm sun and blue skies of Tampa.

Parsons turned to the door. "I'll be in touch."

"You'd better," Mewson said.

Parsons turned back, his body somehow more erect, his face stiff. "Mr. Mewson," he said quietly, "I'm not a bum. My associates aren't bums. We deal honest. We give full service for our money."

Mewson had not been prepared for this kind of reaction to his parting shot, which was almost de rigueur in the circles in which he moved. "Okay," he said in what he hoped was a tone of impatient dismissal. "Just get on with the job. I'm a busy man."

Parsons didn't move. "I don't like to be threatened," Parsons said. "I overreact to threats, Mr. Mewson."

They stood there, frozen in time, and then Mewson heard himself say, "Okay, forget it."

Parsons nodded, as if in acknowledgment of Mewson's apology, and let himself out.

Mewson was stunned by the exchange. He finished his drink without tasting it and made himself another. After a while he realized what had happened. He was simply too used to dealing with ass-kissers. Everybody kissed the Mob's ass. Lawyers, judges, cops, nightclub owners, bikers, dealers, everybody. Yes, sir, Mr. Mewson. No, sir, Mr. Mewson. Because back of Mr. Mewson was Mr. Bartoli, and back of Mr. Bartoli was the whole organization, and *nobody* fucked with the organization.

Except—

Rider woke up with a putrid mouth and a grade-two headache—the dull, throbbing kind. He really wanted some cold water, but there was no spring within a decent distance, so he forced the rest of the pint down in throat-burning sips, gagging at the taste, fighting to keep it on his stomach. Christ, he thought sickly, realizing how easy it would have been for someone to have come on him in the night.

Presently the liquor decided to stay put, and the familiar, disoriented glow of the morning-after buzz suffused his body. He dimly remembered leaving a passed-out Pat Cousins in the motel bed and maneuvering the rattling pickup through the city and over the miles of highway and twisting mountain roads, finally putting the left front wheel in the ditch a mile above his cabin, at which point he had collapsed across the seat, dead drunk.

He had to push the truck off in order to get it started,

forcing it to roll down the twisting, rutted road after a lot of straining. He jumped in and popped the clutch, his face slimy with whiskey-odor sweat. He drove to within a quarter mile of his cabin, then parked the pickup on a grade and made the rest of the approach through the woods.

The forest floor was damp, so he made good time, sliding under, around, and between the heavy foliage.

When he judged he was close to his cabin he slowed, taking more pains. He moved in almost total silence, stopping every ten paces or so to look and listen. When he came out on the ridge in back of his place he stopped for a long time, squatting down and waiting as his breathing quieted. He could see his own roof through the trees, two hundred yards farther on down the slope.

He moved in carefully, listening, totally alert, ignoring the still-untamed hangover, the shotgun off safety, the .45 in his waistband. He looked under the porch, then circled the house and stopped at the edge of the porch, listening again. No thump of shifting feet. No coughing. Only the mountain silence broken by bird chatter and wind rustle. Rider raised up and peered in one of the uncurtained windows. The place was empty.

Satisfied, he went back up the ridge at double time, his breath rattling in his chest, whiskey sweat forming and drying in the cold air. Gotta straighten up, he thought. Gotta get in shape.

He had not really expected an ambush this quickly, but he simply couldn't risk the chance of walking into one like some clown. Killed making all the right moves was acceptable, but nobody wanted to get killed because of a fuckup. The enemy was supposed to give your carcass a quick mental salute of respect, not a sneer of contempt.

He approached the truck alertly, then rolled it off

and drove it into his yard. After the truck was unloaded he allowed himself a half hour and two warm beers to straighten up on while he organized his plans. Then he went to work.

Since there was thick cover on the slope behind the cabin, making it the most likely avenue of approach for an enemy, Rider went to work on that first. With his helper gone he had given up the idea of clearing brush and stringing barbed wire.

He changed into camouflage and put on his shoulder holster and the Magnum revolver. A web belt, holding a canteen of water and a bayonet, went around his waist. He took a faded pack from a hook on the wall and began putting items in it. A claw hammer and a double handful of tenpenny coated nails. A package of brass thumbtacks and another of wooden clothespins. An industrial-size spool of green carpet thread. A paper bag of new flashlight batteries. A spool of electrical tape and wire pliers. As an afterthought he added two cans of beer. He took the Stevens 12-gauge pump loaded with number 4 buck and put two five-packs of extra shells in his pocket.

Outside, he kicked the dirt and leaves away from his hidey-hole and pulled two .50-caliber metal ammo boxes into the pallid sunlight. He lifted the rubber-sealed lids. Inside one box nestled about a dozen yellow plastic tubes with metal screw-on lids. Each tube was marked "NI PAK STICK one and three-eighth inches DIA x eight inches." Underneath that it said, "Warning: High Explosive When Armed."

The other box held a number of plastic bottles filled with a thin red liquid and blasting caps. These were small silver cylinders the thickness of a pencil and about two inches long. Each cap was complete with its green and yellow lead wires, banded neatly with paper tabs. Each tab bore a single number, from 0 to 7. This indicated the delay time in seconds from initiation of current until detonation. It was all commercial stuff, easy enough to obtain on construction jobs, if you knew the right people. Rider had worked on a flume building job the previous summer, and the first time a charge went off, blowing huge chunks of rock out of a cliffside into the river below, he had determined to meet those people. He had traded a box of tools for half a case.

Since then he had used maybe half of that, clearing some stumps from his driveway and shooting ponds for fish. But he had always begrudged its use, in a way. It seemed wasteful to use a limited supply of such handy material in such a prosaic manner.

Surely more exciting, meaningful uses could be found, if one saved the stuff and had any imagination at all.

He realized he was humming a little tuneless ditty as he put two of the sticks, a bottle of priming fluid, and one of the caps back in his hole and covered it up again. He took everything else and staggered off into the woods, overloaded with the two boxes, the pack, the shotgun, and a killer hangover.

Halfway up the slope and between two and three hundred yards behind his cabin Rider stopped and took a beer break. It was heavily wooded in here, the pines and oaks and maple trees dripping moisture on the carpet of wet brown leaves. The undergrowth was a thick tangle of dead tree limbs, brittle winter-killed briars, vines and tangled foliage reaching desperately for the weak winter sun.

Rider finished the beer and began stringing the incredibly strong carpet thread from tree to tree through bent-over nails about knee-high. When he was finished he had a series of fifty-yard lengths of trip thread running in a reasonably straight line along the entire avenue of approach. If they came down this ridge, somebody was going to hit something. Of course, if a nosy bear or deer came exploring, the same thing would happen, but that was out of his control. He remembered a time in 'Nam when a water buffalo had wandered into their perimeter defense at a little hamlet near Chu Lai. When the Claymore went off, everybody opened up, MGs, flares, small arms, the whole bit. Orange tracers crisscrossed through the smoking night air, NCOs cursing, trying to enforce fire control. In the morning came the sheepish grins and embarrassed bullshit remarks when it was discovered they had wasted $40,000 worth of ordnance on some poor farmer's only means of support.

At one end of each run of thread Rider fastened a clothespin to the tree, and at the other end tied the thread off, anchoring it. He whittled a little wooden wedge for each clothespin and attached the other end of the thread to these wedges, which he placed between the jaws of the clothespins.

He now had the clothespins fastened to trees, a wedge in place, and the thread barely taut, stretching to its anchor point. Rider made sure each arrangement worked as it should, with no binding. A slight pull on the thread, anywhere along the line, and the wedge popped out of the clothespin, letting the jaws close.

Things would be much simpler, he knew, if he had some M-1 pull firing devices and about a dozen Claymores. But one must work with the tools at hand. Basically the idea is to simply close an electric circuit, which can be improvised in a number of ways. The trouble with all this Mickey Mouse shit, he thought as he worked, is that it *is* Mickey Mouse. The stuff made for this business has standard procedures and built-in safeties. None of this crap did, so in lieu of that, he finished off the other beer to steady his hands, then went back to all the clothespins and pushed a brass thumbtack into each jaw in such a way that they would come in contact with each other when the wedge was removed. Then, because it was getting close to the ass-puckering part of the job, he went back to the house for more beer, carrying the shotgun.

He returned with the beer and a cardboard box containing about thirty pounds of rusting half-inch roofing nails. He took a number 6 blasting cap and unrolled the twin eight-foot wires, stripping the protective cardboard cover from the two bared ends. He cut one of these wires halfway down and stripped the rubber insulation back on both the new ends. Then he wrapped one of the original bare ends of wire around the upper brass thumbtack and pushed it firmly into the wooden jaw. He did the same with the other original end on the other tack. He reinserted the wooden wedge and took out one of the D flashlight batteries and taped the newly cut wire ends to each pole.

He now had a complete circuit, wire from cap to thumbtack, wire from other thumbtack back to battery, then back to cap. Only the wedge holding the thumbtacks apart kept the circuit from closing.

Rider prepared each set like this, working his way up the line methodically, humming and drinking beer steadily now. He taped each battery and excess wire neatly to the bottom of the trunk and covered the arrangement with leaves. The entire series of booby traps was ready now, with the exception of the main ingredient.

Rider sat down on the ground, open beer can next to him, and removed the top on a stick of dynamite. He poured the red fluid onto the white powder a little at a time, letting it soak down through, turning the powder a pastel pink. When he had done all eleven sticks he finished his beer, then moved all his tools, empty cans, and shotgun well down the slope. He had no intention of farting around up here any more than he had to.

Keeping his mind carefully blank to all the possible fuckups—like a branch falling on a trip wire—he taped two bundles of three sticks each and put them in the bottom of the ammo cans. He put each can by a tree toward the middle of the complex, on the theory that anyone coming off the ridge would be more likely to come through here than the sides.

He inserted each dangling cap into the slot on the side of the plastic tubes, then put the bundle into the bottom of the cans and carefully filled the two ammo cans to the brim with the roofing nails and closed the covers as tight as he could without damaging the wires. He broke off some small branches and covered the cans, making them less noticeable.

He could feel a thin sheen of sweat on his forehead, and he wanted a drink and cigarette badly. Doing this always caused a thin balloon of incipient panic to swell in the chest, a little balloon that could, if allowed, grow and burst in an instant, making the hands fumble and hurry or the legs start running in blind, instinctive flight.

"Shit," Rider said, and went down the hill to his gear. He sat down and opened a beer and lit a cigarette. His hands were all right but his knees felt a little weak. It was just the idea of inserting that silver cap into that slot. That was the time the world would come to an end in a blinding, stunning flash.

He finished the beer and smoke, then went back up the hill and worked outward on both sides of his line. Since he had no more cans or nails, he put the rest of the sticks on the ground, one to each tree, and covered them.

All he was really counting on was a warning. Somebody would have to be almost on top of one of these sticks for the blast to kill them, and it was a big woods out here. The ammo boxes full of nails would be better, of course, but he really had no idea how effective they would be. He suspected most of the shrapnel would blow up, instead of out. But then again, if someone was close enough, it was sayonara, motherfucker. But he would know they were there, which was the main point of all this. No one knew better than Rider how much shooting and blasting it required to produce a casualty or two. After the battle of the water buffalo, the platoon leader had sarcastically informed them, "Never have so many shot so much for so little."

When he was done he went back down the hill, being careful where he walked until he was well clear of the danger zone. He gathered his gear, finished off the rest of the beer—rather than carry it—and headed for the cabin, moving quietly, his hangover only a bad memory.

While Rider had been in the woods sweating over his explosives, ex-Captain Vance Parsons had been less than a thousand feet away at one point.

He had arrived at McGee Tyson Airport in Knoxville that morning on the first flight out of Washington International. He traveled under an assumed name and continued to wear his casual disguise.

Upon arrival, he had purchased a road map of Tennessee and located the small town indicated on the W-2 form. Then he took a cab to the regional office of the National Forest Service and bought a topographic map of the area surrounding his target.

He went back to the airport and had the taxi let him out at the hangar where the fixed base operator was located. He went into the office and made arrangements to rent a Cessna 150, using a pilot's license and medical certificate in his own name because he had nothing else. The aircraft and a flight instructor to give him a checkout ride were available at ten o'clock.

Parsons bought the appropriate sectional chart and, since he had an hour to kill, went to the coffeeshop next door and had breakfast while he studied his maps and charts. He then realized that he would need an even more detailed map in order to pinpoint his target exactly. With what he now had, he had no way of locating a rural route, let alone a specific house, from the air.

He went back to the flight office at ten and shook hands with a gangling young flight instructor. They walked out on the flight line and Parsons preflighted the aircraft, then took off and made one circuit around the airfield. The instructor was satisfied Parsons could fly the plane, and had Parsons taxi him back to the office. Parsons took off again and climbed to 3,000 feet. Some of these mountains were 2,500 feet above sea level, with radio beacons and fire towers on top of them.

He rolled onto a heading of 270 degrees and trimmed the plane until the pressure on the wheel was neutral. It was a clear, cold morning, slightly bumpy. Visibility was unlimited.

He navigated with the chart in his lap, glancing from it to the landmarks below. The silver snake of the Tennessee River wandering through the barren plowed fields, scattered towns, and roads passed beneath him.

Rather than follow a compass course directly to his destination, which entailed allowing for compass deviation, wind drift, and elapsed time, Parsons simply followed the obvious visual aid of the expressway out of the city.

After flying thirty minutes he identified a large town from the chart and turned the aircraft to a southerly

heading, following a secondary road that cut a tortu-
ous path through steep valleys and along the sides of
heavily wooded hills. He was forced to climb another
thousand feet in order to smooth out the increasing
bumpiness of the air from the updraft around the
mountains.

Presently he saw the town he was looking for, a
small, scattered area, homes and commercial buildings spread out on a flat, wide valley floor. From here,
his target was somewhere close, but where? He circled
the place twice, studying its layout and surrounding
terrain. Roads led off in several directions, quickly lost
to view beneath pine trees or between deep cuts in the
surrounding hills.

Parsons had an idea. He looked at his chart, identified the closest general aviation airport, and flew in
that direction.

His new course took him along the spine of a huge
mountain range which stretched away ahead of him
until it disappeared into horizon haze. Glancing at the
chart, he saw that it ran for over thirty miles before
leveling out somewhere in northern Georgia.

He saw the blinking red of the radio beacon poking
its thin finger at the sky ahead of him, and began a
gentle bank to the right, easing off the power and
setting up a glide toward the level country and the
airport. As he did so, he plucked the microphone from
its bracket and, at that exact instant, passed over
Rider's head. Both hunter and hunted were totally
unaware of this. Rider was concentrating on filling an
ammo can with nails and was only subliminally aware
of the buzz of a small plane above him, and Parsons,
because he was trying to locate the small airport
somewhere off his nose, never noticed the tiny group
of rooftops below him, nestled in the hollow of the
mountainside.

Parsons finally located the airport under his left wingtip, a one-runway affair with a blue and white prefab hangar and several planes parked haphazardly in front of it. He saw only one car at the end of the building, but decided this meant someone was home.

He switched the radio to the general aviation channel and keyed the mike. "Monroe Unicom, this is Cessna 1957 Whiskey. Over."

After several tries a scratchy voice replied, "Five Seven Whiskey, this is Monroe Unicom. Over."

"Uh, Monroe, what runway you using?"

"Five Seven Whiskey," the voice replied, "active runway two four. Wind one zero knots. Watch the powerlines, y'hear?"

"Roger that," Parsons said. "I've got the powerlines."

He hung up the mike and spiraled down, then leveled off and entered the traffic pattern in the approved manner. Even though there was no other traffic, there wasn't going to be any daring-fighter-ace shit from Vance Parsons. He had stayed alive for forty-four years by following three simple rules: Think everything through. Trust no one. Take no unnecessary risks.

And there was reason to be especially careful now, because this was going to be Parsons' last job. The ab-so-fucking-lutely last one. He'd said that before, of course, but somehow the money just seemed to dribble away. Parsons didn't care much for drink, and he wasn't a gambler. He'd never had a wife to support and saw no reason to change that now. His problem was business. He had been trying to build some sort of successful endeavor ever since he left the army in '69. He'd invested his accumulated pay from three straight tours in 'Nam in a deal that couldn't fail, and yet somehow it had.

When he was almost broke and getting desperate, he sold what stock was left and flew to South Africa, leaving his creditors holding the bag, which was what they deserved, and enlisted in the SADF with the rank of major.

Two years of running around in Land Rovers wasting terrs had earned him enough to try again, this time a partnership in a nightclub.

And he would have made it, too, but, Christ, everybody had their fucking hand out. The cops, building inspectors, liquor board, everybody. And he should have killed his partner, but back then he still had some respect for the law.

Since then Parsons had worked at a series of "security consultant" jobs in South America and a number of "short-term contracts." Each contract had been a little dirtier, a little messier, than the preceding one.

So here he was, pushing fifty and broke, doing the Mob's dirty work. He was under no illusions. Once you got into bed with those kind of people, they owned you.

But they wouldn't own ex-SF Captain Vance Parsons, by God! One more job, a money job like this one, and nobody would ever see him again. He had a modest little ranch picked out in Belize, already a going proposition. It couldn't fail. Let them find him there if they could.

Parsons allowed himself a tight grin as he turned on final and cranked some flaps.

Five grand for a couple days' work wasn't bad, and wait until they heard the price for the real thing. They'd shit! But they'd pay, too, he was sure of it.

He realized that he was coming in too high, and also realized that his mind had been wandering. Jesus, he thought, daydreaming on final. Now I know it's time to retire.

He pulled the throttle all the way out and put the carburetor heat on, then crossed the controls and slipped the plane down, losing altitude rapidly.

He passed over the powerlines and runway numbers and straightened the controls, letting the plane sink on its own, coming up on the nose in little increments, glancing at his air speed and the blinking stall-warning light.

The main wheels touched the macadam with a squeak, bounced slightly into the air, and then came down to stay with a solid thump. The nose wheel settled down as the speed bled off, and Parsons taxied off the runway onto the grass verge and braked the aircraft by the office/hangar.

He pulled the mixture of full lean and waited until the prop choked down and stopped, then cleaned up the panel and unbuckled his seat belt. He locked the brakes, opened the door, and climbed out.

A slim, middle-aged man wearing glasses, slacks, and a nylon windbreaker leaned in the doorway. He nodded to Parsons.

"Howdy. My name's Fillmore."

"Howdy yourself," Parsons said. "Mine's Gedney." He got a Coke out of the machine standing against the outside wall. He sipped at it while he made small talk with the man for a few minutes, then got down to business.

"I'm thinking about investing in a piece of property around here," he told Fillmore. "I've got a hot tip but I'd like to check this place out by air before I contact this guy." He chuckled conspiratorially. "I don't guess I have to tell you that you can find out a lot about property by a little air reconnaissance."

Fillmore smiled. "No, I guess you don't. I don't know much about real estate, but I flew recon in '51, back in Korea." He pronounced it "Ko-*reer*."

"All I've got is a route number and a box number," Padgett said. "I need to match this route number up with something I can recognize on the sectional."

"Oh, yeah, I think I got what you need. Come on inside," Fillmore said.

Parsons followed him into the small but surprisingly modern-looking office, which obviously doubled as a pilot's lounge. There was a glass-fronted counter filled with sunglasses, flight computers, and other aviation aids. Comfortable-looking chairs were arranged against the paneled walls. Local charts and maps were tacked up on the paneling. An oil stove radiated welcome heat from one corner of the room.

"I reckon this is what you want," Fillmore said, pointing to a black and white county map tacked to the wall.

Parsons looked. It was indeed what he wanted. Years of experience reading maps of all kinds enabled him almost immediately to relate what he was now seeing with what he had studied in the coffeeshop this morning.

"Wouldn't happen to know where Route One is on here, would you?"

"Oh hell, yes," Fillmore said. He put a tobacco-stained finger on the map and traced a faint line no more than four inches long. "Actually that's Bullet Creek Road. Lots of creek roads around here. Runs off the pike from Ashland, goes up the other side of the mountain, and dead-ends in Bullet Creek Community." He gave Parsons a shrewd look. "You buying up in Bullet Creek?"

When Parsons hesitated, Fillmore backed off. "Hell, none of my business. It's just there ain't nothing up there much. A few empty houses the bank or the government owns, but nobody can make a go up there. Too far from the action, I guess."

Parsons was realizing that he must have almost flown over the place a little while ago.

"Listen, Mr. Fillmore, you got any more of these maps?"

Fillmore went behind the counter and rummaged in his desk, then threw a folded map on the counter.

"How much?" Parsons said, reaching for his wallet.

"No charge," Fillmore said. "Glad to help." He grinned. "You ain't the first one ever been checkin' out land around here. 'Bout the only business there is around here, buyin' and sellin' land."

"Well, I appreciate it," Parsons said. He made small talk for a few more minutes, then sauntered back out to the plane, gave it a cursory preflight, and took off.

He climbed back toward the mountain range, but the hills rose faster than the underpowered engine could lift the aircraft, so he flew in a zigzag, gaining altitude. His ears popped and he thought, I know where you are now, m'boy, surely I do.

He leveled off at six thousand feet and flew over the top of the mountain. Using the radio beacon as a reference point, he positioned himself above where his target area should be, then cut his power, pulled on the carb heat, and began a wide spiral down, looking at the mountainside revolving up at him.

Suddenly he saw it, a thin brown strip of road dead-ending maybe a half mile past a tiny cluster of rooftops. He knew that he would never have found this place in the summer. Then the bare, spidery hardwood trees would have been heavy with foliage. He kept going down, clearing the engine several times to keep it from icing, trying to absorb as many details of the terrain as possible.

As he started to run out of sky, he leveled the plane up and fed in power slowly, attempting to keep engine noise to a minimum. When he was far enough away he brought it up to the recommended climb rpm and pointed the nose back toward Knoxville.

He took a notebook and pen from his jacket pocket, put the notebook on the empty passenger seat next to him, and began to sketch in the details while they were still fresh in his mind. He had the glow of satisfaction a man gets when he has made a good beginning on a difficult job. Although he didn't really think this job was going to be all that difficult.

In fact, he thought it was going to be a piece of cake.

X.

What Rider really wanted was a grenade. Grenades were pretty inefficient killing weapons in the open. They were great for clearing out rooms and bunkers and spider holes, but in the open the killing zone was quite limited, generally less than ten yards.

The beauty about grenades on open ground, especially at night, was that, unlike a firearm, which leaves a muzzle flash signature, you could throw a grenade and nobody could tell where it came from. One minute you're walking along and the next minute something hits the ground in front of you and *pow*!— goodnight David, goodnight Chet.

Rider wanted a grenade.

As Parsons was paying for his plane rental at McGee Tyson, Rider was sitting on a poncho in the woods on the other side of the road from his house. He had set up a simple camp here because he had no intention of sleeping in his cabin anymore. They might come this way instead of down the booby-trapped ridge, they might even come by the road or parachute in, but by God he wasn't going to be where he was supposed to be, even if it meant sleeping out in the woods from now on. Which it did. He had his ground sheet, a sleeping bag, a plastic cover in case it rained, the army pack full of beer, and all his guns laid out next to him.

He studied the two sticks of dynamite, thinking. It wasn't any problem to tape them to a handle, and he had some big sixteen-penny nails he could tape around the whole thing for shrapnel. The problem was getting the damn thing to go off when it was supposed to go off. He put the dynamite down and picked up the cap, which was a seven-second type.

He visualized taping the explosive and nails to a piece of wood, then taping a flashlight battery some-where on that. He could trim the wires down on the cap and insert it in the dynamite stick, then twist the lead ends together for safety, since the cap wouldn't fire with the wires touching. When he was ready to use it, all he had to do was untwist the wires, stick one on each end of the battery, and throw the thing. He would have seven seconds' leeway.

Except that if it was dark and he was under extreme stress and his hands were wet with rain or sweat or blood, things might get a little confused, or they might get a little worse than confused if somebody had mislabeled the cap and it was only a two-second fuse. He wished he had some real honest-to-God grenades. Or even a nonelectric cap. Then he could light the goddamn thing off his cigar, just like John Wayne.

He drank his beer in the cold dampness and thought about it.

Parsons had two drinks in the airport lounge, then got a taxi to a motel close by.

He started calling car-rental agencies until he found one that had a four-wheel-drive vehicle available. He made arrangements to pick it up in the morning, then started getting his gear ready for tomorrow.

He laid it all out on the bed, checking it as he went. Hiking boots, brown corduroy trousers, L. L. Bean chamois-cloth shirt, camouflage hunting hat, heavy wool jacket. He hefted the heavy case containing the Celestron forward-recon scope onto the bed, took it out and cleaned the lens, then replaced the cover cap and put it away. He didn't check his cameras individually, but he assured himself they were there, then put them under the bed with the Celestron. He made sure his second wallet with the phony driver's license and business cards was ready.

He checked the spare magazine for his personal defense weapon, an HKP7, then checked the weapon itself, wiped it down with a silicone rag, and put it back in the shoulder rig.

After sharpening his boot knife, he took a shower, deciding not to bother with the foam-rubber-and-glasses disguise. It was only eight o'clock and he was going to go down to the lounge for a drink or two. But no more than two. Absolutely no more.

Tomorrow would be a long day.

Joe Ball was rump-sore and bleary-eyed from driving. He was coming into the outskirts of Watertown, New York. It had been dark for several hours and was starting to spit a light mix of rain and snow.

He drove off an exit ramp below a sprawling Holiday Inn complex, ablaze with lights. He parked, went inside to the desk, and rented a room, puffy-faced from a combination of travel fatigue and nervous exhaustion.

Once inside his room, he locked the door, put the chain on, and collapsed on one of the double beds, his mind whirling.

Tomorrow he would sell the car. He was starting to

have paranoid thoughts about the car. Then he would buy a cheap suitcase, shaving gear, and some more clothes. Then he would take a bus, north, west, anywhere. It didn't matter, as long as he ended up in a city the Mafia had never heard of. Then he would find an apartment and a job somewhere, probably as a salesman with a car dealer. It was really all he knew, and he was good.

He decided that he would take a nap before showering and washing his socks and underwear. As he drifted off to sleep, he allowed himself the comfort of believing that all this would eventually be over, that things would work out for the best. Maybe someday he'd find a connection where he could turn the rest of the coke, a little at a time. He spun on down into the sleep of the just.

Pat Cousins was also in a motel room. After Rider had driven away she had stood in the shabby Trailways station, nervously fingering the wad of bills in her purse, trying to decide where to go. Finally coming to the conclusion that she had no ideas whatsoever, she paid four dollars for a ticket to Chattanooga, and from there took a taxi to the closest motel with a lounge, which turned out to be a Best Western.

She had sat for hours, nursing mixed drinks and trying to develop some idea of what to do or where to go.

As the place filled up, the attempted pickups had become more numerous and annoying, so she had gone to the office and rented a room.

She sat at the desk making notations on motel stationery, attempting to organize her options. After a long while, out of boredom, frustration, and a certain amount of loneliness, she had a burst of inspiration. It was a natural, instinctive decision. She was really not all that sophisticated, and somehow she had completely forgotten a warning casually injected in a conversation several days ago.

Pat Cousins was frightened, confused, and in way over her head. She was only twenty-four years old.

In the morning she would get on a bus and go home to her mother.

Bartoli was spending the evening at home, with his family. He was in the basement rec room with his oldest boy, drinking a rum and Coke. His wife, Ruth, and the two younger children were already in bed. As far as the Hillbilly Connection was concerned, things were in motion, and now all that was necessary was to wait for the results to start coming in.

In truth, he would have preferred to just let the whole thing drop and go back to making money, but there were principles involved here. Matters of honor and respect. Somebody had ripped him off, and then somebody else had wasted his people, and if the thing was left hanging, the word would get around that his shit was weak, and that would be the beginning of the end.

He realized that he was treading on unfamiliar ground and that this was inherently dangerous, yet he really had no choice. It all boiled down to a matter of respect. Somebody fucks with you, you have them put to sleep. It was as simple as that. There was no practical alternative.

He resisted the urge to contact Mewson and see if there was any progress in Washington; or call his office, on the remote chance somebody had shown up at all the places being watched: Ball's car lot, or his home, or the woman's mother's place in Gainesville, Florida. Christ on a crutch, how he wanted their slimy asses! How he wanted that fucking hillbilly's ass!

He became aware of a voice and with an effort focused back on his surroundings.

"Daddy, look, I won, I won!" his eight-year-old son, Mark, was shouting, as he pointed to the video game that had been his Christmas present.

"Beautiful, kid, beautiful," Bartoli said, not even understanding what the child had accomplished.

Mark Bartoli 'had passed 800,000 points on the Centipede game and the computer was going crazy.

The Drunken Chief was sitting on his porch, shivering in his blanket, watching the moonlit valley below and drinking pure, one-hundred-percent bad-ass-kickin' corn liquor.

The old M1 rifle was leaning on the rail next to him, loaded with an eight-round clip. He had three more clips in a pouch.

The Chief was wearing buckskins and, as he drank and watched, he wondered if he had the sickness of the head that comes with old age.

He should have been inside where it was warm, watching the goddamn overpriced color idiot box he had paid for out of his pension and browbeat his modern young relatives to lug puffing up the trail. But no, instead he was sitting outside in the cold, not even the little Honda generator running, all decked out in age-stiff leather and painted up like some kind of punk-rock star.

Waiting.

Because of the dreams, yes. The dreams said the people down below, rotting underground in the field, wouldn't be the end of it. The dreams said the fire wasn't over, not by a long shot. But why was *he* here? It was none of his damn business, is what it was. His bones were old. He had done *his* fight, years ago, and the only thing he ever got out of it was that wonderful rifle he'd managed to smuggle back and a pension a dog would starve on. So why?

The Chief pondered, there in the dark, drinking

moonshine against the cold. He thought of the Crazy One down below, also waiting in the dark and the cold, also drinking, without a doubt. Then he wondered if it was possible for people to get just plain bored with it all. To get fed up with their mindless routine and pallid entertainment and meaningless lives.

Maybe a whole bunch of people would jump at the chance to legitimately run amok, to mix up in some sort of violence at the slightest excuse, to run and shoot and fuck and loot and go out in a blaze of glory. Maybe the dumb heathen Indians had something, after all, he thought. Maybe they knew that the Bible bangers were wrong and there is no heaven. Maybe there was only Valhalla. Maybe the truest, only really noble human instinct is to go down fighting.

Maybe there is really such a thing as Warrior Blood.

XI.

Two days later, at ten in the morning, Mewson opened the door of his room and Parsons walked in.

Mewson, who had spent his time pacing the confines of the room, drinking in the lounge, and trying to reassure Bartoli over the phone that everything was progressing smoothly, watched impatiently as Parsons tossed a large manila envelope on the bed and shucked out of his overcoat.

"Well?"

Parsons sat down. "Anything to drink in here? It's colder than a well-digger's ass outside."

Mewson sloshed whiskey in a plastic motel glass, handed it to Parsons, then sat down in a chair, pointedly waiting.

Parsons downed half the drink, then put it down and reached for the envelope. "I've done air recon," he said. He drew the charts and maps out and handed them to Mewson. "The target area is circled in red. It's isolated. Eight houses, four mobile homes, all abandoned except for the cabin. A little shack higher up on the side of the mountain. Old man lives there, no phone, probably deaf as a post."

He paused for another drink, a sip this time, then went on. "It's rough country up there. Real rough. Very heavy vegetation, even at this time of year. Steep hills, narrow, deep hollows, boulders, clear cuts covered with dead falls, the works. Hard to navigate in, hard to travel in."

Mewson, who was not really interested in topographical details, said, "Okay, it's going to be pure hell. What I want to know is can you do it, and if you can, how long and how much?"

Parsons just looked at him a second, his face expressionless, then went on. "I spent all day yesterday on a forestry service road that runs along the top of the target area, about four miles away. I got a pretty good idea of the layout of the place and the routine, of which there isn't much."

"They're not gone?" Mewson asked, alarmed.

"One person there," Parsons said. He slipped a number of photographic blowups out of the envelope and handed them across. "No woman, one vehicle, an old junky pickup. I'd say the two lovebirds have hauled ass, and the hillbilly is still there." He allowed himself a wintry smile. "Waiting." He picked up his drink.

Mewson examined the photographs. They were of good quality, taken with a 35mm Pentax through the recon scope. They showed the front of Rider's cabin, the parked truck, short portions of the road, everything slightly foreshortened by distance and elevation.

They were basically all the same except one. This showed the front of the cabin like the others, but in this one a tiny figure was visible, halfway down the yard, carrying something on his shoulders.

Parsons leaned over and tapped the figure with his finger. "Your friend Rider, I believe, carrying a case of beer up in the woods, where he's apparently swilling it to kill time until we make our move."

Mewson looked at the picture a long time, Parsons' "waiting" echoing in his mind. A thought surfaced. What if this try turned out an abortion like the last one? What if this Rider decided he was tired of waiting? Annoyed, he brushed the speculation aside and tossed the photos on the bed along with the maps, then looked at Parsons. "I'm assuming we can do business."

"In answer to your questions earlier," Parsons said, "yes. As soon as you can deliver some hardware from our mutual friend, and one hundred thousand dollars."

"One hundred K!" Mewson said, coming out of the chair. "Bleeding shit, buddy, there's only one man up there! We're not asking you to infiltrate Libya and whack out Khaddafi!"

Parsons remained calm and seated. "Mr. Mewson, as we concluded at our last meeting, this isn't in the same league as having a car worked on. This, sir, is murder one, for which they are once again executing people, in case you don't watch the news." He held up a hand as Mewson began an angry retort. "Also, this one man you so casually mention has already killed five of your own people, professionals in their own way, I'm sure."

"Nobody pays that kind of money for a hit," Mewson said. "It just isn't done. Don't let all those half-million-dollar contracts everybody hears about go to your head, Mr. Parsons. It's all bullshit. It doesn't work that way."

Parsons finished his drink and went over to the bottle for a refill. As he was pouring, he said, "I know all this. I know you people put out those big-bucks contracts on people like Valachi and Teresa, then if some poor jerk does manage to put them down, he can go piss in a bucket while he waits for his money."

He turned from the table, drink in hand. "I also know that once I do a job for you, you're going to get the idea that my ass belongs to you. That's why a job like this costs so much, Mr. Mewson. Because it's got to be the last job. After this I disappear." He grinned nastily. "If you people played right, it wouldn't be so expensive."

To stall for time, Mewson said, "What kind of hardware are you talking about?"

Parsons reached in his coat pocket and handed Mewson a typewritten list.

Mewson studied it a second. "I'll have to get an okay on this kind of money from down south. Where can I get in touch with you later today?"

"Bullshit," Parsons said, and nodded at the phone on its stand. "It won't take ten minutes to get your okay, if you really need one, which I doubt." He looked at his watch. "Mewson, this deal is going to cost you one hundred big ones up front. No negotiating and no welching this time. I'll be down in the lounge until one. If you want the job done, you come down anytime before that and sit down and have a drink with me. When you leave you forget to take your briefcase. If that briefcase has got one hundred thousand dollars in used, unmarked money, I'll call you in this room before six tonight and tell you where to deliver the hardware. Then the job gets done within a week. Otherwise, you and your sponsors can go up in the mountains and dig Rider out yourselves." He finished his drink, put on his coat, and went to the door. "One o'clock," he said, and left.

As soon as the door was closed, Mewson went to the briefcase, unlocked it, and transferred $50,000 to his suitcase, leaving $100,000 in the briefcase. Then he called Florida.

"One hundred K, Bob," he said when the connection was made.

"All right," Bartoli said, dismissing the amount. "When?"

"Within a week. I've got to get my contact to deliver some tools. That shouldn't take over a day, so I'd say this business should be wrapped up by the middle of next week at the latest."

Bartoli grunted. "It better be. I don't mind the bread, but things better happen." He paused. "You made that clear to this guy?"

"Oh, sure," Mewson said, feeling tiny beads of sweat start to grease his palm against the plastic of the phone. To change the subject, he said, "This guy cased the place up there pretty thoroughly, Bob. He says Ball and the woman aren't there. Just Rider, off in the woods, boozing it up and waiting for us."

There was a short silence while Bartoli digested this, then he said, "Well, it figures. Anybody but a crazy would run. No problem, though. Now we're back in the ballpark. I'll get our people moving on this end. You move on anything that needs doing up there." He paused again and Mewson listened to him breathing heavily for a second, then Bartoli said, in a low, intense voice, "*I want Rider*. You hear me, Al? I want Rider. Everything else is secondary."

"Yeah, I hear you, Bob. We'll get him."

"Then get on it," Bartoli ordered, and dropped the phone back in the cradle.

Mewson put his phone down and wiped his hand on his pants. He put on his jacket and picked up the briefcase. It was time to have a drink in the lounge.

Pat Cousins was lying on her side in the dark. Her hands were tied behind her back with a tie, as were her feet. They had taken her shoes, presumably so she couldn't kick at the car trunk lid to attract attention. She was also gagged with a wad of toilet paper and a silk handkerchief. It was hard to breathe just through her nose, and she was on top of something hard, possibly a car jack.

It was cold and stank of gas fumes and new rubber.

She had walked right into it, of course. The taxi had left her out in front of her mother's modest home on the outskirts of Gainesville. She'd never noticed the car with the two men in it parked down the street.

Her mother wasn't home, which was not unusual. She'd been looking for the key under one of the flowerpots on the window ledge when she heard the squeal of tires.

Then her arm was being twisted up to her shoulder blade and a stinking, meaty palm was slapped over her mouth. She'd almost fainted from the pain as she was frog-marched out to the car and forced in.

They'd quickly found a deserted side road, probably already scouted out, where they had trussed her and locked her in the trunk.

The twisting drive to the expressway had made her nauseated, and now, in spite of the car traveling in a steady direction, she was still sick. It was the sickness of terror, and she struggled to keep from throwing up, knowing that if she did she would strangle.

She thought of Rider and the cabin up in the hills, both of which she had detested so thoroughly before. Now she wished with the anguish of lost hope that she were sitting on that rickety porch, drinking moonshine and lemonade. Where it was safe.

I'm a fool, she thought, and I'm going to die. She started to cry silently behind the gag, snuffling and snorting through her nose. After a while, she started to pray.

*   *   *

Parsons stood waiting in a field in Fairfax County, Virginia, his breath frosting white in the morning air. The field and the abandoned farmhouse behind him belonged to his brother, who was a GS-7 and worked at the U.S. Treasury Building in Washington.

Parsons' dusty sedan was parked in the dirt driveway in front of the porch. There were five men in it, keeping the motor running for the warmth of the heater. Parsons could see heads moving as they talked and smoked. The radio was playing rock music. Parsons wondered how they could stand the volume in the enclosed space. He drew on a small cigar and glanced at his watch: 8:25 A.M.

The last of the five men had arrived at Parsons' Maryland home late last night. He had called from the airport and Parsons had picked him up.

Immediately after his first meeting with Mewson, Parsons had spent hours on the phone, trying to contact people like the five now sitting in his car.

He knew at least twenty people he could have used, who would have been eager for a short-term job like this. Locating them was something else.

Most people in the business maintain a letter drop, which they check whenever they happen to be in the area. This could be anywhere from every week to once a year, much too slow for Parsons' needs.

So he had spent hours pushing literally pounds of coins into a pay phone, rather than use the one in his home, and had been able to recruit what he needed in less than two days.

The only thing the men in his car knew so far was that they had contracted for a low-risk, short-term assault, and that the job involved a private feud. That and the $5,000 already deposited in each of their accounts was really all they cared to know.

Parsons stamped his feet, trying to force the blood to

circulate in toes starting to numb. He considered getting in the car, rejected the idea as a display of weakness, and looked at his watch again. Eight-thirty. Let's get it, Smith, he thought, and, as if in answer, heard the sound of approaching vehicles.

Parsons' team got out of his car as a dark green van, followed by Harrison Smith's Cadillac, turned off the blacktop and came toward them on the long dirt driveway.

Everybody clustered around the vehicles as they ground to a stop.

Smith got out of his Cadillac, looking puffy-faced and edgy. "You need me to wait while you check this crap?" he asked nervously.

Al Mewson, who had been driving the van, and who was as nervous as Smith, said, "It's all there, Parsons. I helped load it."

"Ain't worried about being cheated," Parsons said. He grinned at Mewson. "Shit, you're paying for it."

"That's right, pal," Mewson said. He moved around the van, beckoning Parsons to follow. When they were out of hearing distance, Mewson said, "When, Parsons?"

"Tomorrow morning be quick enough?"

"That's fine," Mewson replied. "One thing you should know. The woman's out of it. We got her on ice back home, and we've traced the other asshole as far as upstate New York, so all you're to worry about is the hillbilly." He glanced at the van distastefully. "With the army you've got here and enough artillery to fight a fucking war there's not going to be any problems, right?"

Parsons, who intended to sell the artillery as soon as the job was done, grinned again and puffed on his cigar. "No problems," he said, toying with the idea of blowing smoke in Mewson's face.

"As soon as it's done, call me at the motel," Mewson said, and got in the car with Smith, who was gunning his motor impatiently.

Parsons watched them bump over the frozen ruts of the driveway, a smile of contempt twisting the corners of his mouth. Armchair commandos, he thought, then dismissed them and turned to his own command, who were busy unloading the van.

He watched them pry open the wooden furniture cases marked "Fragile: Handle With Care." Like children at Christmastime, they greeted the contents with exclamations of delight and satisfaction.

"Hey, a fucking bloop tube," Ray Shoemaker said, holding up the M79 grenade launcher. He broke it open, squinted down the huge 40mm bore, then snapped it closed and jammed the butt to his shoulder, sighting.

A tall, gangling man in his early thirties, he was a former Green Beret lieutenant, dishonorably discharged for dealing in the Saigon black market. Now he worked as a bail-bond chaser, supplemented with a few odd jobs from time to time. His favorite weapon was a knife, and he was very good with it.

"Here's the grenades that go with it," Herby Allen grunted, pulling a heavy carton out of the back of the van.

Allen was, at twenty-six, the youngest man on the team. He was also the smallest and, in Parsons' opinion, the most unstable. Raised in the backwoods of Arkansas, Herby had not seen combat in Vietnam, but he had spent his entire adult life making up for it, first in the French Foreign Legion, which he had successfully deserted at Djibouti, Africa, then as a gunner on a Corsican smuggler out of Marseilles. Eventually deported back to the States, he made his living from small-time drug deals. Properly supervised and kept away from dope, Herby was a good man, silent in the woods and utterly fearless.

Ex-Sergeant John Hardy was in his mid-thirties, a short, stocky man with a huge, drooping Pancho Villa mustache and two fingers missing from his left hand, the result of an Oklahoma oil-field accident. He had served with Parsons in Vietnam, then left the army in disgust at the way the war was being managed. He had served two years with the Selous Scouts in Rhodesia, and was now working on an offshore drilling rig in the Gulf of Mexico. He didn't really need the money, he just liked to keep his hand in, just in case a real war came along again. He didn't give a shit who he had to kill, but would have preferred it to be communists. Now he grunted in professional approval as he examined a full crate of M61 hand grenades, which were different from the ones that went into the bloop tube.

Frank Vargo was admiring one of the Beretta SC70 short assault rifles. He pulled the action open, examined the chamber, then let it close with a satisfying snap. Vargo, dark and Indian-looking, ran a seedy detective agency in the District of Columbia. An ex-marine NCO, Vargo had been given a medical discharge halfway through his second tour in 'Nam. The only thing that had saved him from a general court-martial was his Silver Star and the fact that his commanding officer had discovered the ears before a reporter did. Vargo had had a footlocker full, strung together on comm wire. He had worked with both Parsons and Harrison Smith in the past, in and out of the country.

The last man in the team was Sergeant Nick Tragger. Tragger was still in the army, a survival instructor at Fort Bragg. He had served with the Air Cavalry in Vietnam, and was the most thoroughly trained person in the team, with the exception of Parsons. His blond hair was shaved close to his bullet head, which jutted up on a massive neck. His arms were covered with tattoos, and his pale blue eyes regarded the world coldly from military-issue glasses. Even now, wearing civilian clothes, he wore army dress shoes. He didn't own any other kind. Parsons' call had reached him in the middle of a thirty-day leave, which he was spending alone and drunk in his mobile home. While on active duty he never drank.

In Vietnam, during a night attack near Da Nang, Tragger's M16 had jammed and his sandbagged hole had been overrun. They found him there, in the morning, sitting on the bodies of seven Viet Cong. Tragger had killed them all with his bare hands and an entrenching tool. Now he lifted the last rope-handled box out of the truck and put it on the ground.

Vargo pried the stapled top off and they both stared down, then Vargo gave a soft whistle. The others came over and grouped around, jostling for a look.

"Anybody familiar with that?" Parsons asked, strolling over.

"No," Vargo said, "but that's what I wanna use."

Parsons took the weapon out of the box and put it on the ground. "The latest thing," he said. "This is a CETME MG82 squad automatic weapon. You can use it on prone with the bipod or from the waist with the sling." He slung the SAW from his shoulder in a combat carry to demonstrate. "It weighs fourteen pounds empty. A two-hundred-round assault pack brings it up to a little over twenty pounds." Parsons squatted and removed one of the green boxlike assault packs from the case. He attached it to the machine gun by the bracket on the left side of the receiver. "The links go in the feed tray open side up. If our arms dealer followed instructions, this little number should have the bolt that gives us a cyclic rate of . . ."

Parsons turned toward the open field and a small, shallow pond, covered with a light film of ice, about seventy-five yards away. He jacked the operating handle back, cocking the piece, then squeezed the trigger. The cold morning air was shattered by a ripping string of explosions, so close together it was one long-drawn-out reverberation. An almost solid stream of empty brass spurted from the breech, and the pond disappeared in a cloud of spray and demolished ice.

". . . twelve hundred and fifty rounds per minute," Padgett finished, turning to them with a smile of genuine pleasure.

"Holy shit. Beautiful," Shoemaker said. The others were silent, still staring at the rainbows shining in the cloud of mist, which was all that was left of the pond. The five-second burst of 5.56mm had literally drained it.

"All right," Parsons said. "Let's get down to business."

They spent the morning firing the weapons for familiarization and zeroing, then went inside the unheated farmhouse to clean them on a blanket.

"Gentlemen," Parsons said, and they settled themselves on the ammo cases and floor.

He tapped a road map of east Tennessee pinned to the kitchen wall.

"This is our area of operation. It's in the mountain country near Knoxville, about a six-hour drive from here. The situation is this." He cleared his throat. "There is an individual living up there who has stolen something from our principal. This individual killed two of our principal's people during the commission of the theft, and three more people sent up there to recover the stolen property haven't reported in. It's assumed they won't."

"Drugs," Vargo said. "Drugs and the Mob." It was not a question and no one commented.

Parsons went on. "Now, this is a simple, in-and-out operation. The area is totally isolated, so there won't be any problems with other civilians or the law."

He pinned the topographic map over the road map and pointed to a red X, using the nose of a 5.56 round.

"This is the target's log cabin. It's on a dead-end road, and it's defensible, but not by one man, of course. In any case, the target isn't living in it. He's off waiting in the woods somewhere, ready to scrag the next bunch of assholes who go stumbling around up there."

Parsons passed the photographs around for the men to examine.

"What's that he's carrying?" Allen asked, turning the picture so it would catch the light.

"I believe that's a case of beer," Parsons said, grinning. "He comes out of his hole every morning for a fresh supply."

"Fucker's gotta be mean, goin' through a case a day," Shoemaker said.

"Must spend half the time shittin' and the other half pissin'," Vargo said, and everybody laughed.

Parsons collected the pictures and passed around copies of the topographical map. "I want everybody to study these, and be serious about it. The more you know about the area the better off you'll be. That's some goddamn rough country up there, and it's easy as hell to get lost, I shit you not."

He paused to light a cigar. "Now, insertion and extraction will be by vehicle and on foot. Looking on your maps, here"—the bullet pointed at a spot on the map—"you'll see a secondary hard-surfaced road about four miles below the target area. I propose to hide the van on one of the many logging roads in the area, then advance on foot up the mountain, which will bring us out on a ridge above and to the side of the target. I'd like to arrive at first light, but I'm not counting on it. I imagine it'll be a real ballbuster trying to move in that terrain at night. It won't really matter, anyway, our target doesn't seem to get up much before ten hundred hours."

"Where will that bring us in relation to this wino?" Tragger asked.

"I'm not sure," Parsons said, "but I think he's on that same ridge. That's the place he should be, where he can watch the road and the front of the house at the same time."

"So we just come off the ridge and take him in the rear," Tragger replied.

"Yeah," Allen sniggered, "just don't trip over no beer cans," and everybody laughed again.

When he had their attention back, Parsons said, "Okay, any questions about this so far?"

Vargo stirred on the floor, where he was trying to shave hair from his arm with his combat knife. "Yeah, I got one, Captain. How come five guys and all this shit"—he waved his knife hand at the room—"for one fucking guy? One fucking drunk?"

"Good question," Parsons said. "I'll answer it in three parts: First, and you should all know this by now, *never underestimate your enemy*. I don't give a shit if this guy is a skid-row rummy, he's managed to waste five people so far and he knows we're coming, and we *are* all going to treat him like he is a combination of Superman and Ho Chi Minh. Everybody got that?"

There was mumbled assent.

"And secondly," Parsons went on, "our principals can damn sure afford all this stuff, so why not use it?"

Everybody grinned at that. They all knew Parsons would sell the hardware once the contract was over.

"And in the third place," he continued, "I'm tired of fucking around here in the cold, so let's get this mess cleaned up and loaded, get your personal gear out of my car and into the van, and then we'll go make us some easy money."

And so they began the mission.

PART TWO

I have rarely met with two o'clock in the morning courage.

Napoleon

Many men die too late and some die too soon. Few manage to depart at just the right time.

Nietzsche

SOLDIER OF FORTUNE

INTRODUCTORY OFFER
9 issues for only $18.95

Save over 29% off the 1 year single copy price.*

☐ Payment enclosed (must accompany order)

☐ MasterCard ☐ VISA

Card # _____ Exp. Date _____

Signature _____

Name: _____

Address: _____

City: _____ State: _____ Zipcode: _____

*Savings based on 12 issue single copy price of $36.

Offer good in U.S. only. All other countries add $7.00 for additional postage. Please allow 6-8 weeks for delivery of first issue. Offer expires 12/31/88. U.S. funds only.

BUSINESS REPLY MAIL

FIRST CLASS   PERMIT NO. 8   MT. MORRIS, IL

POSTAGE WILL BE PAID BY ADDRESSEE

SOLDIER OF FORTUNE

P.O. Box 348

Mt. Morris, IL 61054-9984

XII.

Late that afternoon, Rider sat on the exact ridge Parsons thought he was on, warming his feet by a small fire.

The fire was a violation of security but, what the hell, it was cold out. The sky was heavy with racing grey clouds, and it looked like snow was coming. He was swathed in blankets, and existence had ground down to a matter of holding his bladder as long as possible in order to keep from unwrapping.

He was sitting on a bed of pine boughs covered with a poncho, and he had strung a piece of tarp over his head for a crude roof.

The fire was backed by a wall of green logs in a half-successful attempt to reflect most of the heat back on him, and the wind, which was picking up, was whipping the smoke into his face with increasing frequency.

He finished a beer and tossed the can into a rapidly growing pile of empties, then considered wiping the

SL7 down with the oily rag in the pocket of his field jacket. Fuck it, he decided, instead reaching over and tearing a fresh beer out of the six-pack.

What the hell had it been, three days? Six? A week? Sitting here in the woods, freezing his ass off, drunk and bored and yes, horny as usual, mental images of centerfolds dancing across his imagination in impossible fantasies.

He lit a cigarette and considered his options. Well, hell, he thought, let's face it. He'd started a goddamn war, out of boredom or down-home craziness or whatever, and you didn't fight wars lying on your ass in some fancy motel room watching fuck movies. You fought them in the bush, by God, and on your own turf, if possible.

And this miserable hillside was *his* turf, and he shouldn't even have a fire, for Christ's sake. He shouldn't be sitting here by a fire a blind man could see for a mile, like some kind of candy-ass silhouetted against it with his night vision destroyed and half-drunk.

Disgust washed over him. I will not be taken, he thought. I am not an asshole like Ball.

So it has come down to this, Rider realized. They will come for me sooner or later. They will come for the house, and when they do I will not be in the house. I will either be laid up in some motel, naked and fat and stupid, dulled by booze and easy living, or I will be on this hillside, lean and alert and deadly, waiting for them.

He finished his beer, then watched the fire for a minute, deciding. When the decision came, Rider got out of his blankets and used the last six-pack to douse the fire. Then he urinated and went to bed, shivering.

*   *   *

The Drunken Chief, sitting on his porch swathed in blankets, saw the tiny flicker of fire falter and die. He had watched it go out several times before, but this time was different. This time was not a gradual dimming of an unfed fire. This fire had been extinguished on purpose. And it was earlier than usual. The Drunken Chief nodded in solitary satisfaction. The Crazy One was right. The time was near.

The trip down was longer than six hours. Somewhere in Virginia it started snowing: a steady, no-nonsense, blowing, serious snow, slowing them.

Shoemaker, well traveled on eastern roads, was driving. Parsons sat in the passenger seat, reading road maps and interstate signs. The rest of the team, still in civilian clothes, were in the darkened interior of the van, sprawled on the jumble of packs and assorted gear, smoking or sleeping.

"This shit keeps up we'll have to stop and put the chains on," Shoemaker said, squinting through the windshield between the flapping wipers.

Parsons reached over and turned on the radio. Static-filled rock music poured from all four strategically located speakers. "Shit," he muttered, turning the volume down and fiddling with the knobs until the reception came in clear.

"Get it on," a voice commented from the rear. Parsons ignored it, glancing at the illuminated dial of his hack watch. Five minutes until the half hour. For something to do, he thumbed the pencil light on and consulted the road map again. Christ, it was a long haul diagonally down across the state of Virginia. Four-lane, grass-divided expressway through gentle rolling pastureland, the dark snow blowing, monotony broken every once in a while by green signs with white Day-Glo lettering announcing food, gas, lodging, telephone. Petersburg 36 miles. He decided he would listen to the weather and then volunteer someone from the back to ride shotgun while he got some rest. When they hit the mountain roads he would get back up front and let Allen relieve Shoemaker at the wheel. Allen was used to country roads.

The radio went from music to local news, interspaced with spot ads. The forecast was not good. Increasing cold, scattered snow and freezing rain, some accumulation in the higher elevations. Okay, he thought. Okay, all we've got to do is get up there. If we can't get back out, we'll camp in the van until the roads clear. And if *we* can't get *out*, nobody can get *in* to fuck with us. The more stranded, the better off we are. All we've got to do is get there.

He pushed himself out of the seat and levered himself into the back, letting his eyes adjust so he could sort out the comfortably splayed shapes. The odor of marijuana stung his nostrils. He kicked the sole of a cowboy boot. "Hardy, front and center. Ride shotgun for Ray."

"Right." Hardy crawled forward and Parsons flopped down in his place. He squirmed himself comfortable on the plush brown carpet. "Allen?"

"Yes, sir," came a voice from the dark.

"Put that goddamn dope out and keep it out. If I smell any more between now and the end of this mission you can hitchhike home. Broke. You read me?"

"Yes, sir."

The van droned on into the hostile night.

Rider slept fitfully. He dreamed of wasted beer, great barrels of it being poured on burning hooches to keep all the mamasans and papasans alive. He helped to tip the huge heavy barrels, even though he regretted the waste of all those gallons of beer, glinting in golden waterfalls in the warm Asian sun.

After a while, he dreamed of America and the Mafia.

He dreamed of an America gone soft with luxury and technology. The people taking for granted the highest standard of living in recorded history, expecting as their due and as a fact of nature the existence and availability of push-button lights and heat, of curling irons and VCRs and flashy plastic vehicles and police protection and fire engines and *Star Trek* medicine. Of an America whose citizens have learned that they do not have to pay the price for individual acts of stupidity and irresponsibility. Pregnant? Get an abortion. Quit a job? Get food stamps and welfare. Build a prison? Fine, but put it somewhere else and let *them* pay for it. Cancer from smoking too much? Sue the tobacco company. Steal some dynamite and blow your hand off? Get a lawyer and sue the dynamite company.

Rider groaned in his miserable bed as his dream turned toward the inevitable result of a people surfeited with convenience. The subconscious visions of electrical appliances and legal documents faded into a diffuse misty background as the wolf pack advanced on the sleeping herd.

The wolf pack, saliva dripping from gleaming fangs. All the wolf packs of the world, all down through time, all of them, the pushy, aggressive, unfair, unjust, greedy, violent killers who believe that might is right.

Genghis Khan. Hitler. Lenin. All the Banana Republic dictators who have murdered millions of their own, who have murdered millions in the name of power and ego and greed. All of them, the motorcycle gangs whose numbers and motor roar give them the courage to intimidate a man and his family out for a weekend drive. All of them, the anonymous hooded figures of the Ku Klux Klan burning crosses on the hillside above the homes of frightened black families. All of them, goddamn it to fucking hell, the drunken ignorant son-of-a-bitch who comes home and beats the shit out of his wife and kids simply because he feels like it and is big enough to get the job done and they don't understand they don't have to put up with this shit—

All of them.

The Mafia.

The shadowy, omnipotent Mafia. The transplanted society of friends, Americanized and insinuated into every facet of society. Drugs. Whores. Show biz. Legitimate enterprise. Whose basic business acumen is based on intimidation. Fuck with us, we kill you. You just do what we say.

Rider groaned again and turned under the mound of snow-covered quilts. The dream of the Mafia faded, and he was again in Vietnam, putting out fires. Only this time it wasn't beer he was pouring. He was pissing on the burning hooches. He pissed and pissed, but the fires never went out, and he still had to piss.

Rider woke, his bladder swollen. As he struggled from under the covers a fragment of his dream came whispering back. He gave his poncho-shrouded weapons a clumsy pat. "Fuck you bastards," he croaked. "You don't have any monopoly on killing."

They left the interstate at an exit in northeastern Tennessee. Parsons had the van gassed and the oil checked. He had them put the chains on, even though the snow on the road was melting. He paid cash for the service and consulted his watch: 0110 hours. A little late, but okay.

"About forty miles," he told Herby Allen when they were all back in the van. "From here the roads get progressively worse. Narrower and snakier and poorly maintained. Take it slow and careful. Don't try to pass anybody. We've got plenty of time."

As soon as they were moving on the secondary road, Parsons could see the snow was starting to lie heavy in the tree branches and on the road banks.

"Shoulda brought white cammo or sheets," Vargo grumbled from the back. "Fuck this woodland shit on a night like this."

"No problem," Allen said, his eyes fixed in concentration on the poor visibility ahead.

"No problem, my ass. Telling me woodland cammo won't stand out like a redneck at a peace rally against snow?"

"Snow's white, tree trunks are still dark," Parsons said, hoping to settle the matter before it degenerated into a protracted discussion. He wasn't really sure himself that this was correct, but it was too late to worry about it now. He hadn't considered a snowstorm in planning the mission. As a matter of fact, he hadn't even thought to check the weather forecast. It had been pure luck that the van's equipment included chains.

I'm getting too old for this shit, he thought, then remembered that he'd had the same thought only a few days ago. This would be the last contract. Absolutely the last.

After a while the annoying rattle of the chains against macadam muted to a soft, rhythmic thumping.

"Snow's starting to pile," Allen observed unnecessarily.

Parsons grunted, looking for road signs. He caught a quick glimpse of the lights of a small town between darkened mountains. "Okay, that's our jumping-off point, more or less. After that it's back roads and wagon trails. Soon as we get through town you can start gearing up. Until then, kind of scrunch down under the blankets and stuff just in case the local law is bored enough to check us out."

Parsons had good ID and a cover story, just in case,

but felt confident they wouldn't be necessary. The turn onto the mountain road was before they were actually in the town and there was purposely nothing outstanding about the van. It wasn't new or shiny or garish in any way. They were all dressed in well-worn work clothes. Herby Allen would even fit in with the locals if questioned. Not only did he look and talk like a yokel, he *was* a yokel. There was a lot of thumping and muffled exclamations as the men in back tried to make themselves unobtrusive behind and under the sleeping bags and innocent-looking cartons.

"Here, Tragger," Shoemaker said, "snuggle in next to me, like spoons. I promise not to get a hard-on."

"You do and I'll cut it off, you fairy."

"Listen," Allen told Parsons in a quiet voice. "If we take this sucker alive and you gotta, uh, interrogate him and all, well, if it's okay, Captain, I'll just slide off and prowl his place and stuff, okay? I mean, after we take him, you don't need me for that, right?"

"Yeah, sure," Parsons said distractedly. "Slow down, Allen, slow down now, here's the turnoff, right about now. Here!"

They rounded a descending curve and the town was there, only a few scattered lights showing. The road crossed a sunken railroad bed and continued on through town, then wound its way up into mountains and the North Carolina state line.

Allen cranked the van sharply to the right onto a hard-surface narrow lane which snaked up into blowing darkness. Its surface was unbroken white.

It took them almost two hours to reach the area where Parsons estimated the jumping-off point to be. The van had climbed almost constantly, the chains no longer thumping, but rather crunching in the rapidly deepening snow. They nearly became stuck twice, as Allen eased the van over the tops of hills. His back and eyes were aching from strain. The men in the back had already geared up, with much cursing and fumbling in the tight quarters.

Finally Parsons rolled down his window and began to examine the side of the road with a hand-held spotlight. The blast of cold air that roared in was shocking after the warmth of the interior.

Within another half mile Parsons spotted a deep, rutted, weed-filled logging road that angled off into darkness. At his direction, Herby Allen coaxed the van up it until the wheels began spinning.

"Good enough," Parsons said. They were far enough in that there was no danger of being spotted from the road.

Parsons made a command decision. The original plan had called for them to strike out through the woods immediately, reaching the target area by dawn. But now he decided that it would be ridiculous to go stumbling around in heavy forest in the middle of a blizzard. They would in all probability get lost. They might well freeze to death. Better wait until morning. Christ, he should have checked the weather report! A sense of foreboding flickered through him. Angrily he shook it off. "Change of plans, people. We'll wait out this shit right here in the van and move out at first light."

"A-fucking-men," Vargo grumbled.

They were all starting to shiver.

Parsons rolled the window up and climbed in back to change. "Vargo, up front here and keep watch. Shoemaker can relieve you at 0500. Shoemaker, reveille at first light. Don't run the engine any more than necessary. Rest of you get some sleep."

Pat Cousins was in Tampa, Florida. She was strapped to a gurney, which was in a room in a small, private sanitarium. Her eyes were closed and she was almost comatose from continued injections of sodium pentothal. Her blouse and slacks were rumpled and dirty from the car trunk, her hair was a matted mess, and her face was unhealthy-looking and swollen. One eye was blackened and her lip was split.

There were three men in the room with her. One was tall and thin, wearing the white smock of a lab technician. A stethoscope hung around his neck. He was taking her pulse.

The second man seemed to be Cuban. He was dressed in a rust-color leisure suit, and he lounged in a leather armchair, one leg thrown casually over the arm, smoking.

The third man looked like a prosperous businessman, which in a way he was. This man was standing by the open door, looking out into the hallway.

Heavy footsteps approached, clicking loudly on the tile. They stopped, and a quiet voice said, "She out?"

"Like a light," the businessman answered, and stepped away from the door.

Bartoli came in, shutting the door behind him. The Cuban stood up respectfully. "She better be," Bartoli said. "I don't want her to even think she saw me." He glanced at the form on the gurney with distaste.

He was basically a brawler. He had no real stomach for this kind of business. Unfortunately it was sometimes necessary. And fortunately there were plenty of people who did have the stomach for it.

"You pump her good?" he asked the businessman, who looked hurt, as if Bartoli was questioning his professional expertise.

"No problem there. She's a fucking cream puff. She got diarrhea of the mouth the minute we pulled the gag off. We got her calmed down and had a nice little chat, filled in all the details, went over it a couple times

to catch her in a lie. She passed with flying colors."
The businessman grinned. "Then we fired the second
stage. José here thumped on her for an hour or so.
Same story, only this time with a lot of spit and snot."

"And the juice?"

"Same deal. We been at it all night and everything
hangs together. She's straight, I'll guarantee that."

"Okay," Bartoli said, satisfied. "Now, give it to me
condensed. Just the highlights, okay?" He wanted to
get the hell out of this creepy fucking place as quickly
as possible. All this shit here, the needles and vials and
gleaming chrome and fluorescent lights. Shit!

The businessman dug a notebook out of his pocket
and flipped it open. "Well, okay. Ball found the shit in
the car. They're sitting on it, trying to find a buyer,
when your guys show up. This scumbo Rider, he's
there, too. Ball hired him to wash cars or some such
shit. A fucking bum!"

"Go on, dammit!"

"Right. So your guys haul him along, too, naturally.
No sweat, right? Only when the party starts, this Rider
hauls out a piece and smokes 'em both."

"They didn't shake him down," Bartoli said. It was
not a question.

"No reason to. Hell, a fucking wino bum."

"A bum that shoots," Bartoli grumbled.

"Yeah, well, they dump the car, head north. Trade
the Corvette on the way. Rider talks them into holing
up with him in the mountains."

"And leaves us a note where we can find him,"
Bartoli says.

The businessman wet his thumb and flipped a page.
"So they're up there, happy as pigs in shit, and then
your guys show up." He paused, glancing up. "He
killed them all, Mr. Bartoli. Killed them and buried
them in a field below the house."

"How?" Bartoli exploded, his voice savage.

The businessman took an involuntary step back, startled. "Pardon?"

"How, goddammit? That was three good soldiers. They had firepower. They had balls. How'd he take them? Somebody helping him, what?"

The businessman wet his lips. "She's kind of confused about that. They had her in the car, then there was a lot of shooting. Then the car ran in the ditch and she jumped out and then there was a lot more shooting and then he burned the car. With Johnny Blue Eyes in it."

"He fucking what?" Bartoli yelled, and this time the businessman actually jumped. "Okay, okay," Bartoli said, making an effort to calm down. "Never mind that now. Was he alone?"

"Yes, sir, except for Ball, who apparently wasn't much help."

"Guns, weapons?"

"Yeah, lots of guns, rifles, shotguns, that stuff. Not much help here, though, she don't know a bazooka from a BB gun."

The businessman turned and picked up a small tape recorder. He held it and the notebook out to Bartoli like an offering. "It's all here, phase one, phase two, the juice, all of it."

Bartoli took them reluctantly, as if they were somehow slimy. "Ball?"

"He split after the shoot-out. Too rich for his blood, I guess. She thinks maybe Rider kept a quarter of the junk. Also clipped Ball for some bread, apparently. She don't know where he went. She split a little later. Made a beeline for Mama. That's where—"

"Yeah, I know, I know."

There was a silence while Bartoli digested everything. They all waited respectfully except Pat Cousins, who groaned in her sleep.

"Okay," Bartoli finally said. "I'm gonna take this stuff and listen to it. What I want you to do, you get her"—he jerked his head at the disheveled form on the gurney—"straightened up and cleaned up. Calm her down, feed her, apologize to her for all the rough stuff, then tell her if she promises to keep her mouth shut we'll find something for her to do if she wants to work for us, and if not we'll send her home with a little traveling money. Then when you're sure she won't raise hell, you set her up in the place on Oswald Street. I want a nice long chat with this broad. I intend to find out every fucking detail of what went on with this business. Got it?"

"Got it. Clean her up, get her on our side." The businessman grinned. "It probably won't be hard. I bet she's a money-hungry bitch, anyway."

"Isn't everybody?" Bartoli said with tired contempt.

Joseph Ball was in Albany, New York. At first he had been in a motel, then he had tried to sell some of the cocaine in a bar, and now he was neither place.

Now he was in the meat locker of a slaughterhouse, hanging from one of the hooks that rolled along the curved rail.

It was cold, and Ball was colder than the other men in the meat locker with him because he was naked. The huge frozen slabs of beef and pork had been slid back out of the way to leave a clear space in the center of the locker.

A large vinyl tarp had been spread on the floor and Ball hung directly over the tarp, which was spattered with urine, shit, vomit, and blood.

Ball had vomited when the man in the rubber rainsuit pushed the greased cattle prod up his rectum and switched it on. Then when this same man rammed the chain saw up between Ball's legs, right against his bare testicles, and pulled the crank rope, Ball's bladder went. On the second attempt to start the saw he shit all over himself, at which point he was informed with amused disgust that the saw was out of gas. The blood was from the general workover with an aluminum baseball bat.

Both his eyes were swollen shut, his teeth knocked out, a kneecap shattered, three fingers broken, and his feet were puffed and discolored from the blowtorch.

The man in the rainsuit regarded his handiwork with professional interest. He grabbed a handful of matted hair and jerked Ball's lolling head up. "He's about finished," he announced.

The other man standing at the edge of the tarp nodded. "Thank Christ for small favors," he said. "I hate this example-making shit. I won't be able to eat for a fucking week."

He went to one of the hanging sides of beef and pushed it along the rail until it was nestled against the hanging body, positioning it carefully so that its huge shoulder was level with Ball's head.

Then he stepped around to the other side, fastidiously avoiding the worst of the filth on the tarp. He took a pair of industrial ear protectors from his coat pocket and slipped them on. From his other pocket he withdrew a Ruger .22 automatic. The other man retreated and put his fingers in his ears.

The executioner put the weapon behind Ball's left ear, placing it as carefully as a surgeon would a scalpel, and squeezed the trigger.

The round made a sharp, ear-ringing *wap* in the enclosed space, drilling through the skull and lodging in the frozen meat beyond. Later, the executioner would dig the bullet out and destroy it.

Ball's body convulsed and began to twitch and quiver. Fresh blood dripped out of his mouth in a long scarlet thread. His left eye bulged grotesquely from hydrostatic shock.

When the neural spasms died down, the man in the rainsuit reached up and cut the cord binding the dead hands to the meat hook. The body landed with a squashy *thump* on the tarp, spraying old and fresh body fluids on the rainsuit. Then its legs were pulled around behind the torso, bent backward at the knee joints, and tied to the torso in order to make the smallest, tidiest package possible. The arms were tied to the sides, and the whole horrible mess rolled neatly into the tarp.

Then the thing was stuffed, with much grunting and cursing, into a fifty-five-gallon drum. The executioner had to climb on top and jump up and down several times in order to make room for the lid to go on, like packing garbage in a trash barrel.

When the lid was fastened tightly, they loaded it on a dolly, from which it would be loaded onto one of the packinghouse trucks and delivered to another warehouse several hundred miles to the south, and from there deposited in Long Island Sound. It was not weighted because it was not meant to sink. It was meant to be found. Object lessons were wasted if the finished product was not found.

Several days hence, the New York papers would carry an article on page three: "Victim of Torture Murder Found on Beach." The police would issue a statement to the effect that the deceased was obviously the victim of a gangland slaying. Sooner or later an identification would be made, and that would be the end of it.

Except, of course, to those in a position to know. Among these, the vast army of dealers, pimps, whores, fences, bookies, mobsters, and assorted hangers-on, the word, freshly reinforced, would spread through the underworld grapevine once more. Don't fuck with the Mob!

The killers cleaned up in the washroom. The plastic rainsuit was dumped in a sink and destroyed by acid.

The mangled, recovered bullet was smashed flat and then thrown in the basement oil furnace.

As they washed, they chatted like factory workers after a day on the assembly line. The one who had pulled the trigger wanted to stop at a local bar for a few beers. The one who had worn the rainsuit begged off. He'd promised to take the old lady and the kids bowling, and he was already late.

XIII.

They left the van at the first faint glimmering of dawn. The snow had almost stopped falling, and the scattered tiny flakes that did come down fell straight in the still air.

It was very cold, and breath spewed out in frosty billows from the exertion of wading uphill in the foot or so of powdery white blanket. With the exception of an occasional branch cracking from the cold, the only sound was what they themselves made: muffled thump of feet, breathing sounds, the tiny squeaks and clinks of equipment. There was no talking.

They went up the side of the first hill, clear-cut for timber several years before, in single file. No flankers. They went at five-yard intervals.

Parsons led, compass in one gloved hand. Herby Allen came next, cradling his SC70, eyes searching from side to side, bearing on the leader with only the smallest part of his attention. Then came Vargo, the SAW slung from one shoulder in a combat carry, grenades clipped to his harness, dead cigar clamped in his teeth for macho self-confidence. After a while he put the cigar in his pocket and closed his mouth to stop his teeth from hurting in the cold. This wasn't at all like 'Nam. Hardy slogged stolidly along behind Vargo, feet occasionally slipping on hidden rocks and dead, barkless logs, rifle on his left shoulder, leaning slightly in that direction to compensate for the weight of the spare assault pack slung from his right shoulder. Shoemaker came behind him, burdened with his own gear, weapon, and an M72 light antitank weapon. He had the tube attached to his field pack at the back, and knew that it was going to be a bitch to carry through brush if they encountered any, which he was sure they would. Tragger brought up the rear, a Benelli 12-gauge automatic shotgun in his hands, a bandolier of ammo across his shoulders. An M79 grenade launcher was fastened to his pack. From his shoulder hung a pouch with twelve 40mm grenades. As he struggled through the snow and low brush he constantly checked the column's back trail.

Parsons paused on the crest of the ridge, squatting to keep his silhouette low against the lightening sky, and took a compass reading.

Halfway down the hill in front of him the clear cut ended and the true woods began. They led down the steep slope before him into a brush-choked hollow, then up again to the next snow-laden ridgetop. Pine trees and hardwood, huge round humps of boulders, tangled masses of dead brush and fallen trees, all on a slippery incline that would have to be climbed hand over hand, met his eyes. Christ, he thought, at least thankful they hadn't attempted this in the dark.

He had realized before the mission that, being unfamiliar with the area, they would have to travel in a straight compass line, which would mean crossing hollows and ridges as they encountered them. But having never operated in this particular terrain before, he hadn't realized how damn steep and tangled it would actually be.

It was going to be damn hard just to find a way by compass, he could see that now, too. To follow a straight line by compass, one simply took a bearing, noted some sort of prominent landmark along the desired line of march, and headed for it. Upon reaching this mark, another bearing was taken, and the process repeated. But the key to efficiency in this was distance between bearing marks. The ideal situation would be flat, clear land, with a mountain in the distance for a bearing mark. In that case one could take a reading on the mountain, either right or left, and then put the compass away and forget about it.

But in this shit? Parsons could see that once into the woods he would have to take bearings almost constantly, all the while either sliding down or climbing up the sides of ridges, detouring around or struggling over obstacles.

He sighed, realizing he would have to alter his timetable drastically. No big thing here, but in a combined operation it could have had drastic consequences. Another fuckup, Parsons, he thought dismally, then, in an attempt at humor to bolster his own flagging morale, he thought, Maybe I should have got them to spring for a chopper. Tightening his resolve, he took a reading on a distinctive forked tree on the next ridgeline and led off again.

Two hours and eight or nine ridges and hollows later, they took a break. From here on, the smooth steep side of a real mountain stretched away above them through the winter-bare tree trunks.

Parsons realized that they couldn't stay here long.

The sweat generated by the work of climbing, despite the cold, would soon dry and chill them. It was either seek shelter and build a fire or move on.

They squatted and knelt in a circle, facing out in a tight defensive perimeter. Parsons could feel the unasked question: How much farther?

In truth, he wasn't sure. On the map it was about five or six miles. But the map, unlike reality, was flat. Distance in terrain like this was measured in time, not miles. He estimated they had covered about three miles of ground, but that could be as little as a third of the actual distance to the target.

He knew that the men understood that they were well behind schedule, that the mission was off to a poor beginning. Yet he doubted if any of them had ever been on any kind of mission that went according to plan. There was no coordination with other units to worry about, no necessity to arrive at point B at a specified time, just a stroll through the woods and then a little shooting and looting. Yet he had not properly anticipated the snow or the ruggedness of the terrain, and it bothered him.

Hardy wiped his nose, which was running from the cold, with the back of a sodden glove. "At least there ain't no fucking bugs," he said.

"Or snakes," Vargo muttered.

"Except snow snakes," Shoemaker said, with a sly wink at Allen.

"Now, what the fuck is a snow snake?" Vargo asked in a disgusted voice.

Parsons sighed. He knew the joke, of course, but obviously Vargo didn't, and Vargo was notorious for both his lack of humor and his foul temper.

"It crawls up your ass and freezes you to death," he said. "If you people have time for a bullshit session I guess we've had enough rest, so off and on." He stood up. The others came to their feet reluctantly, brushing snow from their knees, adjusting equipment. And saw the hunter.

They all tensed, frozen in position. Everyone knew what to do. The possibility of this particular situation had been anticipated.

The solitary figure shuffled through the snow toward them, eyes down, single-shot shotgun resting casually on one shoulder. As it approached, they could all see it was a boy, dressed in a ragged plaid jacket and rubber boots, breath pluming in the air. He did not see them until he was about thirty feet away, then his head snapped up, startled, and he stopped, eyes widening in shock.

Herby Allen stepped forward, forcing a tight smile. "Hey. Having any luck?"

The boy didn't answer. His mouth dropped open with incomprehension.

Allen tried again. "Kill anything?"

The mouth slowly closed as its owner seemed to come partially out of his daze. He shook his head, then spoke in an awed voice. "You-uns in the army?"

"Right," Shoemaker snapped briskly. "We're on a training exercise."

The boy's mouth dropped open again. It was obvious he was retarded. Training exercise had no more meaning for him than molecular disintegration.

Tragger, who had seen more than a few war movies in his life, had an inspiration. "A twenty-mile hike," he volunteered.

Understanding flooded the boy's face and he relaxed.

"Yeah," Vargo said, grinning meanly as he jerked a thumb at Parsons, "and this here is our commanding officer, Captain Rambo."

"Shut up," Parsons told Vargo. He squatted down with his back against a tree. His mind was racing, divided by conflicting emotions. He was working to bring the boy closer, yet at the same time weighing the pros and cons of letting him go.

"Security!" he snapped at the men, and they fanned out a little, facing more or less outward.

"Don't pay any attention to him," he told the boy, indicating Vargo, who was leaning against a frozen sapling, pouting. "I'm not a captain. I'm only a corporal and my name is Jones. And we're kind of lost. You from around here?"

The boy's head bobbed up and down, confirming that he was indeed a local, and not from some place like Chicago.

"Well, maybe we could use a guide," Parsons said thoughtfully.

Interest spread across the boy's pimpled, mongoloid features. He walked forward, smiling now, stopping within the circle. "Could I join the army?" he asked.

"I don't know about that," Parsons said. "How old are you?" Christ, Parsons thought, he's a retard! He couldn't possibly give anybody a coherent description of us. All he sees are soldiers. Just soldiers. Probably can't even tell anybody how many we are. Probably can't even count that high.

"I'm eighteen," the boy said proudly. "My name's Hobert."

"Hubert?"

"No, sir. Hobert. Hobert!"

But dammit, the mission. The mission! He can backtrack us, find the van. Let the air out of the tires, damage it in some way, take the tag number.

As they talked, Shoemaker casually rose from a kneeling position and moved behind Hobert. His eyes met Parsons' over the boy's shoulder.

"Well, I don't know about the army, Hobert. Where do you live?"

The boy grinned, pleased that he could answer another question so readily, and pointed down the mountain with the shotgun barrel. He worked his mouth and spat a wad of brown juice in the snow at his feet, then, perhaps realizing he shouldn't be waving a firearm around, dropped the rusty weapon in the snow and pointed again. "Down thar."

"How far?" Parsons asked, avoiding Shoemaker's eyes.

This was too much for Hobert, and his face twisted in concentration and frustration. The silence dragged out, thick with a tension the boy didn't sense.

And I can just see him, Parsons thought, rushing home and babbling about soldiers in the woods, and there sits old Uncle Oscar, who just so happens to be a deputy sheriff, and Uncle Oscar gets up and cranks the old-fashioned wall phone, just like in Mayberry, and calls his buddy Fred, who just happens to be a sergeant in the National Guard. Nod your head, goddammit. Shoemaker already has his knife out. Just nod your head, goddammit! "Hobert?"

Hobert almost snapped to attention at the tone. "Yes, sir?"

"Hobert, we're on a secret mission." Parsons paused, saw that this went over big, and continued, "Now, what I want you to do, son, is pick up that weapon and go straight home. And don't say nothing about us. Nothing to nobody! You got that, Hobert!"

"Yes, sir!"

"And when this mission is over, well, then, I'll come hunt you up, and we'll see what we can do about the army, okay?"

Hobert almost danced with excitement. "Oh, wow. Yes, sir. Yes, *sir!*"

"Good," Parsons said. He could feel the relief in everyone, with the possible exception of Vargo. "Go on now, son. Pick up your weapon and go home."

Hobert scrambled for the shotgun and sidled off down the slope, his face shining, almost tripping several times because he was looking back over his shoulder.

"Don't tell nobody now, Hobert, y'hear?" Herby Allen shouted after him.

Hobert shook his head until tobacco juice and spit flew. "Naw, sir, won't tell, won't never tell," he yelled back.

They watched him flounder on down the mountain in silence.

"Bad business," Vargo mumbled, then turned to Parsons. "Why didn't we at least question him? Find out where the fuck we are?"

"Because he didn't even know where the fuck *he* was, that's why, asshole," Hardy said in disgusted tones.

"Because I decided not to, that's why," Parsons told them all in a cold voice. "Now it's done. Form up and move out!" With that he glanced at the compass and moved off, struggling uphill. The rest followed silently.

The mountain swept up before them. It was nine-thirty in the morning.

Rider woke. "Christ Almighty," he mumbled. His tongue felt like a swollen slug in a jar of slime. His bladder was at the bursting point, and he was cold. The blankets, poncho, and mound of snow over him pressed down with suffocating weight. For a wild second he wondered if he was frozen to the ground.

He surged up out of his bedding, spraying powdery snow, and looked around at a silent white forest. Everything was covered—the remains of his fire, the pile of empty beer cans, the limbs of the trees, the road below. He swayed on rubbery legs as the usual rush of hangover hit him. His bloodshot eyes sought and found the cabin across the road, and he immediately thought of the stove inside it.

"Bullshit on this noise," he croaked aloud. He began to collect his weapons from the tangled mass of blankets, not caring if the hordes of Ho Chi Minh were upon him.

The Drunken Chief had been up for hours, and this morning he wasn't even slightly drunk, or even hung over. He had slept well and felt alert and refreshed. There had been no dreams. He knew with a stoic certainty that the time for dreaming was over. Now it was time to do what his dreams had told him he must do.

He was already dressed in buckskin, the leggings and fringed shirt softened with saddle soap and patterned with intricate bead designs.

He washed his face clean of the old war paint, shaved from a pan on the wood stove, then, looking into the peeling mirror hanging over the sink, he began to carefully repaint his face with an assortment of cheap women's makeup. Yellow lines and red lines and black lines, across his wrinkled brown forehead and slashing down the seamed cheeks. His hands were very steady.

When he was satisfied with the effect, he went to an old wooden jewelry box on his bedroom dresser. Opening it, he carefully removed a single eagle feather. Returning to the mirror, he inserted the feather securely in his braided leather headband, then solemnly surveyed himself. He thought about humming a few bars of an Indian death song, then realized he didn't *know* any Indian death songs, and grinned. May the Great Spirit help those men that will come today, he thought, because they are only greedy mortal fools, and the Crazy One and I are touched by the Gods of Madness. Still grinning, pleased at this bit of poetic idiocy, he slung on the pouch holding ammunition so old it was turning green, added a canvas tote bag over his shoulder, picked up the Garand rifle, and went outside into the cold white morning.

"Down!" Parsons hissed, signaling violently with his arm. They all went on their stomachs with muted grunts and the thump of gear. Parsons was lying at the top of a ridgeline, peering over. He fumbled for his binoculars with gloved hands, put them to his eyes, focusing. The others waited, nerves tense, dividing their attention between Parsons and the silent, hostile forest on their flanks. Parsons motioned them forward on line, and they belly-crawled to the top of the ridge, plowing snow as they came. "The cabin," Parsons silently mouthed, and pointed.

Everyone saw it at once, squatting on a small cleared rise of ground below them through the trees. Smoke issued from the tin chimney protruding from the shingled roof.

"He's crawled in his hole to get warm," Shoemaker whispered hoarsely.

"Wouldn't you?" Hardy asked. His nose was red and running snot from the cold.

"Hold it down," Parsons said. He studied the place through the glasses. Cabin, old truck, woodpile, all covered with snow. One set of tracks leading across the road and up to the porch. Fresh tracks, apparently. All right, he thought. He wakes up this morning with his ass froze, says the hell with it, and heads for a warm fire. We got him by the balls.

His voice was barely audible as he spoke. "Listen up. We advance down the hill, one at a time. Fifty yards and cover. Allen, go!"

Herby Allen came up in a crouch and went over the ridgeline, weapon at high port, safety off. They watched him move down the hillside, slipping occasionally, head swiveling from side to side, until he went to ground behind a fallen pine tree.

"Hardy, go!"

In this fashion they leapfrogged down the hill, one man at a time, the rest covering.

They found Rider's abandoned camp. Tragger rustled around in the snow, held up an empty can of Old Milwaukee, made a face. "Horse piss."

From here they were on a level with the cabin across the road, and had a clear view. Parsons motioned them on line with hand signals, then put his face close to Shoemaker's ear. "We'll wait here. When he comes out on the porch, I'll try to wing him. If I miss, everybody cut loose, then assault the place. SAW stays here and gives covering fire. Pass it on."

Shoemaker passed the word on, then squirmed out of his pack and unbuckled the light antitank weapon.

Because they were facing downhill it was impossible to lie prone and face the cabin with any degree of comfort or convenience, so everyone settled for some sort of sitting or crouching position.

Vargo extended the bipod on the SAW and set it up on the pile of discarded backpacks. This raised the weapon high enough so he was able to sit behind it, cross-legged, and sight on the cabin. His gloved finger caressed the trigger as he swiveled the muzzle slowly across the length of the porch.

The cold began to seep into them again as they waited.

Pat Cousins was sitting on an expensive couch in the living room of a brick split-level, somewhere in the Tampa suburbs. She was alone, but she knew there were guards somewhere in the house or grounds. She was nervously sipping a drink she had made from the well-stocked bar. The whiskey made her puffy lip sting. It had been cleaned and disinfected sometime in the night, while she was still semiconscious from the drugs.

She had awakened in the bedroom of this place and used the shower, dressing in pajamas and a robe she had found, along with other clothes, in the bedroom closet.

A little while ago a silent man had brought her a complete take-out breakfast from some restaurant. She had eaten very little, her stomach still queasy.

She was no longer terrified. It was obvious they weren't going to kill her, and the liquor further calmed her.

Even so, she was startled when the quick rap on the door announced another visitor. She stood up, still clutching her drink, as the door opened and a man entered. He was of medium height, stockily built, starting to run slightly to fat around the middle. He was well dressed in casual style and had dark curly hair and a modified Pancho Villa mustache. She thought he looked very virile, and was further excited because she sensed that this was the Man, the one with the power and the money. His teeth were very white in his Mediterranean face as he smiled.

"I'm Robert Bartoli. And you're Pat?"

Rider was finally getting warm. The coffee on the stove was starting to perk.

The weapons thrown on the bed were turning white with frost as the heat reached them. Rider knew he would have to wipe them down and lubricate them before long. He would also have to bring in some more firewood from the porch. But first he was going to have a few cups of hot black coffee, laced with the last of the jug of corn liquor he had found under the couch. Chores, he thought. Always chores. But all in good time. He poured the coffee, added booze, lit a cigarette, and settled back with a sigh of contentment.

XIV.

Ambushes are murder, and murder is fun, Parsons thought, trying to flex the stiffness from his fingers. Well, this shit wasn't the least bit fun. He could feel his buttocks growing numb and burning as body heat melted the snow into ice water.

They all sat silently, miserably obeying the sacred rules of ambush. No talking, no moving, no smoking, no coughing, while legs turned into unfeeling stumps and time crawled by with agonizing slowness.

Parsons glanced at his watch. Going on two hours sitting here watching that cabin door, probably developing a good case of hemorrhoids in the bargain. He toyed with the idea of having Shoemaker put a LAW round through the place and being done with it. Fuck fooling around with this guy, all this capturing alive and interrogating and all that happy horseshit. Everybody in combat always dreaded the order to take prisoners. Prisoners were dangerous. It was a lot easier

185

and safer to just kill somebody than go fooling around with a bunch of live bodies. A dead man can't hurt you.

Another fifteen minutes of this shit, he thought, and those mob clowns can go whistle for that stash. We'll blow the house and search. If we find anything, fine, and if not, tough shit. Fuck a bonus. This isn't any rain forest down by the equator. Ambushes might be fun, but sitting on your ass in melted snow isn't.

The door of the cabin opened.

Parsons sucked in his breath involuntarily, hurting his teeth with the cold, and wrapped his arm through the sling on the assault rifle.

The others snapped rigid with tension, settling in behind their weapons, fingers rotating safeties off.

Parsons lined the sights up as the figure came out on the porch, turning its back as it bent slightly, starting to pull wood from the pile on the porch.

So that's him, he thought, getting a quick, distant impression of a smallish, slightly built man in baggy camouflage with a navy watch cap pulled down over long stringy hair. He centered the sight picture on the figure's upper right leg and let his breath out slowly, starting the squeeze.

The assault rifle came back at him with its short, snappy recoil as it fired, and at the same instant Parsons knew he had missed because he'd flinched badly, and he'd flinched because at the instant of firing, another, much heavier rifle had gone off somewhere to his left.

Goddamn them! he thought, at first assuming someone in his team had cut loose prematurely, then realized instantly that no one had a weapon like that, and, panic and adrenaline surging, he swung around shouting, "Left flank, left flank," and dived into the snow on his face.

Vargo fired a burst from the SAW into the porch, watched the impacting rounds chase the figure as it scuttled back into the house, firewood chunks tumbling, then picked the weapon up and swung it left, blindly spraying the woods in a long, searching, futile burst.

The rest of them were moving, scattering like disturbed quail as they sought cover against this new threat. All except Tragger, who had been at the extreme end of the line. He sat slumped, head on his chest, his rifle butt in his lap, the muzzle carelessly buried in snow. The only blood visible was a thick rivulet running out of his right sleeve and forming a dark red, syrupy pool next to him.

Oh shit, oh shit, Parsons' mind was hammering as he rolled behind a stand of brush, dropping clumps of snow down the back of his neck.

The woods racketed with small-arms fire as everyone found new positions and began to rake the hillside on rock and roll.

"Shoemaker!" Parsons screamed over the noise. "Put a rocket into that goddamn house right *now!*"

Shoemaker rolled over and snapped the LAW open into the armed position. He would have to sit up or kneel to fire it. "Give me cover!" he yelled, and waited through the ratchety clacks of fresh magazines being inserted, until the volume of cover fire rose with new intensity. God help any squirrel up there, he thought inanely, then came up in a kneeling position, mounting the weapon on his shoulder. He sighted dead center on the cabin and squeezed off.

The launching tube flared yellow at both ends as the rocket sizzled away, trailing sparks and white smoke. The warhead, designed to penetrate tank armor before exploding, drilled through the near-side log wall and hit the huge cast-iron woodstove inside.

The roof of the cabin swelled upward like an expanding balloon. Fire and smoke jetted from the door and windows as they blew outward. The roof settled back, sagging into the blazing shell as the sound boomed off the hills.

Parsons wasn't watching. He was scrambling through the trampled snow toward Tragger. The covering fire slacked off as magazines emptied. "Use that SAW, dammit," he shouted, and was rewarded with a long, ripping burst that sprayed pine needles and tree bark along the ridgeline to the left.

Reaching the body, he jerked it roughly over on its side and lay behind it for cover as he cut the straps loose from Tragger's bandolier of 40mm grenades. Tragger's eyes were only inches from Parsons' as he worked, and they were wide open in amazement. Easy money, easy money, he thought bitterly. Ambushes are fun. Easy money. Shit. He crawled back, dragging the grenades, as Vargo hosed the ridgeline again.

He burrowed in behind the abandoned pile of packs and unstrapped the M79 from Tragger's pack, breaking it open and loading it.

He could hear his breath laboring in his chest in wheezing gasps as silence settled over the hillside. Off to their right now, the cabin began burning in earnest, sending up a huge column of greasy black smoke. No more waiting now, he knew. That smoke would be seen for miles, if all the shooting hadn't already alerted someone.

"Allen," he called softly in the quiet.

"Yo!"

"We've got to get a position on whoever it is up on that ridge."

Silence, as Herby Allen digested this.

"I've got the bloop tube," Parsons said. "Vargo's got the SAW. All we need is one more shot."

Still silence, becoming strained now.

"There's a bonus in it."

"Ah, what the fuck," Herby Allen said, and stood up

from behind a white pine tree. He took one step forward, which saved his life. Bark exploded from the side of the tree where he had just been, followed instantly by the slam of the rifle. "Fuck!" Allen screamed, dropping straight down in a clatter of gear.

"There, there!" Vargo bellowed, and cut the SAW loose in a barrel-melting burst.

But Parsons had seen it also. Not a flash, but rather the muzzle blast of a heavy rifle low along the ground, kicking up snow. He aimed high, trying for an air burst. The grenade hit a tree about six feet off the ground and exploded with a flash and burst of smoke.

"Go! Go! Go!" Parsons screamed, and surged up and over the packs.

They all stormed upward in a slipping, gasping assault, firing from the hip, eyes wild, faces contorted with fear and excitement. The charge stalled almost at the top of the ridge, more from exhaustion than caution, as they flopped to the ground with heaving lungs and trembling, weakened legs.

Parsons staggered into a tree trunk, almost knocking himself out. He ripped a grenade from his webbing, pulled the pin, and heaved it over the top of the ridge as close as he could get it to the blasted tree. He hit the ground as it went off with a muffled, vicious thump. The others rose to their knees, also throwing grenades. "Enough, goddammit, enough," he yelled. "That's enough to kill a fucking rhino!"

The echoes of the explosions died away into petrified silence.

Without being told, Shoemaker came off the ground and went over the ridgetop in a gliding crouch, weapon to his shoulder, eyes glinting.

They watched him until they could see only his head and shoulders on the other side of the hill. They saw the shoulders slump in relaxation.

"Jesus Christ!" Shoemaker said in awe.

Everybody scrambled over the hill and down into the little depression Shoemaker was standing in.

Parsons took the scene in instantly. Shrapnel-shredded bark hanging in strips from the trees, the trampled snow Kool-Aid-pink with great gouts of diluted blood. The blood trail led off down the ridgeline and disappeared in a tangle of honeysuckle at the bottom.

"Looks like he rolled part of the way," Shoemaker said.

"Knocked on his ass by the bloop tube," Hardy grunted in satisfied agreement.

"I'm sure as shit not going down there after him, bonus or no bonus," Allen said, glancing at Parsons defiantly.

Parsons realized everyone was bunched up. "No need to," he said. "He's not going anywhere spilling that much blood. Let's get back to work."

They moved back over the ridge and down toward the burning cabin, still alert, but with a sense of accomplishment.

"An Indian," Hardy said.

"What?"

"An Indian," Hardy repeated. "It was an Indian. He was wearing moccasins. You didn't notice the tracks?" He glanced at Parsons with a sly look of amusement.

"No, I didn't and I don't give a shit. Indian or fucking Mongolian, he's bled out by now. Tend to business."

Parsons was thinking of Tragger. They'd have to take the body, of course. It could easily be identified, through military fingerprints and dental records. They'd have to make at least a cursory search of the cabin grounds for the dope. They'd have to police up the side of the hill for traceable hardware.

The thought of lugging Tragger back down through those mountains almost made him sag with exhaustion. Well, Captain Rambo, he thought, at least it's mostly downhill. We can gut the carcass to make it lighter and drag it out like a trophy buck.

They crossed the snow-covered road one at a time, then fanned out in a skirmish line and advanced up to the blazing pile of tumbled logs. The tar in the roof shingles was causing the black smoke. The old pickup was close enough to the fire to cause the paint to blister and bubble on one side. The heat felt good.

Parsons wanted to get things organized and be out of there as soon as possible. Any second he expected to hear the mutter of an approaching helicopter. He sent Vargo to search the pickup as thoroughly as possible under the blast of heat striking it from the cabin.

Shoemaker and Hardy wandered around the sloping yard, looking for pump houses, containers, bags hung in trees, anywhere that a plastic bag of white powder could be concealed or buried.

It was probably under his fucking bed, Parsons thought sourly. He strolled around the far side of the still-blazing house. Herby Allen followed him, absently kicking at humps in the snow.

"How much bonus?" Herby Allen asked.

"Huh?" Parsons said. He wasn't listening. He was staring at the ground behind the cabin. The snow was rifled from the blast of the rocket, covered with miscellaneous debris, dusted with soot from the stove. But farther out, beyond the ring of melted snow, heading off up the ridge, was a thin trail of red speckles. A blood trail. And tracks. The very distinct tracks of a running man.

"Down-n-n!" Parsons screamed, his throat tearing with the pain of his fury and disbelief, as the saving earth rushed up to meet him. As he hit, landing painfully on the M79, which had been slung across his chest, he heard the familiar deadly *crack!* of a high-velocity round breaking the sound barrier.

Herby Allen stood for a second, then fell slowly backward like a toppling tree, his head blown to pieces in a cascade of blood and bone and brain matter. His rifle, which he had forgotten to put on safe after the charge, went off on full auto as he landed on his back, hands spasming.

A white-hot rage flooded Parsons' brain as he rolled over Allen's body on his way to the cover of the pickup.

He tried to pull the grenade launcher over his head and the strap snagged on his gear. He felt it part as he stiffened his arms in homicidal frustration. He loaded the weapon with fumbling fingers, leaned around the back of the pickup, and fired uphill. Even as it exploded he was on his feet, reloading. He glanced around. Vargo was behind the front wheel of the truck, the SAW lying over the bumper as he waited for instructions.

Shoemaker and Hardy were flat on their faces farther down in the yard, looking confused.

"Up in the woods behind the house!" Parsons heard himself say through a daze of bloodlust. He gestured wildly with his left arm, motioning them forward. "Go! Go! Go!" He felt the weapon recoil in his right hand. He snapped it open, reloaded, and charged up the hill, red-rimmed eyes seeking a target. He didn't know or care if the others were following. "Bastard! Fucking up my last mission! Fucking up my reputation! Killing my fucking people!" He felt his lips pulled back over his teeth in a snarl. "Kill you, motherfucker. Kill you. Kill you!"

"*Kiiiill,*" Vargo screamed as he followed Parsons, triggering sweeping bursts from the SAW into the woods ahead. Saliva from his open mouth whipped back in the wind of his charge.

"Jesus fucking Christ!" Shoemaker muttered as he headed uphill, scanning for movement. Vargo and Parsons had gone apeshit, he thought, and how in Christ's name could anybody come out of that cabin alive? If it *is* him, and not another sniper or relative. Christ, I wanna go home. He glanced over at Hardy, who was advancing next to him, firing short, controlled bursts from the shoulder. Thank God for Hardy!

And then Hardy went down, spinning and falling, clutching at his leg. Shoemaker saw this out of the corner of his eye, but he was busy emptying his magazine at the shadowy figure he'd spotted almost at the top of the slope.

At the same time a grenade from Parsons' bloop tube exploded somewhere in the branches above, and Shoemaker saw a rifle go spinning away. Gotcha, you cocksucker, he thought exultantly, and really started running uphill, trying to reload, ignoring the stitches in his side, ignoring the snapping, breaking tug at his ankle. *Oh no!* he thought.

And then he was lying on his back in the cold, watching clouds of snow swirling overhead, watching tree branches spinning through the air in lazy parabolic arcs, making him dizzy and sick as his ears rang with the afterblast. *Oh no*, he thought again as the ringing increased to the sound of a siren, driving him down into blackness.

XV.

Parsons was on the ground. He had been there a long time, and he was very cold. He was also very deaf. His ears felt numb, and he had experimented by snapping tiny, almost dry twigs, one-handed, against his ear. Nothing. The world was totally silent. He'd cautiously moved all his extremities while he lay there, and was reasonably sure he wasn't wounded. Everything moved, nothing was numb or broken.

He'd done a lot of thinking in the past hour or so that he'd been there, automatic pistol cocked, waiting for *him* to come floundering or creeping or crawling over the hill.

Maybe he was dead, lying just over the hill, killed from the last grenade burst or from his own goddamn booby trap. Serve him right.

But Parsons wasn't about to find out. This mission was over. Parsons had been trying to figure out the casualty rate. It was simple enough, but his mind just didn't seem to be functioning at top efficiency on this balmy, Tennessee-mountain afternoon.

The arithmetic was simple enough, though. Six men. Five of them dead as a wedge, the other wounded. Eighty percent, at least, killed in action. Or, to look at it like the military did, adding both killed and wounded into the equation, one hundred percent casualties. One hundred percent!

Thirty percent was considered enough to demoralize a unit, rendering it unfit for further action. Was this unit demoralized, then?

Parsons looked around, grimacing. He could see Hardy, quite a way down the hill, a dark bundle of camouflage tumbled among tree trunks and scrub brush. Hardy hadn't moved for as long as Parsons had been watching and waiting. Not a twitch. Inert. Motionless. Completely still. Completely dead. The body had seemed to flatten as Parsons watched, like it was sinking into the ground, sinking deeper into the frozen earth as the flesh cooled, the blood pumped out through the severed arteries. Scratch Hardy.

There wasn't any doubt at all about Shoemaker and Vargo.

Shoemaker was higher up the hill than Hardy, and closer laterally. The body was on its back, head downhill where it had been hurled by the blast. Shoemaker was naked from feet to upper chest, stripped of boots, trousers, and gear, which were bunched in an untidy lump under his chin. The exposed skin was raw and peeled-looking, almost like fish scales. Parsons could see a bloody trough in the snow where the body had skidded backward. Scratch Shoemaker.

Vargo had been closest to Parsons when the wire was tripped, sitting spraddle-legged, his back propped up against a pine tree. Since regaining consciousness, Parsons had been studying Vargo. Every square inch of his body had been pockmarked with some kind of ragged buckshot or something. Padgett had never seen anything like it. Would a Claymore do that at point-blank range?

Parsons didn't think so. The shot in a Claymore was round. Whatever had hit Vargo was definitely not round. He could see the hits in the pine trunk, chunks of bark gouged out, leaving white bare holes bleeding sap.

There wasn't much blood on the front of the body. It had all been blown into the tree trunk or around its edges. There was a pink fan of gore behind the tree, dusting the snow like butterfly wings, and the head, of course, or what was left of it. A piece of sheet steel, greenish and blackened and crumpled, was embedded in the tree at the level of Vargo's hairline. It had neatly sheared off the top of the skull. It looked, to Parsons, like the lid of a .50-caliber ammo box. Vargo's brains had slid down over the foreshortened remains of his face, oozing over the chin and chest like some obscene bowl of spilled oatmeal, all grey and shot through with red veins. But it was starting to freeze now, and no longer oozed. Scratch Vargo.

Scratch everybody. Get your head together, Vargo, Parsons thought, and suppressed a sudden giggle with a flash of panic.

Get *your* head together, you incompetent asshole.

Back to the main question. Was this unit demoralized? Oh, surely it was. Parsons felt he could speak for the rest of the unit, because he *was* the rest of the unit.

Yes, General, we are sure as hell demoralized. We have a pocket full of money and a vehicle waiting at the bottom of the mountain, and a whole lot more money at home, and even though it really hasn't been earned, we are so fucking demoralized that all we want to do is get to that van alive, and change into civvies and throw all the rest of the commando shit into the snow and drive to the airport and get that money and head for South America.

Not Belize—that has an extradition treaty with Uncle. Not El Sal—no, that's a fucking U.S. colony. What's that place down there that hides all the Nazis? Paraguay? Uruguay? Somewhere.

All this stuff could just lie here. All the bodies, all the gear. Made no difference now. His reputation was gone, shot in the ass. Wiped out by an alcoholic hillbilly and a throwback to Sitting Bull. He'd never get another job once the word got around. One hundred percent casualties! Captain Rambo's last stand.

I've got to make a move, he thought, wondering if he could even walk. It would be dark in a few more hours. He realized Rider could be anywhere, over the hill, waiting for him to stand up. Or over the hill, wounded or dead. Or backtracking the unit right now, looking for a good ambush site. Anywhere.

"Fuck it," he said aloud, and stood up, swaying. Nobody shot him.

He staggered back down the hill to the smoldering ruins and squatted in them until his boots started to burn. He felt like lying down next to the heat of the ashes and sleeping forever. He unzipped a pocket on his IDF assault vest and took out a pill bottle, swallowing four bennies with scooped-up snow.

He discarded his canteen, binoculars, spare magazines, anything that weighed anything. He remembered all the stories he'd ever read about retreating troops throwing away essential gear. Oh, well, he thought, this mission is over. And then out of left field, This case is closed, King. He wondered where *that* had come from.

Carrying the cocked pistol in his right hand, he stumbled down the hill and back across the road. Bugging out.

* * *

Parsons came off the last hill and saw the clear cut below him. He knew the van was right past it, up the logging road. It was getting late, the sun already behind the mountain at his back. His blood was singing from the speed. He felt like a million dollars, especially since he had realized he could hear again. Van. Warm. Motel. Money. South America.

He decocked the automatic and stuck it back in the shoulder holster. He squatted and rubbed snow in his face. The feel of it was sensual, soothing.

He started off, refreshed, ignoring the twitching in his cheeks and the rubbery sensation in his legs. The van was still there, undisturbed, camouflaged with a dusting of morning snow.

Parsons pulled off his right glove and groped in his pocket for the keys. He had trouble getting the key in the lock because it was stiff with cold, but finally succeeded. He pulled the door open and climbed in, fumbling the key in the ignition. His breath frosted the windshield. Start, baby, start, he prayed, and pumped the gas and twisted the key. The motor turned and caught, roaring to life as Parsons fed it too much gas.

He sensed movement behind him and turned instinctively in panic, staring into the dim interior. A mound of blankets and unrolled sleeping bags was rearing up. They fell away, revealing a grimy, ragged nightmare pointing a long-barrel revolver at his head.

"Now, turn on the goddamn heater!" Rider said.

XVI.

Parsons turned the heater knob, waiting for the bullet.

"Now remove that pistol with two fingers only on the butt and toss it over the seat on these sleeping bags," the hoarse voice ordered. "If you think it's worth a try you're welcome to go for it."

Parsons did as he was told, realizing he wasn't going to be killed immediately. No sense in disarming a man when you could just shoot him. "How in the hell did you get in here?" he asked, mainly for something to say.

He heard Rider give a cracked-sounding chuckle. "No problem. The back doors on this thing weren't locked."

The back doors! Sweet Jesus Christ! Parsons felt like crying in shame and despair. He'd locked the front doors and the sliding side door and assumed—

"It's them little details that get you," Rider said. He sounded almost sympathetic. "Like, I wish you'd keep your hands on that steering wheel, in the ten-and-two-o'clock position. Pretend you're driving."

"What happens now?"

"I'm thinking about that," Rider said.

"Can I light a cigarette?"

"No."

They sat in silence. Parsons listened to his breathing. He heard a small sound behind him and almost flinched, then realized it was a cigarette lighter. His nerves were screaming from speed. A grimy hand reached in front of his face and stuck a lit cigarette between his lips.

"Smoke it like that. When you're done, spit it out on the floor."

Parsons nodded to show he understood and drew in smoke with vast appreciation. The last cigarette?

"What in the hell were you guys shooting at out there?" Rider asked.

"Your buddy. He nailed Tragger."

A pause, then Rider said, "It must have been the Chief. I'll be damned."

"The Chief?"

"Yeah, an old drunk Indian who lives on down the valley. Had to be him."

"He saved your ass," Parsons said.

"I'll send him a thank-you note."

"We killed him," Parsons said flatly, wondering why he was volunteering this information. There was a long pause, making Parsons nervous. "How did you get out of the house?"

"Oh Lord," Rider said, then laughed. "After you singed my ass off the porch, things went kind of confused. I think I grabbed my rifle and kept right on going, up on a chair and through the window, glass, sash, everything. Never even slowed down. Cut the shit out of me. I wasn't ten yards up the back slope when the place went up. Christ! What was that?"

"Sixty-six-millimeter antitank rocket. Throwaway launcher."

"Oh boy," Rider said enthusiastically. "There's more of them back here, ain't there?"

"Yes, three more, in fact," Parsons told him tiredly. He had a sudden premonition, a prevision, something. He thought of all the weaponry and ammunition strewn around Rider's cabin, all the stuff still here in the van which Rider had undoubtedly inventoried like a greedy, spoiled child in the toy department. Then he thought of his shadowy principals, Rider's enemies. Maybe he wouldn't have to worry too much about repercussions from the failed mission. The ranch in South America seemed a shade closer. The cigarette started to burn his lip and he spit it out.

There was the sound of movement, and Rider climbed around the passenger seat and sat down, the revolver pointing at Parsons. The hammer was back to full cock, and Rider grinned at him.

Parsons saw him clearly for the first time in the grimy dusk light flooding through the windshield and flinched.

He'd seen Rider before. He'd seen him in Vietnam and he'd seen him in Africa and he'd seen him in other smoky, dangerous places around the world. Sometimes they were in other units and sometimes he'd commanded them and once he'd served under one. It didn't matter that this dirty, smudged, bloody, unkempt figure in filthy camouflage with the left eye swollen shut resembled no one he had ever known. He had the look.

The one good eye actually glittered with confidence and determination and . . . enthusiasm for the rough business at hand. People like his last command were good at the work, and they had the motivation of patriotism or money, but people like Rider were naturals. They didn't need motivation. The act of combat, of killing or being killed, was motivation enough. Not murder, not assassination, but war turned people like Rider on. The smoke and fire, the detonation of weapons, the adrenaline rushes, the sweep and grandeur and adventure of it all made them come totally, truly alive.

And they couldn't be killed.

They were somehow blind to the possibility of their death, and in some mysterious manner this blindness, this unquestioned confidence in their invulnerability protected them, made them invulnerable.

Parsons had seen it all before. Private Rider sits cross-legged on top of the berm, chewing gum, humming a happy little tune, and calmly, methodically returning enemy fire while rounds crack and snap around him, punching holes through his sleeve, knocking his boot heel off and never touching him, never at all. And Private Smith, gaining confidence from this display, timidly pokes his head over the top and gets a round dead between the eyes. Unkillable. But I'm going to, Parsons thought suddenly.

"Get out," Rider said.

Parsons got out and stood in the snow by the open door, waiting, strangely confident that now was not his time to die.

"Empty your pockets. Put the stuff on the seat."

Parsons had nothing in his pockets but cigarettes, a Zippo lighter, the bottle of Benzedrine, a handkerchief, and five hundred dollars in twenties. He threw it all on the seat.

Rider glanced at the money, then took a number of the bills and handed them back. "Put that in your pocket and take off that assault vest and throw it in here, too."

Parsons peeled off the vest and threw it on top of the rest and stood waiting for more instructions. He was still confident he was going to live.

"Turn around and start walking," Rider told him. "Town's about twelve miles thataway." He gestured with the barrel of the revolver.

Both men eyed each other for a second, unspoken thoughts passing between them.

Then Parsons asked, "Why?"

Rider thought a moment. "Because you are a soldier. I respect soldiers."

Parsons nodded, turned, and started plodding through the snow down the logging trail, his shoulders not in the least tense. He was going to live, he knew it. At least long enough to kill Rider. He could feel the weight of the Randall boot knife against his leg.

Bartoli and Mewson were in the office at the trucking company, waiting. They had been waiting a long time.

Bartoli was getting angry. Mewson was very nervous.

"Go get Pat," Bartoli said.

Glad for any kind of break in the tension, Mewson went into the outer office and crooked his finger at Pat Cousins, who was installed behind the reception desk. Sensing Mewson's nervousness, she followed him timidly into Bartoli's inner sanctum, wondering why he hadn't simply summoned her over the intercom.

Bartoli was at the bar, mixing a drink. They both sat down on the leather couch. Bartoli turned to them. "You know what's going on, Pat?"

She shook her head, not sure of her status here in the nerve center of Bartoli's organization.

"Well," Bartoli said, swirling his drink and staring into it, "we sent a real professional group of people up after your buddy Rider. A real expensive group of real professional people." He favored Mewson with a flat, malevolent look. "And these people were supposed to call in as soon as the job was done. And the phones aren't ringing." He gave the phones another dirty glance, as if the whole situation were their fault. They squatted there silently, defying him.

Pat Cousins felt a queer little flash of pride, which surprised her. "How overdue are they?" she asked, hoping it was the right thing to say.

"Too long," Mewson said, trying, by manfully admitting the probable failure of his plan, to divert some of Bartoli's rage. It didn't work.

"How in the hell could he take out six trained professionals?" Bartoli shouted, slamming his untasted drink down on the bar. He started pacing the office, self-control slipping. "Unless they just took the fucking money and ran," he said, glancing at Mewson.

Al Mewson flinched. "They wouldn't do that, Bob. They're pros. They have a reputation to maintain."

"And I've got a reputation to maintain, too, goddammit! Now, I wanna know what in the hell is going on up there, and I know just the person to send up there to find out, by Christ!"

Mewson could actually feel the blood draining from his face.

Bartoli turned to Pat. "Who is this guy, Pat?" he asked almost plaintively.

"I don't—"

The phone rang. Bartoli lunged at it. "Yeah?" They watched him, holding their collective breaths.

Bartoli nodded several times. "Right. Yes. Right." His face settled, seemed to sag slightly. He replaced the receiver carefully, then pointed at Mewson with a blunt finger. "You. Pack your suitcase. You are going to Tennessee. You are going to rent a car and you are going to drive to a place called Bullet Creek and you are going to find out what the fuck is going on up there. And if you don't come back, tough shit." He paused, breathing hard. "But mark my words, Al. You go. If you cut and run I'll find you and I'll kill you with my bare hands. You hear me?"

"Yes, sir," Mewson mumbled.

"And me," Bartoli said. "I'm going to Miami. My father wants to see me."

As Parsons went down the logging road his brain was churning with options and ideas. There was no question that he was coming back to fulfill the mission. None whatever. It had to be done. The question was how.

He could go into the town, find some kind of shelter, get a few hours' rest, then buy a weapon and hire a ride back up here. Rider had given him enough cash for that. Any kind of weapon would do. A .30-.30, maybe.

He wasn't worried about looking out of place in his camouflage. He knew that half the people around here wore the stuff the season round. But he would need a cover story. A deer hunter, vehicle stuck, lost weapon, something.

But he didn't even know if deer season was in. And sooner or later that mess up on the mountain was bound to be discovered, and somebody would remember the stranger who bought the rifle and had good ol' Billy Joe carry him up here. Of course, if he was in South America by then . . .

He could see the end of the logging road where it intersected the main mountain blacktop. Turn left and go down the mountain to town. But Parsons knew he wouldn't turn left. Because it really didn't matter about anyone connecting him with any massacre. What mattered was that once he got in town, once he got warm and fed and comfortable and safe, he didn't think he could summon the resolve to come back up here. Oh, no. What guts he had left would turn to butter.

And it was now somehow very important that he finish this, the last mission of Captain Vance Parsons. What good was that ranch in the sun if he had to walk it the rest of his days with the bitter taste of shame and defeat in his mouth? The taste of cowardice.

Rider, I'm a soldier! he thought as his boots touched the snow-covered blacktop. He turned right. He walked twenty yards up the road and then went into the bushes, following the logging road back up, only this time off to the side, partially screened by the winter foliage.

He reached down, pulled up his bloused trouser leg, and snapped the bootknife out of its sheath. His full-size combat knife had gone with the assault vest. This one had a single-edge five-inch blade. It was shaving-sharp.

Parsons moved very carefully, very slowly. He had one advantage. He knew where Rider was, and Rider didn't know where he was. As far as Rider knew, he was on his way back down the mountain. If there was a psychologically correct time to pull this, it was now, while Rider was still sitting in the van, congratulating himself, before it occurred to him that Parsons might come back.

Surely he wouldn't leave the comfort and mobility of the van. Surely he was as tired and cold as Parsons was. And when he put the van in gear and moved, Parsons would hear it. And he would have to back the van out, back it out slowly over the uneven humps of the logging road.

Parsons moved about halfway back up the road, then selected his ambush site. There was a small pile of dirt, pushed up when the road had originally been bulldozed out. It was covered with brown frozen weeds now, and it was close to the edge of the road, offering good concealment.

When Rider came backing out, as he had to eventually, Parsons would leap out of hiding, jerk the door open, and use the knife. The timing would have to be very good, of course, but it was the only way he could think of.

He settled down to wait, cradling the knife. He could hear the van from here, idling softly in the cold stillness. He put his gloved left hand inside his jacket to keep it warm and flexible. That was the hand that would snatch open the door.

Things occurred to him. What if Rider stayed there all day? Parsons didn't think he would. There was nothing to drink in the van. He would want to celebrate his victory, wouldn't he? If he did stay, then eventually Parsons would have to come up with another idea, before he got too stiff from the cold to function. What if Rider had relocked the driver's door? Then Parsons would die, pure and simple. You live or you die, he thought. All you can do is take your best shot, and after that it was in the hands of Thor, the god of battle.

He settled down to wait, trying to blank his imagination. Duty would keep him warm.

The warmth in the van was making Rider sleepy. He was waiting until his late adversary had had time to get clear, then he would back the van out of here and take it back up the mountain.

He knew he had a big day ahead of him, in spite of bone-deep weariness. He had to collect all the scattered weapons around his place and hide the van. Maybe he would camp in it. Maybe he would sleep at the Chief's place. The Chief certainly wouldn't have any use for it anymore. He had to find the Chief and bury him or tie him up in a tree, or whatever Indians did. At least the old Chief deserved that. The rest could stay where they fell. Rider was tired of fooling with bodies. It was too much like work.

What he needed now was a drink. Anything in his cabin was gone, of course. He'd already given the van a cursory search and found nothing. But probably there was something in the Chief's place. If not, he'd drive to town. At any rate, that was the first order of the day, he decided.

He eyed the bottle of pills that had been in Parsons' pocket, now in the passenger seat with the rest of his stuff. He snapped off the lid and poured a few in his palm. Carter's Little Liver Pills? Heart pills? The bottle was unmarked.

"Well, shitfire." Rider chuckled. He knew speed when he saw it. White crosses. He swallowed three and put the rest in his pocket.

It occurred to him that maybe Parsons hadn't gone to town. Maybe he was at this moment heading back up to Rider's place, looking for a weapon, hoping to ambush Rider when he pulled down the road. Well, he sure as hell wouldn't have any trouble finding something.

The hell with this, Rider thought. He needed to get his ass in gear. He needed a drink. If the officer type wasn't clear by now, he'd run over his ass. He pulled the van into reverse and started to back carefully down the logging road.

Parsons heard the muted rumble of the idling motor change as Rider put it in gear. He hadn't been waiting ten minutes. He felt his lips pull back over his teeth in a feral snarl. Now, you cocksucker, he thought.

He heard snow crunching under the tires as the van backed slowly down the trail. Parsons gripped the knife tighter, tensing for the spring as his adrenaline surged. Before there was time for another thought the back of the van was even with him, then instantly the side, and Parsons lunged out of hiding, screaming, snow and frozen mud spraying from under his boots.

He had a microsecond vision of a white blur peering at him from behind the rolled-up window, and then his left hand found the door handle and he snatched at it savagely. The door flew open and he released it, aiming a vicious straight-handed thrust at Rider's exposed side, at the same time grabbing a handful of camouflage jacket.

As Parsons punched him in the side, Rider reacted, too late, by instinctively floorboarding the gas pedal. The van shot backward, engine roaring. Its momentum swung Parsons forward, inertia pinning him against the open door, preventing him from stabbing Rider again. His snow-slick boots scrabbled on the running board, seeking purchase. The only thing keeping him attached to the vehicle was his death grip on Rider's jacket.

Rider was still gripping the steering wheel with his left hand. His right clawed the .357 out of the shoulder holster. As it cleared leather, the unsteered, careening van slammed into a tree. Snow from the loaded branches cascaded down in a swirling avalanche.

Parsons was swung inward again, landing halfway in the seat, almost on top of Rider. There was a confused, grunting struggle. Parsons' left hand was locked around Rider's gun-hand wrist. Rider had grabbed Parsons' knife hand, and they struggled silently for a moment, sobbing and straining with effort.

Rider realized that Parsons was far stronger than he was, that the contest would end quickly, as soon as Parsons succeeded in jerking his knife arm free from Rider's weakening grasp.

With a scream of desperation Rider launched himself out of the seat, out of the van, carrying Parsons with him. The impact of the fall broke them apart. Rider tumbled over Parsons' head, doing a complete, uncoordinated flip, landing on his back and rolling up on his knees, disoriented, still gripping the revolver.

Parsons bore in from somewhere, snow-covered, a wild-eyed angel of death, kicking the weapon out of Rider's hand. It went spinning off, burying itself in a snowdrift.

Rider scrambled away, coming erect, seeking distance from the combat, seeking time to bring the spinning world back into perspective. He was brought up against a pine, the rough bark digging into his back, his legs weak and trembling. He ripped the Gerber combat knife out of his sheath and faced his enemy.

Parsons, who had slipped in the snow from the violence of his kick, was just regaining his feet.

He staggered erect. The men faced each other, chests heaving, breath blowing out in frosty billows. Rider was aware of a long string of spit dribbling from his mouth. He wiped it away on his sleeve. The movement brought a twinge of pain in his left side, a warm, ripping sensation. He realized, with casual shock, that Parsons had hit him with something more than his fist. He thought, without much real emotion, that he was going to die now.

"Well," Parsons said. It was a statement of satisfaction. His breathing was starting to return to normal, a result of staying in shape.

"I let *you* go," Rider said, and was immediately sorry he'd said it. It sounded too much like whining, or begging, and he hadn't meant it that way.

Parsons eyed him out of cold, marble eyes. "This is my last contract," he said, as if that explained everything.

In a way, it did, because Rider gave an imperceptible nod, as if he understood completely. Then he grinned and waved the point of his Parkerized blade. "Mine's bigger than yours."

"But I'm in better shape. And better trained," Parsons said. He eyed the spreading stain of blood on the side of Rider's coat. "And if you keep talking you'll bleed out before you have a go."

Rider's free hand groped up to his side, as if in confirmation, and plucked at the stiffening, soaked material of his jacket. He nodded again. "Got a point there." He grinned his crazy grin, and Parsons was proud of him. "So let's do it," Rider said, and pushed himself away from the tree.

The Drunken Chief was tired. Plumb goddamn give out, in fact. He wasn't just getting too old for this shit, he *was* too old for this shit.

It hadn't been too bad this morning, coming down off his ridge, setting himself up in ambush for the gringo honky white-eyes idiots he knew were coming. It was all downhill there. The cold had got to him some, waiting, but the occasional nip of corn liquor had kept his old blood circulating, after a fashion.

But, as usual, he'd forgotten. Forgotten that real combat involved three percent fighting and seven percent waiting under tension and ninety percent covering ground. Covering short sections of ground in frenzied, desperate spurts and covering long sections of ground in a plodding, fatigue-numbed daze. Well, he could still handle the three percent of it, but the rest was playing hell with what laughably passed for his constitution. Brains only went so far if the traitorous body was going to let you down.

He'd called the shots perfectly. Everything had gone like a ballet he'd choreographed. All the dancers had moved in and out of position on cue. All the bodies had moved as expected. Except his own.

It had let him down the first time he had to move fast. After he killed the first white-eyes, he knew that he had one more free shot and then they'd have his position spotted. So he fired his second round from the

ridgetop, blindly, and then rolled off it, gaining his feet
and tearing the top off the quart jar of chicken blood,
splashing it around wildly as he stumbled away in a
zigzag, lurching course downhill. And not a second too
soon. As he had known it would, the top of the ridge
exploded in a storm of steel and explosives before he
was ten yards away. But it had been far enough.

He'd been there, in the bottom of the hollow, lying
concealed among the tangle of honeysuckle, hugging
his rifle to his chest, when they reached the ridgetop.
He had listened to them mumble and curse and laugh,
waiting for one of them to have a brainstorm and
suggest that they beat up the foliage downhill with
grenades and automatic fire, just to make sure.

But they hadn't, and it was like the young ones
said—cool—except that in rolling off the hill he had
twisted something, or pulled it, or busted it, and it was
getting worse now, much worse, and the Drunken
Chief knew that in a very short time he would have to
be rotated to the rear as walking wounded. Or limping
wounded, he thought sardonically.

Anyway, he'd lain there, shielded by the broad, shiny
leaves of the honeysuckle, and listened to the sounds of
combat, the thump of grenades, the stutter of machine
guns, the crack and snap of individual weapons, until
the cold had seeped in through his greased buckskin in
sufficient quantities to force him up out of hiding.

He'd been just below the ridgetop, sprayed with the
blood of his own chickens, when he heard the combat
renew, the snap again of small arms, the muted thud of
grenades, the yelling and screaming, and then, like a
giant cracking his knuckles in the crisp air, the dry
whack of high explosive, followed by silence. For a long
time.

And then, the Chief thought disgustedly, to the
shame of any Indian worth his salt, or any soldier, for

that matter, he had nodded off, simply wrapped up in his blanket, and fallen asleep, like some goddamn old man, and sometime while he slept, Rider had passed below in full view of him and, following him, one of the Krauts, while he snoozed away.

He had awakened eventually, some Indian sixth sense had awakened him, in time for him to glimpse the Kraut receding into the dim woods below him, and the Drunken Chief, summoning his last reserve of energy, had followed.

And so it came to this.

The Drunken Chief limped out of the forest, breath rasping in his sunken chest, and eyed the clear cut below, and the sawmill road, and the stalled van, back-ended and bumper bent against a tree, and the two figures, squared off against each other next to it.

He recognized Rider from three hundred yards— the slight body and the long black unkempt hair and sloppy beard—and he knew that, whatever was going on, he could not hope to intervene personally, not on these frail, ancient legs, so he sat down cross-legged in the cold snow and tried to control his ancient breathing and took up a hasty sling on the equally ancient M1 Garand and sighted in on the distant figure confronting Rider.

As the flat crack of the clean miss rang out, both men momentarily froze, torn between the instinct to hit the ground and the necessity to keep facing each other.

Parsons compromised, without thinking, by turning his head to look in the direction of the rifle's report as it came echoing down the hillside. It was his last mistake.

Rider lunged in mindlessly and, just as Parsons was turning back in sudden realization, drove the blade of his knife through the mercenary's throat.

It went in up to the handguard and Rider left it there and whirled, diving for the shelter of the van, scrambling in and crashing between the seats, fumbling frantically for one of the assault rifles in the dimness of the back.

Parsons stood there for a moment, dumbfounded, as dark red blood poured out around the knife hilt protruding from his throat like an obscene goiter. Then his eyes widened in panic and he made a sound like a toilet flushing and turned and began a shambling, staggering run. He tripped over a bush and fell down, then started twisting in the snow like a hook-impaled worm, his hands beating futilely at his neck. Presently the twisting stopped and his legs began twitching and quivering in the dance of death.

I let you go, Rider thought as he watched him from around the right front tire of the van where he was now crouching. He had come out the back, slamming a magazine into the SC70. He scanned the sparsely vegetated hillside where the shot had come from.

A figure was making its way gingerly down the slick slope, a rifle slung over its shoulder.

When Rider was sure who it was, he muttered, "I'll be damned," and came tiredly out of concealment.

As the buckskin-clad, blanket-wrapped figure limped slowly up to him, Rider sat down in the snow and eased his back against a tire, rifle across his lap. He was starting to feel sick and woozy. He fished a cigarette out and lit it with trembling hands. "Evening, Chief."

The Chief nodded, glanced at the now-motionless figure a few yards away, then looked back at Rider.

"Can you drive?" Rider asked, and the Chief nodded again, then grunted. "Ugh. Me drive good."

"No time to bullshit around now, Chief," Rider said, his voice starting to sound weak and distant in his own ears. "I'll find out what I owe you later. Right now I seem to have developed a leak, and if I climb back in this van I'd appreciate it if you could kind of plug it up and get us hid up on the mountain somewhere."

The Chief smirked. "I'll build a fire so I can heat an arrowhead and cauterize the wound." He limped forward and helped Rider into the back of the van.

Bartoli was sitting in a cocktail lounge in Miami. It was the first bar he had passed as he came from the meeting with his father. He was sitting in a booth as far back into the dim recesses of the place as he could get.

His two bodyguards, who normally would have sat with him, had sensed his foul mood and diplomatically left him alone in the booth. They lounged at a table on the other side of the room, nursing drinks and keeping a casual eye on the entrance.

Bartoli felt the last of the perspiration drying on his forehead as he took a healthy slug from his double Tom Collins. It was warm outside, but not that warm. He'd started sweating in the Old Man's air-conditioned living room, but now his dismay was turning to rage.

He'd listened humbly, of course, as the old Don strode up and down the imported Persian rug, ranting in his hoarse voice and using his cane to punctuate his points. Yes, Papa; no, Papa; certainly, Papa. Well, bullshit!

The thing has come full circle, Bartoli thought bitterly.

At first it had been the Mustache Petes, in the old days, strewing the public streets with bodies in their interminable wars and rivalries. Okay, that was too much, too obvious, and the second generation, Luciano and his contemporaries, had been right to organize, move into legitimate business, and keep a low profile.

But now things had gone too far in the other direction, he thought as disgust and frustration welled up inside him like a great sour bubble.

Now everybody wanted to be some kind of fucking executive. Christ! Ninety-nine percent of these wise guys had never even made their bones. When rough stuff was required they all used unconnected punks. Long-haired dopeheads. Motorcycle crazies. Nobody wanted to get their hands dirty anymore.

Bartoli drained his glass in convulsive gulps and signaled the waitress for a refill.

And so what happens when you run an outfit like this?

Everybody loses respect for you, that's what happens. Look at the dope business. The goddamn Colombians running wild, taking over everything. And crazies like this fucking hillbilly, sitting up there and thumbing his nose at them.

Bartoli's hands tightened around his glass until the knuckles turned white. He made a conscious effort to calm down. It wasn't very successful. He had tried to explain this to the Old Man, point out what was happening to the organization, and why, all to no avail.

The discussion had degenerated into a shouting match, and ended with the old Don ranting and raving, spraying spit in Bartoli's face as he sat there like a chastened schoolboy. Absolutely no more of this cowboy shit! The thing was done. Finished. Written off. The other Dons knew all about it. Sooner or later the wrong people would find out about it. It would get in the papers. In *Newsweek*. "Bloody Nose for Mafia in God's Country." They would make a TV movie about the whole mess. The public would be prodded out of their lethargy. Big money would have to be spread over the troubled waters. And if that happened, heads would roll, the Old Man pointed out, his thin chest heaving with emotion, the tip of his walking stick trembling under Bartoli's nose.

Bartoli felt the sweat start on his forehead again, in spite of the air-conditioning. He realized he was gritting his teeth. Well, fuck it, he thought. Fuck them all. Nothing had changed. Just because their shit was weak didn't mean his was. This just complicated his problem, that was all. Now he'd have to finish this business quietly, so the stink couldn't blow all the way down to Miami. Or up to New York. But finish it he would, he thought with a dull, building rage that was so intense it made him nauseous.

Two days later, most of the snow had melted, but the wind was picking up. It moaned down through the trees on the steep slopes and gusted across the road, drying the slushy mud and rocking Al Mewson's rental car with each fresh blast.

Every time that happened his hands tightened on the steering wheel in convulsive fright. He was driving slowly, carefully, almost in the center of the dirt track, his eyes darting nervously to the right where the shoulder of the road dropped off with stomach-clenching suddenness. Occasionally the vehicle would drift far enough over to allow him a quick view down into vine-choked hollows a dizzying distance below. There were no guardrails, even on the hairpin curves.

He came to a fairly level, wider place at the top of a knob and pulled over, putting the car in park with the motor running. He jammed the emergency brake down savagely, feeling his tension ease slightly. As soon as his fear of sliding down into one of those horrendous hollows eased, the other, greater fear came rushing back. He knew he was close to his destination, and what he had to do when he reached it.

Mewson's legs felt weak. He picked the stainless-steel flask off the seat and had a long pull, waiting for the whiskey to calm him, then recapped the flask and got out of the warm car. The wind snapped his coattails against his legs and he reached up just in time, as his snap-brim hat started to take off.

Jamming it tighter on his head, he took out a large white handkerchief. Feeling foolish, his hands starting to numb, he walked around the car and tied it to the radio antenna. Better foolish than dead, he thought miserably. He had no real confidence in a flag of truce—that shit only worked in grade B movies—but it was the only thing he could think of. Al Mewson was scared shitless.

He got back in the car, shivering, only partly from the cold. The dark specter of his own mortality hung around him like some morbid shroud. For the first time in his long association with Robert Bartoli he sincerely wished he'd never heard of the man.

Before this mess everything had been so removed, so abstract. The business was conducted like any other, in oak-paneled offices and the controlled dignity of court-rooms.

He looked around nervously at the dismal, frightening scenery, feeling very alone. Things were no longer abstract for Al Mewson.

He pulled the transmission back down into gear and fed it too much gas. The rear wheels spun briefly before catching and his heart did a minor barrel loop.

In a short time the road leveled out even more, and suddenly he knew he was there. The cleared ground on the side of a hill, the short, sloping driveway, the gutted cabin. He had no clear plan, no instructions to guide him. Basically he was here simply as punishment. But he knew also that he'd better not go back to Tampa without some new information, something. He turned the car around, ready for a fast getaway, and cut it off.

Gritting his teeth, he got out, taking the keys with him. He walked up the muddy driveway, his sidewalk-slick shoes slipping in the frost-rimmed mud. The wind moaned, flapping his London Fog overcoat.

Even to his unpracticed eye it was clear the cabin had been destroyed by explosives. Debris was scattered in a huge radius around the main ruins.

Warily he circled the shabby pickup, his shoulders stiff with tension. He saw the first body.

Mewson stared at it open-mouthed, gulping. The head was a shattered, bloody mess. The torso had a weird, flattened appearance, like it was already trying to sink back into the earth from which it had come. It was also obviously frozen to the ground.

Mewson couldn't tear his eyes away from it. Ashtrays and rocks and other inanimate objects didn't move, but inanimate objects weren't *supposed* to move. People were supposed to move, to walk and gesture and breathe and talk, not lie there cold and stiff with their mouths stretched open, full of snow.

The only things in motion were a few wisps of unbloodied hair, waving in the wind, accentuating the total lack of any other animation.

Mewson felt the terrible thought coming, and couldn't stop it. That could be me! his mind shrieked.

Before he realized it he was halfway back to the car in a crabbing, panicked run. He forced himself to halt, breathing in huge gulps of cold air, looking around wildly.

Regaining a margin of self-control, he willed himself back up the driveway. He passed the body, not looking, and made a wide circle around the cabin.

His attention was drawn to the trees near the top of the hill. They looked somehow bedraggled. One of them was leaning almost parallel to the ground, held up only by other trees. Reluctantly he approached, and almost immediately saw two more dead men.

This pair was in even more horrible shape than the one below. They were mutilated almost past the point of being human. Gagging, he saw that the leaning pine had been nearly severed at ground level by more explosives.

Mewson had had enough. Blindly, his eyes watering, he began stumbling back down the slope.

He almost walked over another corpse. Compared to what he'd already seen, this one looked almost peaceful. He gave a little moan as he skirted the thing, heading for the car.

He snatched the door open and fumbled the keys into the ignition. He realized, in a numb, almost detached way, that he was teetering on the edge of mindless, headlong, running panic. One sharp sound would do it. If the car failed to start, if it didn't drop into gear smoothly and immediately, anything, cool Al Mewson, lawyer, smooth operator, man of the world, would find himself flying through the hostile woods, sobbing in terror, careening off trees, pissing his seventy-five-dollar pants, slobbering all over his imported silk tie. The car started and Al Mewson pulled carefully, sanely away, congratulating himself on his self-control, trying to ignore the feeling he was being watched.

He never noticed the cabin on the hill farther down the valley, its weathered drabness blending in with the greyness of the terrain. He never knew he was still alive because Rider, watching through the Chief's binoculars, thought he might be an FBI agent.

It wasn't until he reached the first sharp, right-hand curve that he realized he'd forgotten to close the door.

And it wasn't until he was back in his motel room on the outskirts of Knoxville, with a bellyful of whiskey and tranquilizers, that he remembered something odd about the battlefield. Something was missing. All the weapons were gone.

PART THREE

He either fears his fate too much
Or his deserts are small,
Who dares not put it to the touch
To win or lose it all.

                    Marquess of Montrose

XVII.

The Drunken Chief poked the fire up and threw another piece of wood in. He turned back to Rider, who was slouched on the Chief's ratty couch, naked to the waist, his chest encircled with gauze bandages.

"Listen, you asshole. You couldn't take five of them by yourself. If it hadn't been for me you wouldn't be here. I saved your white ass twice, no, three times, if you want to count sticking a plug in that extra cunt hole you got there."

"Hey, I been meaning to thank you for that, Chief," Rider said. Grimacing, he put the reassembled automatic shotgun on the floor next to the already cleaned SAW. "By the way, how come you was in the right place at the right time, anyway?"

"Never mind," the Chief grumbled. "You wouldn't understand if I told you. The point is, if you couldn't handle five of them up here, on your own ground, what the hell makes you think you can take a whole gang of them on their own hunting grounds, huh?"

Rider took another drink of corn whiskey. "Anyway, I owe you one. Or three. Whatever."

"The only thing you owe me is another twenty dollars for that jug you're sucking on," the Chief said. "Now, answer my question."

"Well," Rider said. He held up his hand, ticking points off on his fingers.

"One. I mighta been on my own ground, as you call it, but they had a helluvan advantage. They could come anytime, and I didn't know when. They like to wore me down, waiting. So if I go down there, we reverse the situation, right? Surprise is on my side, right?"

"Oh, sure. They'll all be asleep and you'll wipe 'em out."

"Two." Rider said. "I'm armed to the teeth now. I got a honest-to-God, bipod-mounted machine gun. I got a bloop tube. I got, uh, I got rockets, Chief. Antitank weapons."

"Which you've never fired."

"No problem," Rider said brightly. "They got directions right on the tube. In little pictures. An idiot could figure it out."

"You shouldn't have any problem, then."

Rider ignored him. "Three."

"Never mind three," the Chief said disgustedly. "You said it all with two."

"Eh?" Rider said in feigned innocence. A sly, smug expression crept over his face.

"I got, I got, a *bloop tube*," the Chief mimicked. "I got, oh boy, golly, *a machine gun*." He snorted in contempt. "Go ahead and bullshit yourself, if you want. Don't try to bullshit this old man. You should have seen those bloodshot things you call eyes light up when you said machine gun. You're like a six-year-old in a toy store. Holy shit!"

Rider's expression went from smug to embarrassed. "Well, hell," he said defensively. "They've had their try. Two of 'em, in fact. What am I supposed to do, sit up here on my ass for the rest of my life waiting for the next one?"

"The best defense is offense, right?"

"Exactly!"

"And no point in all that hardware lying around up here rusting, right?"

Rider nodded enthusiastically. "Yeah. Yeah, Chief, you wouldn't believe the ammo in that van. Grenades. Claymores. A starlight scope, for Christ's sake!"

The Chief watched Rider take another drink and give a shudder of satisfaction. "There is only one big difference between running a private war up here and running one in downtown Tampa. Have you thought of that?"

"What's that, Chief?"

"The police. What do you think they are gonna be doing while all these machine guns and rockets are going off?"

Rider thought a minute. "Fuck the police!" he answered.

Thus was his mission planned.

Mewson was back in Bartoli's office, haggard from a combination of exhaustion, jet lag, and hangover.

He'd just finished giving his report, including the missing weapons. Now he cleared his throat and plunged in, before he lost his nerve.

"Uh, I know I'm not in good graces now, but I've got something more that might be pertinent to all this."

"You're fucking right about that," Bartoli said sourly. "What's this latest brainstorm?"

Mewson shifted uneasily on the couch. "I took a little side trip on the way home. To Atlanta. Old college buddy. He's got a practice there. He's a clinical psychiatrist."

"And?"

"I gave him a hypothetical scenario about a hillbilly running amok. About a hillbilly who's a Vietnam vet and who leaves his address casually lying around for the wrong people to find. About—"

Bartoli was coming out of his chair. "You told this fuck about us?"

"It's cool, Mr. Bartoli, it's cool!" Mewson said desperately. He flashed a sick grin. "The guy thinks I work for the CIA."

Bartoli slowly subsided back into his chair, his vein throbbing. "Go on, dammit."

"Well, I'm not going to throw a lot of psychological gibberish around that I don't half understand myself, but"—Mewson hesitated, then spit it out in a rush—"my friend thinks there's a good chance this guy will pay us a visit."

Bartoli leaned forward over his desk, tense. The vein was prominent again, but Mewson saw with relief that Bartoli's emotion was no longer directed at him personally.

"He'll come down here? After us?"

Mewson nodded. "He says it's probable."

When Bartoli said nothing, Mewson added, as an afterthought, "And he does have all that hardware."

A savage light was growing in Bartoli's eyes. The warnings and orders of others faded from conscious consideration. He was too busy thinking of the logistics of going to the mattress, a literal euphemism for an out-and-out war footing.

People. Yes, he could get the people, no problem. And the hardware. He'd have to lay in a supply of food, a bunch of cots, some refrigerators. There was plenty of room in the empty offices upstairs, and if that wasn't enough, there was always the warehouse and maintenance garage next door. His mind was awhirl with details. His blood was soaring. He was feeling like a general. Like Napoleon or somebody.

It was as if his mind, so long frustrated, so long indecisive, had been waiting for this. Once Mewson had planted the spark of this idea, it had fanned with incredible swiftness into a roaring conflagration.

It never occurred to him that Mewson might be wrong. This was right. It felt right. It was logical. Rider was coming.

XVIII.

The winter dragged on in the hills, mostly wet and cold, with occasional periods of even colder weather, mixed with halfhearted flurries of snow. The scenery became progressively bleaker, the bare ground a sea of mud or a carpet of wet, rotting leaves.

The stiffness had gone out of Rider's knife wound, the small, healing scar surrounded by a lump of deformed muscle.

He had made a concession to tidiness by dragging the bodies on his property into a hollow and covering them with dead brush. Parsons' body he had buried, because it was so much closer to the road.

Rider was on the wagon. He allowed himself half a water glass of booze every evening, after the day's work was done. He had been substantially dry for almost two weeks now.

The day's chores had mostly consisted of road work, climbing the hills, covering ground, getting in shape.

Rider and the Chief had booby-trapped all likely approaches to the Chief's cabin.

They had set Claymores and buried a series of two-by-four blocks drilled to accept a short length of PVC plumbing pipe. Each pipe was loaded with a 12-gauge shotgun round, the whole device resting on a thumbtack, which acted as a firing pin when somebody stepped on it. They had placed sixty-three of these VC-inspired devices around, twenty of them on the trail that led to the cabin from the road below.

"What about your relatives?" Rider had asked while they worked.

"They blow the horn before they come up," the Chief had grunted, and that had been that.

The van was concealed under cut brush at the end of the road. Rider had checked the oil, gas, and antifreeze, removed the snow chains, and generally reorganized the gear in the back. All the weapons were in the Chief's cabin.

Rider had practiced with everything but the light antitank rockets. There were only three of them, and once armed, they had to be fired, so he contented himself with studying the nomenclature and memorizing the simple pictograph instructions.

He counted his money, money taken from Ball, money fished from the bloody pants of the men sent after him. What he had on hand was a bit shy of $1,100.

He gave $500 to the Chief and tried to give him the remainder of the white powder that had already cost eleven lives.

The Chief didn't want it. "What am I gonna do with that shit?"

Rider didn't know. He left it where it had been, under some fifty-pound bags of fertilizer stored in his outhouse.

One evening Rider downed more than his usual

spartan quota of alcohol. While he was doing that, he carefully packed an army duffel bag with the items he thought he might need in the immediate future.

He had to repack it several times, because he kept putting in too much equipment.

The Chief watched all this without comment, a sardonic smirk on his brown, wrinkled face.

Rider would build two stacks, one to take, one to leave with the Chief.

The items he wanted were wrapped in sections of an old blanket to cushion them and inserted lengthwise into the duffel. Invariably the duffel would be bulging, with no more room, and there would still be more things to go in.

Rider would take another drink and study the situation intently, then with a sigh unpack and begin again.

The same thing happened the third time. "The hell with it," Rider muttered. He put on his coat, took the flashlight and a shotgun, and went down the hill to the van. He came back with another bag, this one an overnight travel satchel.

In the end, he settled for two LAW rockets, the SAW with two assault packs, the M79 grenade launcher with ten 40mm grenades, his own M2 carbine with homemade silencer, one SC70 short assault rifle, five hand grenades, a spare pistol, a pair of binoculars, and the starlight scope. He kept his Ruger Magnum revolver and shoulder holster, and decided to carry the Benelli 500 shotgun.

The pile to be left included several Claymores, one LAW, hand grenades, a stack of assault rifles, and an even dozen assorted handguns.

The Chief eyed it all greedily. "I bet a man was to sell all that he'd have enough to get a twenty-foot satellite dish."

"Wouldn't do that, Chief," Rider told him. "Everything there is illegal as hell, except the handguns."

"Well, just them, then."

Rider shrugged. "Fine. But you better dig up all that shit we got strewed around this hill before you get a bunch of TV technicians wandering around up here. One of them might trip a Claymore. It'll cause talk." He hefted the bags, grimacing. "Tell you what. When I get back—"

The Chief's face went flat and serious. "You won't get back, asshole."

Early the next morning, Rider awoke, dressed, and staggered outside with a bag on each shoulder. He headed down the hill toward the van, pushing brush aside with his load, staying off the mined path.

The Chief came out on his porch, a cup of steaming black coffee in his hand. "Hey!" he yelled, and Rider paused halfway down the hill. "If you can't get on the national news with all that hardware, you're a chickenshit pussy!"

Rider managed to raise his right arm through the strap of the duffel bag and give the Chief the finger.

The Chief retreated back out of the cold. He poured more coffee, then added a shot of moonshine. He sat down and propped his slippered feet on a stool and sipped his drink. "Hot damn," he said aloud. "Hot damn!"

Bartoli and Son's was no longer carrying on the pretense of a trucking firm. All legitimate drivers and mechanics had been given extended vacations, with pay.

The rigs had been neatly lined up against the chain link fence at one side of the asphalt parking lot.

Bartoli had a huge homemade map of the installation tacked to his office wall. It showed the entire compound, surrounded by chain link fence. The office and attached warehouse backed on Tampa Bay itself.

The asphalt parking lot fronted on Industrial Drive, the entrance guarded by the security booth.

Across the road a number of weathered wood-frame houses squatted sadly, their occupants, all black, stoically enduring the roar and rattle of trucks serving the machine shop and chemical supply business on each side of Bartoli's.

Bartoli studied his map with satisfaction and confidence. He still felt like Napoleon.

The offices upstairs had been stocked with cots, refrigerators, frozen dinners, booze, ammo, the whole wad. Six Cubans were up there, armed with submachine guns and grenades and a starlight scope. One of them was watching out the front and one was watching out the back, toward the bay, at all times.

One of the houses across the street, after a minimum of persuasion and a maximum of cash, had been vacated by the occupants, and now contained four free-lance hit men, recruited from Miami, armed with Mini-14s and shotguns.

One of the parked trailers against the south fence, facing the machine shop, was also occupied by two of Bartoli's men. Peepholes had been drilled in the cargo doors and were manned constantly. An orange drop cord, servicing the heater, TV, and coffeepot, stretched from the trailer to the maintenance garage.

This arrangement effectively covered three approaches to the cluster of buildings. It was the fourth, north side that Bartoli was concerned about.

The metal-sided Brighton Chemical supply building was higher than any of the structures on his own lot. Because he could think of no better solution, he placed a man with a walkie-talkie in a car, permanently parked at the end of Industrial Drive, on the far side of Brighton's.

All his people had been given a description of Rider

and the van he would possibly be driving, as had the street people of the area.

Bartoli was, even in the midst of his personal bloodlust, hedging his bets, paying a token sort of attention to the way things *should* be done.

If any of the pimps, whores, dealers, motel clerks, parking-lot attendants, pawnbrokers, or assorted other creatures of inner-city blight should happen to spot Rider or the van, they would earn a fast C-note by making a simple phone call.

Then one of Bartoli's minions with connections to City Hall would make another simple phone call, and the police would, as they had many times before, be allowed to do Bartoli's dirty work.

Arrested in a stolen van full of automatic weapons and explosives, Rider would then be safely in jail, where he would conveniently hang himself, thus ending the whole mess, with a three-paragraph story on page four of the local paper.

If Rider wasn't spotted, and the thing had to be resolved with a pitched battle on Industrial Drive, then Bartoli could always point out how he had tried to do things the right way. Was it his fault if some poor deranged Vietnam vet with a trunkful of dynamite tried to blow up his honest trucking company? Probably, because the media were always depicting innocent businessmen with Italian names as gangsters.

Bartoli stood in his office, studying his map, planning, anticipating. The automatic pistol stuck in his belt made an uncomfortable bulge, but he was loath to remove it. It was a symbol of his resolve.

He knew that time was running out, that he couldn't maintain this position of preparedness much longer. It was expensive, and routine business was suffering. People were starting to get antsy, including certain people in Miami and New York, who were well aware of what was going on.

People were starting to talk. All this for one man? Was Mr. B's shit getting weak? Had he snorted a bad line?

Today, Bartoli thought. Please make it today. Let's get this little shitface in a cell and put a wire around his fucking neck.

But he knew that he really didn't want Rider in a cell. He wanted Rider out there in his parking lot, on his knees and bloody, begging, as Bartoli ended this vendetta in the way it must be ended now. With the blood of his enemy on his own hands.

Rider was off the mountain and at one of the numerous combination junkyard/garage/used-car lots in the area. Places like this constituted a fair amount of the local industry, along with sawmills, timber cutting, moonshining, marijuana growing, and welfare.

This one was in open, rolling fields, an acre of rusting, window-shattered vehicles, centered around what used to be a farmhouse. Several dilapidated truck beds, minus wheels, bunched together on a patch of soggy, snow-splotched ground, waited patiently until the beer cans they were filled with were worth more than fifteen cents a pound. Rider had contributed more than his share to this pile of treasure over the years.

Now he carefully maneuvered the van along the muddy track that substituted for a driveway, trying to avoid the greasy motors, transmissions, and rear ends that sprouted everywhere like mechanical flowers.

He stopped in front of the porch, which sagged under the weight of rough lumber shelves stacked with alternators, starters, and other artifacts, and unnecessarily blew the horn. If the racket the dozen or so mangy, baying hounds were making didn't alert the owner, he was probably dead.

In a few seconds the proprietor appeared, unshaven and pulling on a ragged coat over grease-slick overalls.

Rider got out, ignoring the dogs, but warily alert for piles of their droppings. "'Lo, Bud."

"S'happening," Buddy acknowledged. He eyed the van speculatively.

"Like it?" Rider asked.

"Nice," Buddy admitted. In this part of the world, anything that ran and didn't have the muffler off was nice.

He walked around it, looking. "Sellin' or tradin'?"

"Trading, I guess," Rider told him.

"Paper?"

"No," Rider said. He had burned the registration and other documents. They wouldn't have helped him, anyway, and they might have caused problems in the long run.

But it didn't really matter. The local people were amazingly considerate of the DMV or, for that matter, any other branch of government, local or federal. Most of them went to great lengths to avoid increasing the already staggering load of paperwork the bureaucracy labored under.

As a result, motor vehicles were regularly bought, sold, and traded without benefit of inconveniences like titles or registration. No notaries were involved, and license tags were switched from vehicle to vehicle with cavalier disregard for the finer legal details.

Most cars, trucks, tractors, and even boats had passed through so many actual owners that it would have taken a task force of Justice Department lawyers six months to track down the last legitimate owner.

So Buddy didn't even raise an eyebrow when informed there would be no pesky paperwork to fool with. He simply revised his estimate of the van's value slightly downward.

"What I need," Rider said, "is a car that has the right paper and tags and that will get me to Florida and back. If you guarantee that, I don't give a shit how bad you screw me. I won't even make you kiss me."

Buddy grinned and directed a stream of Skoal and spit at one of the milling, sniffing dogs, which shied away, then eagerly inspected the deposit. "I do believe I got what you're lookin' for," he said.

Rider followed him around the house to the back, where there were a number of fairly decent-looking newer cars.

"That one, that one, and that one," Buddy said, pointing proudly. "All run like a top, all got good tags, and the paper's right. You got a license, all you need's a bill of sale and you're as straight as J. Edgar."

Rider got into a Dodge Dart and cranked it up. The motor ran smoothly. While he was listening to it, the dogs, which had followed them around the house, were joined by three mongoloid-looking children, who stared at him solemnly.

These dirty urchins represented Buddy's other major source of income. Since the government paid a certain amount of money for the maintenance of disabled children, and since Buddy was married to his second cousin and this union had invariably produced various kinds of genetically defective young, it had become obvious to Buddy early in his marriage that fucking was not only fun, it was profitable, too. A really retarded kid could be worth upwards of $500 a month. The three watching now, Rider knew, were bringing in a total of $1,100 in computerized federal checks twelve times a year.

Rider also knew that Buddy wasn't the only one running this sorry scam, and although it mildly disgusted him, he'd been around the world enough not to make indignant value judgments about such things. Buddy loved his children. It was a sorry old world, and everybody got by the best they could. He'd read somewhere that everybody was born with a cock up their ass and somebody's hand in their pocket. Politician, business executive, general, somebody's. He'd believed it automatically.

He finished giving the Dodge a cursory check, looked in the trunk to make sure it wasn't rusted through, then followed Buddy into the living room/office to consummate the deal.

There was no point in a road check. Rider wasn't enough of a mechanic to spot any subtle major defect, and Buddy, like most of the others around here, was honest. If he said the car was good, it was good. The other side of the coin was, of course, that if Buddy threatened to kill somebody, he meant that, too.

Rider transferred his gear from the van to the trunk of his new car, trying not to grunt with the weight of the bags. He failed, but Buddy said nothing, impassive, bristled face working up for another spit.

Rider drove away from the farmhouse. One of the children lifted a hand in farewell. Rider waved back, drove to the main road, and pointed the car's nose toward the expressway.

XIX.

His timing was bad. He bypassed the outskirts of Atlanta at the worst possible time, the four-o'clock rush hour. On top of that it was raining.

Forty miles of eight-lane bumper-to-bumper driving had left his shoulders stiff with tension. His eyes ached from peering through the clicking wipers at flaring taillights and clouds of misty spray thrown up by the roaring tires of the big rigs. And he felt like shit.

His stomach was churning and his mouth already brackish from cigarette smoke. Ah hell, he thought, what's the rush? He had driven by several exit ramps which advertised motels, but Rider was looking for a Holiday Inn. Because the rooms are nice and I can afford it, he rationalized, trying to ignore the waspish little voice that kept telling him yes, asshole, and a Holiday Inn is sure to have a lounge, too. Eventually he spotted the towering sign he was looking for. He took the correct exit and drove under the sheltered arch by the office.

The female clerk kept eyeing him suspiciously as he registered, noting the too-long hair and beard, the scruffy clothes. Eventually the still-impressive wad of twenties in his wallet mollified her to the point that she condescended to take his money and give him directions to his room.

Rider threw his suitcase on one of the double beds and dug out his solitary set of decent clothes: a pair of dark slacks, turtleneck pullover, and imitation-leather dress jacket.

The weapons bags were still in the trunk, where he intended to leave them. You could carry paranoia just so far.

It still made him uncomfortable, though, to be so far from his primary armament. He had a .45 automatic nestled at his back under his coat, with two spare magazines in his coat pocket.

The Magnum and shoulder holster and two hand grenades were in the suitcase, covered with his clothes.

He made sure the door was locked, the safety chain on, although it was inconceivable the enemy could track him here. Unless they had watched him come down off the mountain, maybe found the van at Buddy's and learned what kind of car he was now driving . . .

Paranoia, paranoia, Rider chided himself. Nevertheless, he jammed a chair under the doorknob and took the pistol and a hand grenade into the bathroom when he went to shower.

Later, he stood in front of the vanity mirror, trimming great hunks of his beard off with a pair of scissors. When it was as close as he could get it, he shaved slowly and painfully, leaving a thick black mustache.

He regarded the finished product in the mirror with fascination. He looked like some kind of goddamn religious fanatic—thin white face, hollow cheeks, the eyes radiating a weird glow. Jesus! Beard or no beard, no wonder the broad at the desk had been eyeing him!

He began to wonder if she had possibly called the law. What if they were going through his trunk right now? Jesus God, they find that stuff in there and I'll have the Atlanta SWAT team on my ass! he thought wildly. Or maybe even the Delta Force!

Rider shook his head violently. The still-too-long black hair swirled. Settle down, asshole! he thought savagely. His pulse rate was up and his palms sweaty.

But he knew what was wrong. All that getting-in-shape bullshit. It took a full month to work all the booze out of the system, and he was right in the middle of the thing, all that poison oozing out of his pores, making him stink like a wino, making him nervous and jumpy and paranoid. Well, by God, he knew how to cure *this* particular problem.

Rider got dressed in his city clothes, stuck the .45 in his belt, put his coat on over it, and headed for the lounge.

It was a lounge just like the last hundred motel lounges Rider had been in. Imitation-leather-fronted bar, whiskey bottles in front of a mirror, tiny tables intimidated by the chairs surrounding them. Jukebox. There was a small bandstand to one side of the room, but it was deserted. Apparently it wasn't Saturday night.

Rider, into his fourth mixed drink, wondered what the hell night it *was*. Matter of fact, he didn't even know the date. He was pretty sure it was February, though.

He studied his reflection in the bar mirror. The back lighting made him look even worse. Kind of like Charlie Manson, Jesus save us.

But he was feeling better. For a while there, in the

room, he'd been afraid he was turning chickenshit. Because, in a way, he didn't want to go to Florida. He knew he should go, he knew he had to go, but he'd been strangely reluctant.

He'd considered all his other options on the drive here, and some of them had started to seem seductively attractive.

Sell his lousy two acres, buy a legit van, and head for Canada. Homestead up there, be a real hermit.

Take the dope and drive to California, trade it a little bit at a time for high-class starlet pussy.

Sell all that beautiful hardware he'd inherited. Rider didn't know much about selling dope, but he damn sure knew some people who would give big bucks for the stuff he had in the Dodge's trunk.

Take the money and—what? Drink himself to death?

He'd figured it all out, sitting in this shithead bar in Atlanta. He would go down to Florida and show some people what happened when they fucked with Elvira Rider's youngest boy.

Because he wasn't scared of Florida, and he wasn't scared of the Mob, and he wasn't scared of dying.

He was scared of the law.

He was scared of going to jail.

In jail he would be helpless. He wasn't that big or strong, and in jail they had guys with muscles as big as bowling balls doing life and a day with absolutely nothing to lose.

And they didn't have to kill him. With a weapon, Rider knew he was deadly. Without one, he would be helpless, just another punk for the bullyboys to shove around.

And that was why he'd been so nervous in the motel room. If they caught him here, on the way to his rendezvous, with all that stuff, he'd go to jail, sure enough.

And that wasn't in the game plan. Not to rot in some

cell, forever walked over by some muscle-bound moron just because he didn't have a weapon. Same thing could happen in Florida. As soon as the shooting started, the place would be crawling with cops.

So, Rider reflected over his drink, that idiotic answer he had given the Chief had been correct. The only thing he could do was get in, do the job, and somehow get out. If he couldn't get out, he could make the cops kill him. All plans are simple, Rider thought, once you make some hard decisions and have the balls to stick by them. He surreptitiously swallowed more bennies, then shoved his glass to the edge of the bar. "Make it a double," he told the uniformed bartender. He was feeling great again.

"How about it, tootsie?" Rider said. He started to grin, remembered his teeth, and changed it to a smile, which he realized was probably a smirk instead.

"I'll pass," the cocktail waitress said. Then by way of uneasy apology, "I'm tired, y' know?" She didn't want to tell him he reminded her of Charles Manson.

"No sweat," Rider told her. He hefted the bag of overpriced beer he'd talked the bartender out of and staggered into the parking lot.

As he approached the stairs leading up to his second-story room, he noticed two cars parked close together with some people milling around them. Drunks, his mind cataloged.

When he was closer he saw that he was partially correct. The two large biker types confronting the teenage boy and girl were obviously cranked up to the max.

"Get back in the car, Larry," the girl begged, tugging on the boy's arm. He shrugged her off and swung back to face his antagonists.

"I don't want no trouble, Franky," he said, the tone a

mixture of adolescent bravado and fear.

The one whose name was Franky wore a denim cutoff jacket, decorated with emblems. He raised a muscled, tattooed arm and pointed at the girl. "You go, man. The bitch goes with me!"

"I'm not your *girl* anymore, Franky!" she screamed, and started tugging on the boy's arm again.

Franky's partner rolled his shoulders in his leather jacket. "Let's stomp this motherfucker's ass and get out of here, bro," he said, glancing around nervously. He saw Rider.

Rider carefully put his bag of beer on the asphalt and smiled at him.

Franky turned his head and saw Rider also. "You want parts of this or you wanna get the fuck in your room, huh?"

"I guess I want parts of this," Rider told him.

Franky and his partner were too far gone on pot, wine, beer, and Quaaludes to have even a vestige of caution left. All they saw was a runty drunk poking his nose in private business. They split, moving in from opposite sides, intent on violence. Franky's lost love was momentarily forgotten.

Black leather jacket was reaching for his knuckle-duster trench knife, grinning, when Rider pulled the .45, thumbed the safety down, and shot him through the leg.

The round removed three inches of upper thigh-bone, passing through and ricocheting off the fender of one of the cars. Leather jacket stood there a second, a stupid look on his face, then the leg collapsed and he fell on his face.

"Oh shit," Franky said, and turned to run. Rider caught him side-on, breaking his pelvis and blowing a silver spray of change out of his pants pocket.

Larry and the girl stood petrified with horror.

Rider was horrified, too. What are you doing? a part of him screamed plaintively. What about Florida? Are you fucking crazy!

He looked around wildly. Everything was still deserted, the huge parking lot almost empty. The echoes of the shots were still bouncing off the buildings.

He gestured with the gun. "Go," he told the teenagers. "Get the hell out of here!"

They scrambled into the car, staring back in openmouth disbelief.

The car cranked up and roared out of the parking lot, rubber screaming. Rider picked up his bag of beer and threw it in his car. He fumbled for his keys, got in, slammed the door, started the motor.

Leather jacket was on his back, rolling from side to side, both hands desperately clamped on his leg, trying to stop the flow of blood that was rapidly forming a dark lake under him. Franky was lying on his side, propped up on one elbow, almost as if reclining on a couch watching television. Instead, he was watching Rider's car pull out of the parking lot.

"Son of a bitch shot me!" he muttered in dazed wonder.

Rider took some secondary roads, got lost, then found his way back to the interstate.

About dawn he started to relax. Time, distance, and some beer had eased his tension. He wondered how in the hell that little deal had gone down. It had all happened so damn quick. He was there, they were there, he had a gun, bam!

He stopped at the Florida state line and bought more beer and a large can of V8 juice. He soaked the paper wrapper off the V8 juice in a rest room and used it to wrap his beer can in while he was driving. Best not to take a chance of getting stopped for drinking.

He kept thinking about the business of last night.

Getting mixed up in shit like that when he had to get to Florida was abso-fucking-lutely stupid. No, worse than that, it was abso-fucking-lutely certified fucking crazy.

Lieutenant Ronald Fortune of the Metropolitan Atlanta Police Department was leaning against the counter of the Holiday Inn registration desk, questioning the clerk.

"I could tell he was a nut," she was saying. "It was his eyes. I mean, he looked pretty wild, y'know, with the hair and all. But we get people in here all the time with *hair*." She used the word as if it were some unnatural condition she was forced to put up with.

"Didn't happen to notice what kind of car he had?" Fortune asked her.

"I don't check cars," the woman said. "They put the license number down, I take the money, that's it. Sorry."

Fortune's partner came in from outside and Fortune went over and conferred with her in a corner of the lobby.

"Interesting stuff up in that room," she said.

"No shit. A .357 Magnum with shoulder holster, goddamn hand grenades, a mess of hair in the sink, dirty clothes."

"But nothing to help with an ID."

"No," Fortune conceded. "The tag he gave checks out, though. Reported lost eight months ago. We're running the hardware now. It'll take a while."

"Nobody saw anything from the rooms?"

Fortune gave her a tired, disgusted look.

"Well, I bet you this," she said.

"What's that?"

She looked at him, a strange smile playing around her mouth. "Woman's intuition, Toots. Whoever this guy is, I hope to God he kept on going."

XX.

Drinking works like this.

The first night is up to the gods. Depending on what kind of shape the drinker is in, when he starts, what he drinks, and how much he is used to, determine whether he is passed out at eleven o'clock, puking at two, or getting wild at dawn.

In any case, all the drinker need do is stay awake and keep drinking. He will soon reach, somewhere in the second day, a state of quiet, functioning insanity. Motor responses will be adequate. The drinker will be able to drive, insert keys in ignitions, carry on civilized conversations with teetotalers.

It is the mind that gives way first. Common sense and judgment evaporate, and if the individual is unstable to begin with, the effect can be devastating.

Take this situation and prolong it into the third day with the aid of amphetamines.

Wired for sound.

*   *   *

The sun rose on Rider as he drove north. By the time he reached Tampa it was almost noontime, and the famous Florida sunshine was making its pallid winter strength felt as it filtered through the windshield.

He was humming inside as he cruised over a long white concrete causeway, Tampa Bay sparkling off to his left. His right foot kept unconscious time to the solid rock blaring from the radio.

The smell of Florida filtered into the car through the rolled-down window. Saltwater tides and the odor of things that grow in swamps. Even in February, a heavy, flowery, rotting smell, totally alien to the cold damp pine Rider had come from.

He felt great. He was buzzing and humming, the speed he'd taken at the lounge in Atlanta still racing through his veins like an electric river.

He wanted a drink from the bottle of Boone's Farm he'd picked up on the way, but was afraid to blatantly tilt it up in all the traffic.

He came off the causeway and took an exit ramp, slowing the car to the legal speed.

Within a mile he found a shopping center and cruised through, then parked and locked the car. He left the pistol under the seat.

A visit to a barbershop used up a half hour. He came out with a considerably lighter head, his neck and shoulders itching under the jacket.

Naturally there was a watering hole in the shopping center, a place called the Beer Witch. This was, after all, Florida.

Rider didn't want any more beer, and the Boone's Farm didn't seem to be doing him a whole lot of good. He settled for a glass of something called Night Train, a twenty-percent wine. By the time he'd finished it he knew he'd found a winner.

He got directions to Industrial Drive from the long-legged, miniskirted, artificially friendly barmaid. He found out he was only four blocks over, but that Industrial Drive was about eight miles long. He did not ask about Bartoli's trucking company.

Instead he used the phone book and looked it up, fixing the street number firmly in mind.

When he left, he took a bottle of Night Train with him.

The waitress moved to the end of the bar where she could watch him make his way across the parking lot. She wasn't real good at identifying cars, but she thought maybe it was a Dart or Duster or something like that. It was too far away to read the tag, but it was definitely not Florida.

She went back down the bar and rummaged in her handbag, then looked at the picture a long time. Probably from a driver's license, and poor quality. A lot more hair and beard, too. But what the hell? It could be. Nothing ventured, nothing gained. She picked up the phone.

Rider went the wrong way when he found Industrial Drive. As soon as he realized his mistake he turned around at a Kentucky Fried Chicken and got back on the narrow, two-lane asphalt road.

After a few miles and a much larger number of traffic lights, the fast-food restaurants, service stations, and middle-class motels began to give way to small business establishments.

Rider saw that the road was curving around the bay or whatever it was, and now railroad tracks were on his right, close behind metal-sided buildings and cheap frame houses.

He passed a switch engine pushing several boxcars, its diesel engine roaring. Kerosene fumes added to the other odors. Must be fun to live here, he thought. Occasional pedestrians on the ancient, grass-cracked sidewalks were either black or Hispanic.

Suddenly he saw what he was looking for. It was unmistakable. On the left, maybe three blocks down. Large metal building, smaller attached brick building. The cabled trailers parked neatly on the near side of the fenced lot gave it away.

Rider checked a street number quickly. Yeah, this had to be it.

He didn't want to drive by it now. He slowed the car, looking for a parking place or a turnaround. A burned-out house, a grass and sand yard. He missed the driveway, bumped over the sidewalk, cut the motor with the car facing in the direction of his target.

He couldn't see much from here, the trailers were in the way. He took the cellophane cigarette wrapper from his pocket and counted his stash. Five white crosses left. What the fuck. He took all five, washing them down with a healthy drink of Night Train.

He was sitting there, playing with the binoculars, as the two black men came down the sidewalk. They slowed at his car, then stopped.

"Hey, my man, what's happenin'?" one said, approaching the window with a businessman's smile. Anything this spaced-out white dude wanted, he could supply.

Rider showed him the .45. "Fuck off, slick."

The black businessman immediately realized that what the spaced-out white dude wanted was to be left alone. So he supplied that, with an even brighter smile. "Okay, baby, it's cool! No sweat, my man!"

He diddly-bopped on down the sidewalk, towing his stupefied companion along in his wake. Shee-it! he thought. Getting so an honest on-tro-pee-noor couldn't make a little gold off the tourist trade no more. They were all getting crazier and crazier.

Bartoli was in his office, feet up on the steel desk, drink in hand, brooding.

He couldn't keep this red-alert shit going on much longer, but there was one nagging problem he could resolve right now, by Christ. He punched the intercom.

"Pat, I'd like to see you, please."

"Yes, Bobby," she answered from the front desk. Even the flat metallic speaker couldn't disguise the cloying intimacy of her voice.

Bobby! he thought. When the fuck had he ever told her she could call him Bobby? He wasn't in the mood to play games. When she came in he didn't even take his feet off the desk.

"Ever been to Vegas?" he asked.

Her face went blank with momentary surprise, then lit up in excitement. "Are we going?" she said. It was almost a squeal of pleasure.

"Not we," Bartoli said. "I—"

The door burst open. It was Al Mewson. "Bob! We got a call from a bar on Blanding. I think it's him!"

Bartoli sprang out of his chair, spilling his rum and Coke all over his lap. "Where? What! Where?"

Mewson's face was flushed with the blood of possible victory, of possible vindication in his boss's eyes. He'd predicted this, hadn't he?

"We're not sure," Mewson sprayed out. "But it looks good. Real good, Bob. Broad called in an hour ago, and it just now filtered down to us. Brown car, might be a small Dart, out-of-state tag for sure, and the description fits."

"Where?" Bartoli shouted. He threw his cup into the trashcan.

"About four—"

The door opened again, more gently this time. It was one of Bartoli's bodyguards, his face tight with urgency. "Mr. Bartoli, it's your father. He's here."

Oh shit! Bartoli thought in agonized confusion, his

attention swirling from Pat to Al Mewson to the latest messenger.

He burst out of his office, slamming the door shut, and confronted the figure limping with merciless determination down the fluorescent-lit hallway, flanked by his own bodyguards, cane tapping.

The Drunken Chief was in the bushes behind his house, the M1 rifle leaning against his leg, watching the activity below. He didn't notice the weight of the binoculars.

They had started earlier this morning, at first a nondescript van with a couple of people in work clothes, just poking around.

Then a newer van, and more people, dressed in brown and black coveralls. With shovels.

And now, a little while ago, the helicopter. It had come in low, down the valley, its rotors fluttering and muttering. A Huey, but a black Huey, with no markings. None at all.

It squatted in Rider's front yard now, blades drooping, as people milled around it. Some of them were dressed in camouflage and full combat rig, obviously perimeter security.

The others were in civilian clothes; high-class assholes, the Chief could see. He had been watching the television ever since Rider had left, and so far nothing, so he couldn't understand what the hell was going on.

But he knew one thing. This wasn't the Mob. This smelled like Government. The bad part of Government. The secret part.

After a while, as he watched, the people in the coveralls started carrying heavy black plastic bags up to the helicopter. The Chief had watched enough television during the Vietnam War to know what they contained.

The Chief wasn't stupid. It was pretty obvious who had dealt themselves into the contest, although it wasn't clear why yet.

But he could find out. He didn't think they would shoot without talking first, and the Chief could talk a lot better than he could shoot.

He figured it was obvious they knew he was up here. He didn't think it advisable to let them come up and hit a boobytrap. It might give them a negative attitude.

So the Chief washed his face, changed into respectable clothes, tied a piece of white rag to a stick, and headed down the hill.

He left the rifle behind.

XXI.

It was getting late. The sun was starting to get low on the flat horizon, sinking behind the buildings to his right. Rider threw the empty wine bottle on the floorboard and started the Dodge.

Time to do something.

He went back the way he'd come, then took the first left. One block over, then left again, and he was on a street that paralleled Industrial Drive. He drove until he judged he was directly opposite the trucking company, then pulled over to the side of the sun-cracked asphalt.

He surveyed the tactical situation through dilated pupils, with amphetamine screaming up through his feet and turning his legs soft, his bowels to jelly, his arms into pillars of oak, his brain into a computer, and his eyes into infrared scanners that missed nothing.

To the right: scattered houses, wood-frame, paint peeling, yards littered with scabby cars, some rusting on cinder blocks in time-frozen stages of repair, wheel-less tricycles, plastic toys, trash. Porches with people on them, black people, watching him with casual, noninvolved interest.

To the left: open fields, brown waist-high grass, glitter of shallow water. Beyond the field, maybe a hundred yards, the grey gravel embankment of the railroad tracks, then the faded green-and-red-shingled roofs of the sharecropper shacks.

Beyond that, Industrial Drive.

Beyond that, Bartoli and Son's Trucking Company.

Rider wanted to get over there, at least to the raised railroad bed. From there he could look between the shacks and see his target. Maybe he'd start his attack from the tracks, maybe run somebody out of one of those houses and use that. But a wooden house wouldn't stop return fire very well.

The main problem was getting across that field with all his gear. The thought of dragging all that heavy shit through the saw grass and mud made him tired just thinking about it.

He started the car and drove a little farther down the traffic-free street. Almost immediately it curved back to the left, crossing the railroad tracks and apparently dead-ending at Industrial Drive.

As he approached the crossing he stopped. From here he had an oblique view of Bartoli's warehouse and office, maybe a half mile away to his left. He raised the binoculars, focusing. A tingle of excitement ran up through him, riding on the speed. Awful lot of cars in front of that office. Cadillacs. Lincoln Continentals. A Mercedes. Well, well.

He considered the possibility of driving the car up the tracks. It looked like it could be done. And if he got stuck he'd just get out and drag his stuff the rest of the way. That sure beat crossing the field.

His mind made up, Rider backed up a car length,

preparatory to swinging hard over the crossties. And then he noticed the train.

It was the switch engine, pushing a line of cars toward the crossing. It was moving at not more than ten miles an hour. Now he'd have to wait until it passed. He was fuming with impatience. Now was the time. Bartoli was sure to be in that building. It looked like a regular summit meeting.

As he watched the line of cars approach, the small spark of an idea surfaced, then instantly burst like divine revelation. Why not, by God!

Burning with inspiration, he stuck the pistol back in his waistband, slung the binoculars around his neck, and got out of the car. He went to the trunk, opened it, and hauled the two heavy bags out, putting them by the side of the car. Then he leaned against the fender and nonchalantly lit a cigarette as the string of cars rumbled closer.

Several empty boxcars went by, side doors gaping open, then a flatcar loaded with steel reinforcing bar, then two shiny aluminum tank cars.

Rider was so busy watching the engine pushing all this that he never noticed the stylized flames painted on the sides of the tank cars, along with various other written warnings.

There was a man in a hard hat with a walkie-talkie leaning on the railing of the walkway that encircled the massive body of the engine. He watched Rider without much interest as the engine started to pass over the crossing.

His attention quickened, though, as Rider pushed himself off the fender of the car, walked quickly toward him, and swung aboard the train.

The man in the hard hat hurried down the catwalk to meet Rider, his face tight with indignation. "Hey, ace, what the hell—"

Rider stuck the .45 between the man's eyes, which crossed as they tried to focus on the bore at a range of three inches.

"Into the cab. Now!"

Rider followed him back down the catwalk. The brakeman glanced back over his shoulder at Rider, then slid the metal door of the cab open. Rider shoved him inside unceremoniously, then stood in the door, the pistol held casually at waist level. The safety was still on.

It looked like the cockpit of a 747. The engineer sat on a metal seat at the other side of the cab, arm resting casually on the windowsill as he watched down the tracks. He pulled his head back in at the noise of the door sliding and looked around. His mouth dropped open. "What's this shit?" he sputtered.

"This," Rider said, "is a hijacking. Stop the fucking train."

The engineer tore his fascinated gaze from Rider's hand and took a quick look at his eyes. He stopped the train.

"Now," Rider said, still standing in the door, "back this thing up until you're even with my car and the crossing." He watched carefully as the engineer did as he was told. It was simple enough, basically a throttle, brake, and forward and reverse lever. Not even a steering wheel.

When they had stopped at the crossing, Rider had the man in the hard hat climb down and lug his bags up on the catwalk next to the cab. Then they continued back on down the tracks.

A radio speaker started squawking somewhere in the cab. "I've got to answer that," the engineer said.

"No, you don't," Rider told him. He located the CB installation above the huge windshield and switched it off. The engineer and the man in the hard hat glanced uneasily at each other.

As the engine reached a point that was again opposite the trucking company, Rider was gratified to see that the combination of the track bed and the engine gave him enough height to see over the roofs of the shacks. The Bartoli trucking company was framed in the cab's window like a picture.

As soon as the engineer got everything stopped again, Rider gestured with the pistol. "Okay, boys. Everybody out. Have a nice day."

The two men thought it would be a hell of a nice day if they managed to live through what was left of it. They wasted no time scrabbling out of the other door and down to the ground, disappearing along the sides of the cars.

Rider got his bags and emptied them on the floor of the cab. Wading through thousands of dollars' worth of ordnance, he slammed the outside door shut and locked it. He knew he didn't have much time. As soon as the train people got to a phone he would have SWAT teams crawling up his ass.

He went to the other window and raised the binoculars. At a distance of two hundred yards the optics brought everything into his lap.

Oh, yes. Lots of fancy cars parked in front of the brick office. To the left, raised garage doors. He could see fifty-five-gallon drums stacked three high against the inside wall of the garage. He wondered what was in them. He wondered what would happen if he put a 40mm grenade into them.

A guard shack at the front gate, uniformed attendant sitting in a folding chair in the doorway. There were several men leaning against the sides of the parked cars, all dressed in suits. Chauffeurs and bodyguards, he decided.

He noticed movement in the upper left-hand window of the office building. The window was open. In a second he caught a quick glimpse of a rifle barrel.

Rider was filled with a sick, gleeful, guilty anticipation. He always experienced this feeling just before he instigated killing, like a little boy who has made up his mind to do something daring and naughty and forbidden. Well, he was about to be real naughty. He put the binoculars on the control console and started rummaging through his gear.

A bandolier of shotgun shells went over his head, then a canvas shoulder bag half filled with 40mm grenades for the bloop tube. The .45 in his waistband. Two spare pistol magazines in his left coat pocket, a fragmentation grenade in the right.

He inserted a doubled magazine into the SC70 assault rifle and tapped it in place, leaning the rifle against the side of the cab. The already loaded automatic shotgun went next to it. He put a loaded magazine for the rifle in each of his back pockets. He was starting to feel like a pack mule.

He broke the bloop tube open and loaded it, putting it on the console. The CETME MG82 SAW, assault pack attached, went next to it. Then he picked up one of the rocket launchers.

Kneeling down, he armed it and rested it on the edge of the cab window, sighting in on the window where he had seen the rifle. He wondered about backblast in the enclosed space. He carefully put the weapon down, clanked over to the other door, and slid it open. Then he went back to the window and sighted in again.

He could hear his breathing and the muted rumble of the idling diesel. His hands were very steady. He was calm and happy. Party time. He squeezed the round off.

Harvey Stubbs was damn glad it was winter. Summertime would have been unbearable, sitting in a car in the open like this.

There wasn't much traffic along here at this time of

day. An occasional truck or van. Earlier a police car had cruised by, but the cops had ignored him. Probably got their hands in Bartoli's pocket, he thought.

In a little while the traffic would pick up some, as the small shops scattered widely up and down the street finished the workday.

He couldn't see the railroad crossing from here. The last of the old nigger sharecropper shacks blocked his vision. Stubbs thought of them in this way because he was black and had been born in one. He had a vast contempt for the people who lived in them.

His stomach rumbled and he glanced at his expensive watch. About time for them to relieve him.

The walkie-talkie on the seat next to him squawked. "Yeah?"

"Everything okay?" a scratchy voice asked.

"Ten-four. It's cool. Hey, I'm getting hungry."

There was a pause, then, "Never mind that now. Pull down the street to the crossing. We can see a brown Dodge down there. Dominick wants you to check the tags."

Oh balls, he thought. He thumbed the mike button. "What's the stress?"

"We got a possible make on our friend. He might be driving a brown—"

The radio cut off. At the same time Stubbs was jarred by a muffled boom behind him. He jerked around in the seat. The corner of the office building was shrouded in a blossom of smoke. He could see things flying through the air.

It's going down, he thought in disbelief.

George Gamble thought the whole thing was a crock of shit. They'd imported him from Miami, and all he'd been doing so far was sitting in this cockroach-infested dump staring across the street at Bartoli's office.

He had a table pushed up under the front window,

and he sat in a kitchen chair next to it, drinking beer, watching the asshole over there in the guard shack watch him back.

Bippo and Paulas were sprawled in ratty easy chairs behind him, watching soap operas on a portable color set, the only item in the whole place that wasn't falling apart. Rizzo was in one of the bedrooms, sleeping or jacking off or whatever it was he did in there when it wasn't his turn at the window.

Gamble couldn't understand how the others could sleep on those nasty beds. He'd dragged his own personal mattress into the kitchen and slept on that, but it still gave him the creeps. They all laughed at him because he sprayed bug killer around his bed every time he lay down.

There was absolutely nothing to do. The television sucked. Not even cable, the place wasn't hooked up for it. Just soap operas and game shows and sitcoms. Christ!

He sighed and played with the walkie-talkie button, then with the safety on the Mini-14, both lying on the table in front of him. He took a drink of beer.

He was still facing the window and, as he tilted his head back to swallow, he saw something fly overhead, something headed for Bartoli's office. Before he even had time to realize it wasn't a bird, it hit.

There was a flash and a tremendous flat *whack* as the entire left side of the building vanished in smoke, brick dust, and flying debris. Gamble could feel the heat and shock wave roll over him. He jumped up, spraying beer all over the table, grabbing for the rifle.

"In back of us!" he yelled to the other two soldiers, who stared at him in confusion, the television forgotten.

Gamble ran past them, down the short hallway toward the back door, and collided with Rizzo, who had stumbled out the bedroom door, eyes blinking.

"Get the fuck out of my way!" Gamble snarled, and shoved him into the wall as he went by.

Bippo and Paulas snatched up weapons and headed toward the rear bedrooms, intending to shoot out the windows there.

"Holy shit!" Rizzo said as they thundered past. He went back into the bedroom to get his own weapon. He thought he might need it.

The rocket hit the front of the building on the upper left-hand corner, about six feet below the window Rider had been aiming at.

The two men standing there had almost no time to react. Dominick Valenziano, Bartoli's cousin, was standing behind the man with the radio, looking at Rider's car with binoculars, when he saw the flash of the igniting rocket in his optics.

He dropped the glasses and stared, and there it was, heading toward them, eating distance with frightening speed, trailing a ribbon of white smoke. He gave a strangled cry and dived for the center of the room. The man with the radio froze.

The warhead blew a twenty-foot hole in the brick wall. The floor of the room buckled upward, catapulting the man with the radio out the window. He landed on the trunk of a Cadillac parked below, mercifully unconscious, his back and both legs broken.

The other men in the room froze with shock, their ears ringing from the blast. The place was filled with smoke and plaster dust.

Valenziano pushed himself up from the floor, his nose streaming blood, and looked around wildly for the stairs. They were being rocketed from the railroad tracks, and he knew the submachine guns they had here were impotent at that range. It was time to consult with the General.

* * *

Pat Cousins was back at the reception desk. She'd scuttled out of Bartoli's rear office the minute the old man with the cane had barged in and he and Bartoli had started yelling at each other in Italian.

The explosion blew the wall across the hall out. It knocked her out of the chair and into the corner of the room in an untidy sprawl. She stayed there, curled up in a petrified ball, whimpering in fear and confusion.

There was pandemonium in the hallway by Bartoli's office. One second everyone had been standing there in painful embarrassment, Mewson and Bartoli's men eyeing the Old Man's bodyguards uneasily, shuffling their feet and giving little subdued coughs, and the next everyone was running or screaming or crouching as the shock wave rolled down the passageway in front of a choking, blinding cloud of dust and smoke.

Suddenly there were a lot of handguns out, and the Don's men were charging into the office to protect him.

Bartoli came crashing out through the milling mob, his face livid with fright and anger. "What the fuck was that?" he screamed.

A disheveled, bloody figure loomed up out of the haze. It was Valenziano. He grabbed Bartoli by the lapels of his coat with grimy hands. "Somebody's shooting rockets at us from the train tracks!"

Bartoli tore himself out of the man's frenzied grasp and turned to Mewson, who was flattened against the wall, eyes glazed. Bartoli's voice rose in pitch. "Rockets?" He seized Mewson by the tie and jerked him forward, their faces only inches apart. "Rockets?" he screamed.

"Y-y-you knew!" Mewson babbled. "Parsons' stuff! The list—I gave it to you. I told you!"

"Ah, goddamn!" Bartoli snarled, and flung the lawyer away. Think, his mind was racing. Act like Napoleon!

He pulled his pistol and stood in the swirling hallway. The Old Man went by, face white with fear, hustled along by two protectors.

"You see!" he yelled at Bartoli in accusatory falsetto. From somewhere outside, the stutter of automatic weapons drifted in, followed by the dull *crump* of an explosion.

"Get my pop out of here!" Bartoli screamed unnecessarily. "Dom! Take a couple of the boys and go out the back. Circle around and get that motherfucker!" He looked around. No Dom. It was all confusion and smoke and noise. Then he started to understand the difference between a streetwise hood and Napoleon Bonaparte.

People started to boil out of the building, piling into the cars. It was like kicking over an anthill, Rider thought, grinning.

He had the SAW stuck out the window, bipod extended. All he had to do was drop the thing, and it would hang there, caught on the metal legs.

He took out the security booth first, with a two-second burst. The outhouse-size structure destructed in a blizzard of .223-caliber ball and tracer. The uniformed guard, who had been on the phone trying to reach Bartoli, staggered out of the wreckage, dying.

Rider started working on the cars, to prevent escape. He swept the muzzle back and forth over the parking lot, firing short bursts. The tracers tore chunks out of the asphalt, evaporated windshields, destroyed tires, punctured radiators. Hubcaps went flying, spinning from the impact.

A grey Mercedes careened around, motor roaring, riding on a cloud of smoking rubber as it powered toward the entrance. Rider led it and squeezed, riddling the expensive machine. It crashed into what was left of the security booth and stalled, clouds of steam billowing up. The front door opened and the driver fell out on his head. The back door opened and an old man crawled out, scrambling on all fours like a crab, clutching a cane.

Rider fired into the trunk, trying for the gas tank, trying to start a fire that would block the gate for the other cars.

The back of the Mercedes lifted up and settled back in a ball of orange fire, the trunk lid turning over gracefully in the air. The crawling figure was engulfed in the flames.

Suddenly the cab of the switch engine was filled with the clatter of impacting rounds. Pieces of metal ricocheted around viciously, chipping paint, shattering gauges in a spray of glass. One hit the ceiling, hit the far wall, hit the floor, and took the heel off one of Rider's combat boots. His whole foot went numb.

Without thinking, he screamed and swung the muzzle left, pivoting the weapon on the windowsill, raking the back of the house where the fire had come from. Raking it back and forth, forgetting his training, holding the trigger down in a barrel-melting sustained burst of fire that perforated the place in a storm of woodchips and ancient paint.

Paulas, at one of the back windows, died instantly, his head exploded by a tumbling .55-grain slug that blew his brains out his nose and mouth.

Sonny Bippo, next to him, became an instant believer in the doctrine of superior firepower. As Paulas sprayed him with the horrible mess that had been neatly contained in his head an instant earlier, Bippo threw his weapon down and turned to run. The second sweep of Rider's continuous burst chewed over him. He dropped to his knees and coughed a scarlet stream of blood all over the faded linoleum floor, then fell on it.

Gamble took rounds through both shoulders, plus a

sliver of wood in his left eye. The cheap pine walls were no protection at all. He turned away from the window and started for the front of the house.

The SAW locked up from the heat. Rider dropped it and swept the grenade launcher up from the control console. He put a 40mm projectile into the open back door of the house. It hit in the hallway, almost between Gamble's legs. The flash-bang tore his trousers and testicles off and tumbled him into the living room, where he lay charred and smoking.

Rizzo had been headed halfheartedly toward the rear when the hail of steel came sweeping through. He turned and ran for the front door. He hesitated there, torn between terror and duty, when the grenade went off, and Gamble came back-flipping out of the hallway in a cloud of greasy smoke.

Enough for Paolo Rizzo. He went out the door, across the dirt yard, and started to cross the street, then stopped. It looked bad over there. Car windows shot out, tires flattened. One car blazing, squatting like a bonfire on the rubble of what used to be the guard shack. A huge, ragged hole in the front of the building, still hidden by dust. Miami looked pretty good to Rizzo right at that moment in time. He started moving down the line of wooden houses, heading up Industrial Drive, when he realized he was still holding his Mini-14. And it occurred to him that they might be watching him from the office. How would it look if they saw him bugging out?

With this in mind, he moved until he could see part of the engine between two of the houses. The engine and the tank cars behind it.

He raised the semiautomatic and emptied his twenty-round magazine in their general direction as fast as he could pull the trigger. His eyes were shut.

Then he put another house between him and the target as fast as his legs would move. He realized he wasn't alone. The people who lived in the houses were on the sidewalk with him, all moving toward a line of flashing blue lights he could see up the street.

With wonder, Rizzo surveyed the old men, old women, and kids carrying babies and personal possessions and each other, all streaming away from the scene of the fighting. Like the old combat footage he had sometimes watched on television, the jerky, grainy films from World War II, Korea, Vietnam. This looked just like that. He threw his rifle away and joined the refugees.

Rider didn't even realize Rizzo had shot at him. He was too busy burning up his own ordnance.

The threat from the house seemed to be neutralized. Who the hell would have ever thought anybody would be in there? To make sure, Rider put another grenade through a fuel-oil tank squatting on rusted legs along the side. It was almost empty, but there was enough left to start things going. The dry wood house began to burn.

Satisfied, Rider directed his attention back to the main business. He looked through the binoculars. There were people crouching behind some of the cars, and automatic weapons stuttered at him from the lower window. He laughed. He wasn't worried about a submachine gun at two hundred yards. But it was time to get things moving again. He picked up his last LAW rocket tube and sighted in on the open doors of the maintenance garage.

There was a sharp *clang* as a high-powered rifle round snapped by his ear and hit the far side of the cab, followed by the sound of the shot. Rider ignored it and squeezed off.

This time he aimed a little higher. The rocket went whizzing away, and hit true. It exploded in the garage, blowing fifty-five-gallon drums of burning motor oil out the door. Stacks of used tires, gas tanks, lubricating grease, lumber, cleaning fluid, and other combustibles sailed around inside, starting other fires. The thin metal sides of the building bulged outward toward the chain link fence separating it from the machine shop next door.

The acetylene tanks for the cutting torches waited a few seconds, protected by their thick sides, then they went, too, in a series of slamming explosions that drove the front of the building into the parking lot on a wave of fire and crumpled siding.

The blast whirled a tank of oxygen into a steel column, knocking the valve off. With 2,500 pounds of compressed oxygen escaping from a three-quarter-inch hole, the 150-pound tube shot across the parking lot like a runaway steel balloon, snatching the support away from the trailer Bartoli's sentries were still hiding in. The front of it thumped to the ground like a leg-shot buffalo, and the two men inside began trying to force its cargo doors open. In a few seconds their efforts became panic-stricken. It was getting very, very hot.

Rider laughed gleefully at the spectacular results he had achieved. But he had to get out of here. Looking over his shoulder, he could see a line of police cars and fire trucks pulling into the clear space along the road on the far side of the field. Blue and red lights were flashing. Somewhere a siren moaned, and the *whoop-whoop* of an ambulance.

He picked the SAW back up. It was still hot. He worked the bolt, and it moved freely, ejecting two live rounds. Then the assault pack was empty. He mounted the other one, then put the shotgun over his shoulder and slung the SAW by its sling.

Clanking with weaponry like a robot of the future,

Rider came out of the engine's cab and climbed carefully down to the bottom of the embankment. He didn't want to break his ankle.

Wildly fired rounds from the building pinged and smacked and snapped around him. The only thing he was worried about was the guy with the high-powered rifle. He'd softened them up, by God, now it was time to start the assault.

Skirting the heat from the now-roaring building, keeping a structure between himself and the sniper, Rider began his attack. He wished he had a drink of Night Train.

XXII.

Rizzo's wild burst of fire had come nowhere near Rider. It had, though, put four holes in a six-foot, horizontally spaced group along the side of the tank car nearest the switch engine. One of the holes was almost directly centered on a poorly stenciled notice in black paint which read, "CAUTION! VARSOL—A Petroleum Product—FLAMMABLE!"

The four holes were emitting a solid stream of thin, brownish liquid. This liquid poured out onto the heavy gravel of the railroad bed, soaking through and filling the ditch below. Then the liquid ran down the ditch until it found a convenient low place in the yard of the burning house.

Eventually the depression in the yard filled up. The overflow began a thin trickle past the corner of the house, where a piece of burning wood fell off into it. The trickle began to burn.

The fire worked its way upstream. Soon the depression was a small lake of fire. The fire continued its mindless way up the ditch, until the railroad embankment was ablaze, casting a flickering red glow off the bottom of the aluminum tanks in the fading daylight.

The fire stopped there momentarily, unable to force its way past the pouring stream of Varsol. But the heat expanded the liquid in the tanks, increasing their volume. So as the level in the first tank went down, the holes spurted flammable liquid at a growing rate. The more Varsol that poured out, the higher the fire burned. The higher it burned, the faster it poured Varsol. Like a snowball rolling downhill.

The fumes in the empty top of the tank got hotter and hotter.

Varsol is a low-grade kerosene. It is used mainly as a degreaser and thinner for certain types of paint. It is not considered dangerous, assuming reasonable precautions are taken. It is flammable, but not explosive.

A government pamphlet on improvised munitions contains this information: Anything that will burn will explode, under the right conditions.

The fire kept building.

Taped recording, edited for the six-o'clock news:

DISPATCHER: Tac Two, what's your ten-twenty? Over. [*Static*.]

PILOT: Uh—this is Tac Two. We're right over the action. Over.

DISPATCHER: Tac Two, can you see anything? Over.

PILOT: Yeah, we see all sorts of *bleep* burning. Looks like World War II down there. Over.

DISPATCHER: Stand by. [*Static*]. Tac Two, what's burning? Over.

PILOT: Lots of *bleep*. We got Bartoli's burning. Going real good, a three-alarm job. Car burning in the parking lot. And there's a train burning [*static*] a train burning on the tracks. Over.

DISPATCHER: Can you, ah, see people moving? Over.

PILOT: Ah, negative on the people. Might be, but it's hard to see. Too much glare and smoke.

DISPATCHER: Roger the smoke. What's your altitude? Over.

PILOT: Never mind my altitude, *bleep*. We ain't in the Air Force, and I ain't going no lower.

DISPATCHER: The captain says [*static*] ah, we need to know what's going on. Over.

PILOT: Then let the captain [*static*] hustle his *bleep* in there and find out. What's in those tank cars? Over.

DISPATCHER: Stand by.

The black smoke from the burning maintenance garage gave Rider some concealment as he moved across the road, lugging his weapons.

He glanced back over his shoulder. The wood house was going up nicely, and the tank cars were sitting in a lake of oily fire. He wondered if they would explode.

He could see police cars, SWAT vans, and fire engines five hundred yards up the road. Apparently they were going to cordon the area off and move in after the fireworks died down.

People were shooting at him from the office, so he went prone in the ditch and hosed a line of tracers across the front of the building.

Two men came scrambling out of a trailer with its front wheels knocked off. They ran toward Rider, trying to escape the heat from the garage, and a burst from the SAW cut their legs out from under them. They squirmed around on the asphalt, screaming.

The office itself was starting to fill with the smoke of burning oil and tires. Bartoli had sent several of his men out the back door and down the narrow space between the side of the building and the chain link fence that separated it from Brighton Chemical.

They popped around the corner just as Rider came

out of the ditch in a running crouch. He dived for the shelter of a bullet-riddled Lincoln in a hail of 9mm slugs.

The two men emptied their magazines and ducked back around the corner to reload. Rider came after them, sweeping the front of the office as he ran.

The men thought Rider was still behind the car, so they almost ran over him when they came back out. One of them got off a wild burst before he was knocked spinning and bloody into the fence. The other one was almost cut in half as high-velocity projectiles hammered into him at a range of five feet.

Then Rider was under the shattered window, panting, as a rifle barrel poked out, followed by the white blur of a face. Rider sat down with a thump and swung the muzzle of the SAW up and squeezed the trigger. The face disappeared in a halo of red and the SAW ran dry.

Rider threw it away and unslung the shotgun. People inside the building were shouting in confusion as he took the fragmentation grenade from his pocket, pulled the pin, let the spoon fly free as he did a fast three-second count, and threw it into the room.

It went off immediately, blowing what glass was left in the window out on a cloud of grey smoke.

Rider stood up and poked the Benelli inside and shot a stumbling, screaming figure that was the only thing left moving. Then he climbed in himself.

Two men had come out of the back of the building and two more had come out the front, trying to catch him in a crossfire while he was still crouched below the window.

They were too late. They saw him disappear inside and immediately decided that since Rider was *in* and they were *out*, they would just as soon keep it that way. They started zigzagging through the wrecked cars, heading for the tangled gate.

And then 60,000 gallons of overheated kerosene decided to blow.

There was a blinding glare and a tremendous, earth-shaking *whap* as the first tank car went. The force of the explosion drove the switch engine ten yards down the tracks, covered in blazing Varsol. It picked the other tank car up, stood it on end, and detonated it with an eye-stunning flash and a thunderclap of sound.

A mushroom-shaped pillar of fire boiled upward, raining streamers of incandescent fuel like comet tails. House windows shattered and the shock wave drove the running men in the parking lot down in a battered confusion of bruised flesh.

Pieces of aluminum tank car cartwheeled in the air and came down, bouncing off the road, and more houses caught fire from the raining fuel. Water in the drainage ditch began to steam as the wave of heat rolled outward from the center of the inferno.

Rider never even felt it. He was too busy killing people in the office building. He shot anything that moved in the smoky haze, he shot through doors and walls. He kept shooting and plugging fresh shells into the Benelli and sending screaming, terrorized, colliding figures to hell on the orange muzzle blast of double-aught buckshot.

They shot back. The dim hallway was streaked with the flashing stutter of submachine guns stitching holes in the thin walls, blowing chunks out of the floor, ricocheting around like crazed insects.

Al Mewson came out of Bartoli's office propelled by Bartoli's imported shoe. He was clutching an M16 in numbed hands, his face frozen in the rictus of terror. Buckshot tore through his silk vest. He went down screaming, arms windmilling.

Rider took rounds through his trousers, through his jacket, through his left earlobe. A 9mm round hit the stock of the Benelli, shattering it, a fragment hit Rider in the left elbow. His arm went numb. The shotgun was empty.

But there were no more targets, except one.

Down the hallway stood a stocky figure silhouetted against the open back door, a pistol hanging from its hand. It was their first meeting, and they knew each other intuitively.

Rider dropped the empty shotgun and pulled the cocked .45, thumbing down the safety. He grinned at the figure confronting him through the haze of smoke and dust. "Shall we dance?"

But Bartoli didn't want to dance. He didn't want to start the ball. He didn't want to get the show on the road. Bartoli ran.

He turned and bolted out the back door. He threw his pistol down and hit the chain link fence halfway up in a great surging, panicked leap, and started climbing.

He threw his right leg over the top of the fence, ignoring the pain as the barbed wire pierced his flesh. He was going over the fence and into the bay and then he was going to swim across the bay and stay alive forever and ever.

With his one leg over the fence he felt something hard hit him in the rectum. He looked down and Rider was there, grinning at him, the .45 jammed up Bartoli's ass. Their eyes locked, Bartoli's pleading, Rider's gleaming with alcohol and Benzedrine and insanity.

And then Rider moved the weapon back just enough to take the pressure off the muzzle so the piece could fire, and pulled the trigger. And pulled the trigger. And pulled the trigger. Until the gun was empty.

Rider went back inside to Bartoli's office, stepping over Mewson's sprawled corpse. There were rifles and grenades and boxes of ammo lying around on the desks and chairs. There was a liquor cabinet.

Rider took a bottle of Bartoli's expensive whiskey and held it under his bad arm and unscrewed the cap with his good hand. He took a nice, long drink.

Pat Cousins was standing in the doorway. Her hair was matted and tangled, her clothes torn and wrinkled, her support hose ripped and shredded, her face bleeding from flying glass. She was covered with a layer of smoke and plaster dust. Her eyes were wild. She looked at Rider with a mixture of confusion and awe.

He grinned at her. "Hi, Pat."

Her mouth worked. "You," she said. "You!"

"Yeah, it's me," Rider said. He took another drink, then put the top back on the bottle and tucked it under his bad arm. He knew he wouldn't be able to climb the fence Bartoli was still hanging on, so he picked up one of the grenades.

When he did, Pat turned and stumbled up the hallway, tripping over bodies. She was making a high, quavering noise, something like a teakettle starting to boil.

Now, what the fuck is wrong with *her*? Rider wondered.

He went to the back door, pulled the pin on the grenade, and rolled it up against the fence with an underhand throw. Then he stepped back inside for protection.

The grenade went off with a flat crack and flash. Peering out the door, he waited for the dust to settle, then saw with satisfaction that it had blown a crawl-size hole through the links. It had also abused Bartoli's inert body to a considerable degree, but Rider wasn't interested in that.

He figured it was time to take a swim. He'd use one of the wooden pallets for a lifeboat, and if the water was cold, he had his bottle to keep him warm.

EPILOGUE

It was a large, expensive, colonial brick house in McLean, Virginia, which for all practical purposes is a suburb of Washington, D.C.

The huge columns at the front gleamed whitely, illuminated by low-level lights placed strategically around the perfectly manicured lawn. A number of well-waxed luxury cars were parked in the circular driveway. Every fifteen minutes or so a private-security vehicle cruised by the residence.

Inside the house it was quiet. The domestic help had retired for the night, so when the door chimes rang, the Master of the House answered it himself.

He admitted his Assistant and led him into the den, where the General and the Politician were waiting.

Everyone got down to business immediately. The Assistant settled himself in a chair and began talking, referring occasionally to a notebook. "Bartoli is dead, along with about thirty presently unidentified bodies.

Quite a few wounded also. All the casualties seem to be Bartoli's people."

He glanced up, saw that he had everyone's complete attention, and continued. "Property damage is about a million dollars—"

"What about Rider?" the General grunted impatiently.

The Assistant smiled. "Oh, the police have him, all right. Crazy bastard was a half mile offshore, floating on a wooden pallet and drunk as a lord."

"What about the woman?"

"They've got her, too. They've got *everybody* who was still walking or crawling after the shooting stopped. They're holding them all incommunicado until they sort it all out."

"Will they cooperate or will we have to lean on them?" the Politician asked.

"They seem inclined to cooperate," the Assistant replied. "I get the impression that they're happy to have Big Brother taking the responsibility."

The General lit one of his large, stinking cigars. "I don't like it," he said. "Too many people know too many things. What if we activate this character and he goes berserk in a shopping center with a sophisticated weapon? A weapon we gave him?"

"We've already been over this, Barney," the Master of the House said. "That won't happen. Rider will be supervised."

The General blew cigar smoke. "Bullshit."

"If that *does* happen, Harrison Smith will take the fall," the Politician told him. "The trail will stop there, believe me."

"Harrison Smith is a scumbag," the General said disgustedly. "A traitor to his country and a mercenary son-of-a-bitch to boot. Just because we've got him by the balls and he's looking at twenty years doesn't mean he won't roll over on us the first chance he gets."

"Mr. Smith will never get that chance," the Master of the House said. He said it in a manner that silenced everyone for a moment.

The Politician fidgeted uneasily. That kind of talk made him extremely nervous. To brighten the mood, he said, "And the woman won't be a problem. We'll give her National Security Act speech number twelve, scare the shit out of her, and send her home to Mama. She'll keep her mouth shut."

"Will that goddamn old Indian or hillbilly or moonshiner up there scare, too?" the General asked skeptically.

The Assistant laughed. "I don't know if he can be scared, but he sure as hell can be bribed. We've got the bomb squad clearing the place of booby traps. As soon as they're done, the Army Techs are going to start installing a state-of-the-art satellite dish, plus a solar generator, plus the biggest fucking color television console made."

"Jesus," the General said. "What a way to fight a war."

"But it *is* a war, isn't it, Barney?" the Master of the House asked him quietly. "And we're fighting a bunch of psychopaths, right here at home and down south. They're swamping us, Barney. The Colombians with the coke, the big-city street gangs getting so organized that they've branched out cross-country, the biker clubs hand in glove with the Mafia. Christ, Barney, we've got to do *something!* Due process just isn't working. We need a few psychopaths of our own." He smiled a cold, deadly smile. "A series of strategic strikes against key groups and installations. We're not going to lock 'em up or deport 'em or any of that tired old shit. We're just going to kill them. A war of attrition. Like you'd kill cockroaches. As fast as they come out of the woodwork we stomp 'em down!"

He paused for breath, his eyes shining. "We've got

researchers looking for potential recruits. Rider is the first. If he can kill over forty people with the junk he used, just think what he could do with some real gear!"

The General had already thought about it, at length. He looked at the men around him, the nervous Politician, the dedicated Assistant, the Master of the House, whose eyes burned with the light of fanaticism.

All patriots, though, in their own way. And martyrs, too, the General realized grimly. Because, sooner or later, this business would be exposed, and all their heads would roll.

But in the meantime, maybe they could do some good. Stem the tide for a while.

The General sighed and leafed through the file on Rider. The first of a new natural resource, maybe. Natural killers, trained and turned loose by the government like antibiotics, to attack the virus that was bringing America to its knees.

The General put his doubts firmly aside and began to plan the details of the coming war.

BESTSELLING BOOKS FROM TOR

THE BEST IN HORROR

Buy them at your local bookstore or use this handy coupon:
Clip and mail this page with your order.

Publishers Book and Audio Mailing Service
P.O. Box 120159, Staten Island, NY 10312-0004

Please send me the book(s) I have checked above. I am enclosing $_____
(please add $1.25 for the first book, and $.25 for each additional book to
cover postage and handling. Send check or money order only—no CODs.)

Name _____

Address _____

City _____ State/Zip _____

Please allow six weeks for delivery. Prices subject to change without notice.

THE BEST IN SUSPENSE